HEIR TO THE THRONE

*Welcome to the world of the Carradignes,
a family of wealth, power and scandals
of royal proportions!*

PRAISE FOR KASEY MICHAELS

"Using wit and romance
with a master's skill, Kasey Michaels
aims for the heart and never misses."
—*New York Times* bestselling author
Nora Roberts

"If you want emotion, humor and characters you
can love, you want a story by Kasey Michaels."
—National bestselling author Joan Hohl

"Kasey Michaels creates characters
who stick with you long after her
wonderful stories are told."
—*New York Times* bestselling author Kay Hooper

PRAISE FOR CAROLYN DAVIDSON

"Davidson wonderfully captures gentleness in the
midst of heart-wrenching challenges, portraying
the extraordinary possibilities that exist within
ordinary marital love."
—*Publishers Weekly* on *The Tender Stranger*

"From desperate situation to upbeat ending,
Carolyn Davidson reminds us
why we read romance."
—*Romantic Times* on *The Bachelor Tax*

KASEY MICHAELS

This *New York Times* and *USA TODAY* bestselling author of more than sixty books is the recipient of the Romance Writers of America RITA® Award and the *Romantic Times* Career Achievement Award for her historical romances set in the Regency era. Kasey also writes contemporary romances for Silhouette and Harlequin Books. Her next release from Harlequin, a lively Regency short story, will be out in June 2003 as part of a special historical bridal collection, *The Wedding Chase.*

CAROLYN DAVIDSON

Born and raised in Michigan, Carolyn chose a writing career at the age of ten. Since being published in 1995, she remains fully committed to telling stories of life and love in another century. With the support of her family and the community of writers who surround her, she has written eighteen books for Harlequin. Carolyn welcomes mail from her readers at: P.O. Box 2757, Goose Creek, SC 29445.

Please look for Carolyn's next Harlequin Historical, *Tempting a Texan,* available in March 2003.

KASEY MICHAELS

CAROLYN DAVIDSON

HEIR TO THE THRONE

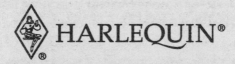

HARLEQUIN®

TORONTO • NEW YORK • LONDON
AMSTERDAM • PARIS • SYDNEY • HAMBURG
STOCKHOLM • ATHENS • TOKYO • MILAN • MADRID
PRAGUE • WARSAW • BUDAPEST • AUCKLAND

ISBN 0-373-83520-5

HEIR TO THE THRONE

Copyright © 2002 by Harlequin Books S.A.

The publisher acknowledges the copyright holders of the individual works as follows:

HER ROYAL PAIN-IN-THE-HIGHNESS
Copyright © 2002 by Kathie Seidick

A KING WITHOUT A COUNTRY
Copyright © 2002 by Carolyn Davidson

CONTENTS

HER ROYAL PAIN-IN-THE-HIGHNESS   9
Kasey Michaels

A KING WITHOUT A COUNTRY   145
Carolyn Davidson

THE CARRADIGNE ROYAL FAMILY

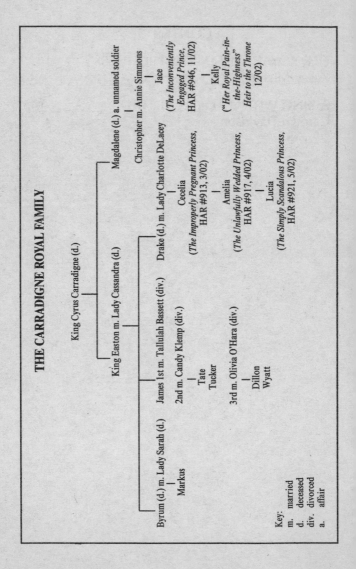

King Cyrus Carradigne (d.)

Magdalene (d.) a. unnamed soldier

King Easton m. Lady Cassandra (d.)

Christopher m. Annie Simmons

Jace
(*The Inconveniently Engaged Prince*,
HAR #946, 11/02)

Kelly
("*Her Royal Pain-in-the-Highness*"
Heir to the Throne
12/02)

Drake (d.) m. Lady Charlotte DeLacey

Cecelia
(*The Improperly Pregnant Princess*,
HAR #913, 3/02)

Amelia
(*The Unlawfully Wedded Princess*,
HAR #917, 4/02)

Lucia
(*The Simply Scandalous Princess*,
HAR #921, 5/02)

James 1st m. Tallulah Bassett (div.)

2nd m. Candy Klemp (div.)

Tate
Tucker

3rd m. Olivia O'Hara (div.)

Dillon
Wyatt

Byrum (d.) m. Lady Sarah (d.)

Markus

Key:
m.   married
d.   deceased
div. divorced
a.   affair

HER ROYAL
PAIN-IN-THE-HIGHNESS

Kasey Michaels

To Ron Hosmer, terrific fan and all-around good guy, who has more of my books than I do.

CHAPTER ONE

KELLY CARRADIGNE CLOSED her book, turned her head slightly, pushed her glasses higher on her nose, and dared to look out the porthole window of the private jet carrying her over the Larella Mountains.

She was a scientist. An educated woman. A highly educated woman, and not one prone to silly superstitions.

However, this rational, intelligent woman did have a niggling little voice in the back of her head that told her that air flight wasn't really possible...and that the only reason this sleek white machine remained in the air was because she did not look at the ground.

Not that she hadn't flown before this international trip to Korosol.

She'd flown several times. An air sickness pill, downed with a glass of wine, had always been enough to get her to walk down that long passageway to the plane, pat its metal side as if to say, "Hi, it's me. Be nice," and then actually *voluntarily* step inside what, in her heart of hearts, was nothing more than a tin sausage.

"It's on a hook, it's on a hook." That's what she'd think, comforted by that knowledge—or the combination of the air sickness pill and a glass of white zinfandel.

But she had never before flown on a private jet. Private jets were small. Very small, at least to Kelly. Because, to Kelly, any airplane shorter than a city block in length just couldn't be safe.

Maybe she should read another book on aerodynamics, and let her scientific self bone up on lift and thrust and flaps and cruising speeds, and all that sort of thing. Or just page through some official safety statistics that showed that more people were wiped out on the drive to the airport.

Or maybe she'd go back to pretending the plane hung in the air, safe on a great big hook.

Oh, this was silly. She was a grown woman, flying across Europe, on her way to the miniscule kingdom of Korosol, where she would be crowned queen—of a country she was afraid to look down on as she soared above it, for fear she might meet it nose first in a tin sausage.

Kelly laughed. Giggled, actually. All right, maybe that last glass of wine had been enough for her to see the absurdity of her situation. Kelly Carradigne, heir to the throne of Korosol, and on her way to her coronation. Pretty classy stuff for a girl who hadn't even gone to her senior prom.

"You find our mountains amusing, Your Royal Highness?"

Oh, damn. Kelly turned away from the porthole window and looked across the small plane at the man who would be any romantic girl's dream.

Thing was, Kelly Carradigne wasn't a romantic

girl, and Sir Devon Montcalm, captain of the royal guard, only looked like a romantic dream. Once he opened his mouth, it was midnight, and the coach had turned back into a pumpkin.

But she wouldn't think about that, think about how attracted she was to this man who also drove her crazy.

So, what could she think about instead? All right, she had one. Did pumpkins grow in Korosol? Kelly didn't think they did. Because they probably didn't have Halloween in Korosol, or Thanksgiving and pumpkin pie. And there'd be no Fourth of July celebrations, or even a Groundhog Day.

She may as well be flying to the moon.

"Forgive me, ma'am," Devon Montcalm said with a nearly imperceptible nod of his handsome head. "I should not have addressed you without being asked."

Yeah. Remember that. Don't speak unless spoken to—and if you think I'll ever speak to you unless I have to, Captain Montcalm, you have a couple more thinks coming, buster. Because I don't like you. Except when I do like you, which is why I don't like you. You make me nervous. You make me want you to look at me as a woman. A desirable woman.

Yeah, that was going to happen...

Kelly returned his slight nod, pushed at her glasses once more, then directed her nervous gaze back to the mountains below the airplane.

Well, that was stupid, she thought, mentally kicking herself. *If he thought you were proud, or arrogant, or soon-to-be queenlike, that would be one thing. But the man probably thinks you're too shy or dumb or whatever to be able to string two coherent words together.*

He saw straight through her, she could sense it. He knew she was shy, nervous. He probably even knew that she wore glasses only to hide behind, not because she needed them to see.

So, was he laughing at her? Or pitying her? Boy, she hated him...when she wasn't dreaming about him.

Kelly turned away from the window again—did the mountains look closer?—and then cleared her throat as genteelly as she could.

"These would be the Larella Mountains, wouldn't they, Captain?"

"They would, ma'am," Devon replied, with yet another small inclination of his head.

It amazed Kelly how the man could go through all the motions of a loyal subject speaking to his soon-to-be queen, and yet still make her feel as if he were insulting her. He had to really be bent out of shape that such an unlikely, and unsuitable woman had been chosen to be his next queen.

She didn't blame him.

"Perhaps you could be so kind as to tell me something about them?"

"It would be my pleasure, ma'am," Devon replied, folding his hands in his lap. His very well-shaped hands, with long straight fingers, neatly clipped nails, and with a brushing of golden hair on the back of each hand. The man had the hands of a pianist, not a soldier. Not a royal bodyguard.

Pity he was here, instead of wowing all the folks playing "Chopsticks" at Carnegie Hall, and four thousand miles away from this airplane.

But she'd miss him then, so that wouldn't work.

"The Larella Mountains, ma'am, are actually an extension of the chain of mountains that—"

"Do you have to call me ma'am?"

"Yes, ma'am," Devon said, his expression as close to noncommittal as an arrogant man could make it. "When I first address you in any conversation, I address you as Your Royal Highness. After that, because the term can become cumbersome, you are addressed as ma'am. After your coronation, you will be addressed as Your Majesty, then ma'am."

"Ma'am. I'm twenty-five years old, Captain. Are you telling me I have to go through the rest of my life being called ma'am?"

She saw one corner of Devon's mouth twitch slightly. Ah, so he was human, and saw the absurdity. Either that, or he was happy to know that he'd be getting her goat every time he called her ma'am.

Probably the latter. Still, the half smile made her like him more, even as she felt herself becoming angry.

What was the matter with her? She'd always been so logical. Oil and water didn't mix, she knew that. Neither did love and hate. Well, nothing that intense. Like and dislike? That sounded better.

But it didn't explain her feelings for Sir Devon Montcalm, or silence her dreams at night.

Kelly lifted her chin, knowing her cheeks were growing pink, but felt just brave enough with white zinfandel on board to say, "I think, Captain, I would prefer it if you were to address me as Your Royal Highness at all times. Then, after my coronation, you may continue with Your Majesty. Ma'am, Captain, is henceforth...banished."

Then she ruined it all by looking across the airplane at him and asking, "I can do that, can't I? I mean, can I really do that?"

Any trace of amusement disappeared and the captain's hazel eyes turned to ice. "Yes, ma'am—Your Royal Highness. If it is your wish."

Sonofagun, Kelly thought, settling back in her seat once more. It was true. Power has its privileges. Except that she wasn't sure she'd ever get used to being called anything remotely "royal."

But it was nice to be listened to...especially when, to date, she'd never had anyone listen to her. She couldn't even get a real person on the line when she'd called the telephone company to ask about her bill.

Now she had a country. Her country. All hers. A country, and a lot of people who were her subjects. People who would listen to her.

So why did she want to have the next person who listened to her be the pilot, who'd she tell to turn this jet around and head back across the Atlantic Ocean?

Kelly closed her eyes and sighed aloud.

"Yes, Your Royal Highness?"

Kelly fought down the urge to growl, low in her throat, like a petulant tigress.

She turned her head on the small pillow she'd been offered earlier by the flight attendant, and looked over at Devon Montcalm, the glory and the bane of her existence.

Over six feet tall, with soft brown hair cut military short. Hazel eyes fringed with dark lashes. Storybook handsome. A by-the-book loyal subject of her great-uncle, the king, who had been knighted by that same king for his loyalty and service. By rights, she should call him Sir Devon.

The devil she would. She had to start asserting herself at some point, rid her mind of silly dreams, or else she'd be writing "Kelly loves Devon" in all her notebooks, then drawing silly hearts all over the page instead of working on her latest experiment.

"I didn't say anything, Captain. I...I yawned."

"Yes, Your Royal Highness. Forgive me. I just thought perhaps you might like me to tell you more about Korosol before we land in Korosol la Vella. That is the capital city of our country, Your Royal Highness, and the royal palace is located there."

"Difficult as this might be for you to believe, Captain, I had already assumed that the royal palace would be located in the capital city of the country. Logic is logic, be it the scientific lab or geography, and I am very logical. Ask anyone."

"Yes, Your Royal Highness."

He was laughing at her. Without cracking a smile, the miserable, arrogant man was laughing at her. Each time he said "Your Royal Highness" he made it sound like an insult, a joke at her expense.

Well, at least both of them wouldn't be writing "Kelly loves Devon" in their notebooks....

"You're less than pleased that my great-uncle, the

king, has named me his successor, aren't you, Captain?''

"It is my duty and my pleasure to serve my king, Your Royal Highness.''

"Oh...bullfeathers,'' Kelly said in exasperation as he avoided answering her.

She was currently reading a historical novel set in the American West—ergo the "bullfeathers." If she hadn't finished with the historical novel set in England last night, she might have said "bloody hell."

That would have gotten him!

Kelly put one hand to her cheek, the cheek closest to the captain, who would see the embarrassed color run under her skin. "Captain...could we please be honest with each other? If only until this plane lands?''

"Wherever and whenever, I perform as commanded, Your Royal Highness.''

"You perform like you've got a key stuck in your back!'' Kelly said, losing her temper. Look what he'd made her do. She *never* lost her temper. Well, not often. "Look, Captain, I'm here, I'm staying, and you'll have to get used to it. I'll have to get used to it.''

"You could have refused,'' Devon said coldly. "Everyone else did. I never saw so many people who could refuse a crown and a title.''

"Everyone else being my cousins? My brother? Yes, they all refused. I'm the scraping-the-bottom-of-the-barrel princess, aren't I?''

Now there was a book title—*The Scraping-the-Bottom-of-the-Barrel Princess.*

Catchy title. She'd read the book.

"It is not my place, Your Royal Highness, to question the choice of my king."

His remark brought her back to attention. She'd have to stop letting her mind wander, her imagination wander. Especially when Sir Devon Montcalm was around.

"Yet you do, don't you, Captain?"

"You want honesty, Your Royal Highness?"

"Yes, Captain, I want honesty. As long as I know, and you know, then perhaps we can call some sort of truce until I can convince my great-uncle that your, I'm sure, considerable talents are best employed anywhere that doesn't include having you as my personal bodyguard. Tell me, does Korosol have an embassy in Antarctica?"

Devon raised one expressive eyebrow. "What happened to the shy and stammering girl I met not so long ago in San Diego?" Then he belatedly, and pointedly, added, "...Your Royal Highness."

"The poor tongue-tied thing has had two glasses of wine and an air sickness pill, I suppose," Kelly answered honestly. "Besides, I'm shy in social situations, Captain, and always have been, even if I am confident in my workplace, with a belief in my own abilities. I admit that, because it would be pointless to deny a fact. But this conversation is far from social, wouldn't you say?"

"Are we then in your new *workplace* now, Your Royal Highness?"

"We're in a tin can hanging over a bunch of mountains, Captain," Kelly said, surprised at the bite in her tone. "What we say here and now has absolutely no relevance to whatever is waiting for me in Korosol la Vella, or how I will behave once I am there. So how about we clear the air? I'll start."

She started with a lie, on her end, but probably not on his: "I don't like you, Captain, and you don't like me. Correct?"

"I'm sorry you've taken me in dislike, Your Royal Highness, because—"

"Kelly! My name is Kelly. I need one person, just one person in Korosol, who remembers that, who makes *me* remember that. If you're going to be my shadow, then you, God forbid, are that person. Therefore, I need you to understand that I'm not a royal princess, or a queen. Those are titles. I don't want to be a title. I want to be a person. *Kelly.*"

"You, ma'am, are Korosol."

Kelly pressed both hands to her temples, trying to keep her head from exploding.

"No, Captain, Korosol, as you well know, is a country. I am a scientist. I am a genetic engineer, a microbiologist and a *person.*"

"I cannot forget that you are a scientist, ma'am. Your research has saved my king's life."

"You admit that grudgingly, Captain," Kelly said, lowering her hands. "Not because my uncle is benefitting from my research, but because you'd rather it had been anyone else in this world that had discovered a way to help your king."

"Our king, Your Royal Highness. Our king, who learned of your occupation and presented generous, anonymous grants to further your studies, your experiments, your research into the virus that has so weakened his royal majesty's heart. One hand washes the other, ma'am, and you owe our king, just as he owes you.''

"Which brings me to why I'm on this plane," Kelly agreed, sighing. "I couldn't have developed my theories, had my small breakthrough, without those generous grants, Captain, and I know that. I also know that my work is far from complete. My research has given my great-uncle more time, but not a cure. Not yet. That lies in gene therapy that will strengthen and rebuild every weakened heart. I'm only one small part of the eventual cure, but my work is important.''

"I agree that your work is ambitious, Your Royal Highness.''

"Ambitious? No, Captain, ambition has nothing to do with my work. It was, and is, the focus of my life. Remember that, Captain, as you call me Your Royal Highness and look at me as if I'm as super- fluous and annoying as an extra inch at the end of your nose—stuck there, but definitely not wanted. I don't know what Korosol expects from me, but I know I am not going to spend all my time making polite conversation at endless receptions, and cutting ribbons and patting little children on the head as they hand me bunches of flowers. I still have *work* to do, Captain, and I'm going to do it.''

He looked surprised. It was nice to get a rise out of the guy, who always seemed so cool, compe- tent...and remote. Still, it was better for him to be remote, than to have him realizing that she'd gotten a dumb schoolgirl crush on him. That could be real trouble!

"You plan to *work,* Your Royal Highness?"

"This surprises you? I don't know why."

"You're to be queen of Korosol, ma'am. You will have…duties…responsibilities."

"So much for thinking he might believe I can walk and chew gum at the same time," Kelly muttered under her breath, then said, "Yes, Captain, I intend to work. My great-uncle has already agreed to setting aside space for a fully equipped research facility for me somewhere on the castle grounds. Frankenstein built a monster in his castle, Captain. As I already have you, I don't need another monster, so I will continue the work I was doing in San Diego."

Devon Montcalm blinked. He actually blinked. "You're to be queen. You'll have everything any woman, any person, could ever want. And you want to *work?*"

"Sorta blows your mind, doesn't it, Captain?" Kelly said, feeling strong, and in charge, and pretty damn *good* about herself. It was a new feeling, but she liked it. She gave her glasses a small shove back up on her nose. This princess stuff wasn't all bad.

The captain was silent for some moments, clearly lost in his own thoughts. "I apologize, Your Royal Highness," he said at last.

"I…I beg your pardon?" Kelly wanted to tap at her ear, just to be sure she'd heard him correctly.

"I said, ma'am, that I wish to apologize. I…I've underestimated you."

Instead of being pleased, Kelly found herself growing angry again.

"Oh, I get it. You thought I grabbed the brass ring and figured I could spend the rest of my life jetting off to Paris to buy designer clothes and…and dancing all night and…and lying on some couch while somebody peeled grapes for me. You thought that I was nothing more than some royal opportunist? Admit it, Captain. Didn't you think that of me?"

"Yes, *Kelly,* I did," Devon Montcalm said just as the flight attendant approached and asked them to please fasten their seat belts, as they were on their final approach to Korosol la Vella Airport.

Kelly looked at Devon out of the corners of her eyes as she checked her seat belt—as if she'd ever unfasten a seat belt while flying in a tin can.

He'd called her Kelly. Very pointedly called her Kelly. Just as if she'd gotten through to him, and now, finally, he was beginning to see her as a person. Her *own* person.

Was this a good thing, or a bad thing?

"Will you do that again, please? Call me Kelly?" she asked him as the attendant went to the back of the airplane to fasten her own seat belt.

"I serve at the pleasure of Your Royal Highness," Devon said quietly. "Do you know what that means, Kelly?"

She shrugged, suddenly the nervous "social" Kelly again, because now they were talking man to woman, and she'd never done that very well—actually, she'd never done that even close to very well.

"I…I guess it means you open doors for me and

make sure I don't step in mud puddles, although you don't wear a cape so you can't really do the Sir Walter Raleigh thing. Frankly, Capt—Sir Devon, it all seems like a sad waste of your talents.''

"Yes, it would seem that way, wouldn't it," Devon said, staring at her. "You don't know, do you? His Majesty didn't tell you?"

"Tell me what?" Kelly was beginning to feel decidedly uncomfortable, which had a little to do with their swift descent into the Korosol la Vella Airport, and a lot to do with the look on Devon Montcalm's handsome face.

"Perhaps I should not say."

"Perhaps you should, Captain," Kelly said, holding her breath in the hope that would slow her suddenly pounding heart. "In fact, I do believe I am ordering you to tell me whatever it is I don't know."

"That, Your Royal Highness, would take years," Devon said, and his rare smile made her stomach do a small flip that had nothing to do with her fear of landings.

"Captain, I repeat, consider this an order. Why are you here? I know I was told you were my bodyguard, but I thought that was because nobody wanted to say you were a baby-sitter. What's the truth?"

He looked at her for long moments, then nodded his head as if coming to a decision. "All right... Kelly. One moment of candor, for the woman, rather than my next queen. You will, of course, remember Prince Markus?"

Kelly nodded. "Prince Markus? I've had so many

names thrown at me, it seems. My cousin—some sort of cousin, some sort of relation?''

"The son of King Easton's oldest son, the late Prince Byrum. The prince and his wife, the Princess Sarah, died on a safari to Africa last year.''

"All right, I remember now. The king had three sons. Prince Byrum, and Prince James, who left for America years ago, pretty much cutting his ties to Korosol, and Drake, who moved to America and died at least twenty years ago. Oh, and one sister, of course, the Princess Magdalene, who was my grandmother, although my father's aunt and uncle raised him in America, away from the stigma of his illegitimate birth.''

"Yes, and Prince Christopher was formally adopted by these relatives, making both your brother and yourself legitimate heirs to the throne of Korosol.''

"Jace was ninth in line, and I was tenth. As I said, the scraping-the-bottom-of-the-barrel princess. But Prince Markus? He was first in line after his father, wasn't he? Did he voluntarily give up his position of heir? I really should have paid more attention before I left San Diego, but I was so busy, packing up my lab notes and arranging for everything to be shipped here.''

"You mean when you were not scribbling formulas and equations on every napkin, bit of paper and a few walls, or hiding your head in a book? You paid attention to very little, ma'am—Kelly—or else you would know that King Easton has the right to pick any heir he wishes, and that Prince Markus, who thought he would mount the throne after his father died, clearing the way for him, is not a happy subject of the soon-to-be queen of Korosol.''

"Oh, wait, I remember now. Wasn't it Prince Markus who hired some horrible gossip columnist to spread rumors about everyone? About my brother, Jace, and his Victoria? I'm sorry, it must be those air sickness pills, they've clouded my brain. Jace would have torn Prince Markus apart piece by piece, if he'd found him. But he returned to Europe, didn't he? Will he be in Korosol?''

"I doubt he'd be anywhere else, ma'am.''

"Oh, joy, we're back to ma'am,'' Kelly said on a sigh. "I take it we're getting very serious here?''

"Prince Markus is, in my opinion, not a well man. He is a man twisted by hate and ambition. Ever since King Easton announced that Prince Markus would not be his choice to succeed him, and launched his search in America for a suitable heir, Prince Markus has been acting…strangely.''

"He's madder than hell, you mean,'' Kelly said, nodding her head. "Do you blame him?''

"I do, considering the fact that I believe, yet cannot prove, that Prince Markus had a hand in the untimely deaths of his parents.''

Kelly felt her blood run cold. Funny, she'd thought that was only a saying. But now she knew that blood could run cold, or all her nerves had frozen, or something. Did it matter? "Are you saying…?''

"I cannot say anything, Your Royal Highness, not for certain. But there are suspicions. What is more than suspicion is Prince Markus's attempts to discredit every candidate King Easton considered as his heir. Including your brother, through the woman he loves.''

''Yes,'' Kelly said, shaking her head. ''That was terrible, although everything is all right now. So now you think Prince Markus is going to come after me?''

''What do you think, Kelly?''

''I think he's going to have to dig pretty deep to find anything to exploit in my background. I'm as dull as a wooden spoon.''

''Child prodigy, graduated from college at seventeen, and now a brilliant scientist with several degrees. A woman whose life has been dedicated to science. Yes, there is little there to exploit, although the prince probably, as I did, indeed as the rest of the world must do, believed that you were gladly giving all that up to be a queen. The alternative for the prince, of course, if he cannot discredit you in some way, would simply be to remove you, who are the last remaining barrier to Prince Markus ascending the throne.''

''Re...remove me? As in *kill* me?''

''I see we've come to the same conclusion, Kelly—Your Royal Highness.''

Kelly slunk down in her seat, as far as the seat belt would let her. ''You were right, Devon,'' she said, unconsciously using his first name. ''I'm not at all suited to be queen of Korosol. I mean, it's got to be pretty hard to rule a country while you're hiding under a table...''

CHAPTER TWO

SIR DEVON MONTCALM, his alert hazel eyes hidden behind mirrored sunglasses, stood on the tarmac in the cold October drizzle of a gray Korosolan fall day, and watched as Her Royal Highness, Princess Kelly Carradigne accepted an armful of roses from three curtsying schoolgirls dressed in native costume.

The children curtsied and, God help them all, Princess Kelly curtsied back to them.

So much for the instructions he'd hastily whispered at her as they came down the small flight of steps from the airplane and he saw the ad hoc welcoming committee that must have been added to the official itinerary after he'd received his last listing of welcoming ceremonies.

Devon closed his eyes for just one moment, silently cursing both the idiot who'd deviated from his careful arrival plan and his future queen's lack of protocol, then became vigilant once more.

They should have taken another airplane, a commercial flight, one that would be attached to a folding umbilical that would provide safe passage directly from the plane to the terminal, without exposing Her Royal Highness to either the elements or the many advantageous firing positions for would-be assassins.

He scanned the rooftops of the terminal and a few hangars close to the terminal, and saw nothing, nobody. That meant that either his men were doing their jobs very well—or that nobody was doing their jobs very well.

Could Prince Markus have "gotten to" any of his men? Bribed them, promised them high positions in his new hierarchy when he became king?

Devon couldn't know. But he had to act as if he did know. He had to—to be blunt about the thing—behave in a completely paranoid way, as if there were a bogeyman hiding behind every corner, ready to leap out and strike.

Her Royal Highness was still smiling at the little girls with the flowers in their hair when Devon grabbed her elbow and said, gruffly, "I thought you didn't want to do this sort of thing, Your Royal Highness," as he came close to pushing her forward, toward the terminal.

"But they're so sweet," Her Royal Highness explained, looking back over her shoulder at the giggling schoolgirls—even waving at them. "But I am getting wet."

"I know. I could have held an umbrella over your head, but I find there's more firepower in keeping my hands free to reach my Beretta."

Her green eyes grew wide. "Your—? Your *gun?* You're carrying a *gun?*"

"No, a peashooter. I especially like wadded-up spitballs for ammunition," Devon said sarcastically as he curtly motioned for one of his men to hold open the doors, then escorted his princess inside the small, one-story terminal. "Of course I'm carrying a gun."

"But…but we were on an airplane."

"A private jet, Your Royal Highness, and property of Korosol. As the captain of the royal guard, I have a few privileges. They even give me *real* ammunition."

"Well, good for you," she said, pulling her arm free of his grasp before looking at her surroundings. "Oh, there's more people in here. And more flowers."

"Korosol is known for its flowers, Your Royal Highness," Devon told her, his alert gaze still scanning the crowd, looking for anyone who seemed nervous, or too intent…or even anybody smiling too widely. Anyone. Prince Markus could have hired anyone.

"Since we seem to have left Kelly and Devon on the plane, go back to ma'am, please. You were right, Your Royal Highness is too long."

"Yes, I do believe that's what I said, ma'am," Devon grumbled as he took hold of her elbow once more, expertly guiding her toward the knot of dignitaries here to welcome their next monarch.

Along with the dignitaries, there were several photographers, all snapping photographs and yelling at Kelly to look this way, look that way, wave.

Devon wouldn't be surprised if one of the pushy photographers asked her to sit up and beg, or catch a ball in her teeth. He hated the media.

"Who are all these people?" Kelly asked, speaking out of the corner of her mouth as flashes lit up the small terminal. "Please don't tell me they're all relatives."

"These are various ministers of the royal council, ma'am, and their wives. Please keep smiling, and allow me to make the introductions. And don't curtsy, for God's sake. Nod. Just a small, regal nod, and a smile and handshake. Now, let's go. I want to get you out of here as soon as possible."

"Oh, you can count on that, Captain. I also want to get through this greeting stuff quickly. I...I need to use...to use the facilities."

Devon blinked, completely nonplused by her statement—as well as entranced by the embarrassed color that had run into her cheeks.

She needed a *bathroom?* How the hell was he supposed to handle *that?* Being bodyguard to King Easton was one thing, but there was no way he could follow the princess into the nearest ladies' room.

He called over one of his men, told him to get the photographers and reporters out of the terminal. The last thing anyone needed was to see front page photographs of the new royal princess heading into the ladies' room.

Didn't the damned woman know any of this, *sense* any of this? From now on, her every move would be photographed, commented on. Judged.

And he was supposed to protect her—both her royal person and her reputation. How was he going to do that when she curtsied to children and used public rest rooms?

Still slightly distracted, Devon led Kelly down the long line of dignitaries, rushing through the remainder of the introductions as he cudgeled his brain for a way around his latest dilemma.

That's when he spied Miriam Kerr, King Easton's goddaughter.

Miriam had been in San Diego, tutoring Prince Jace when it was thought he'd be the heir, but she'd flown back to Korosol weeks earlier.

Now she was here, at the airport, and Devon had never before been so grateful to see her.

"You remember Miriam Kerr, ma'am?" he asked Kelly as they finally got to the end of the line, where Miriam, as a daughter of one of King Easton's royal advisors, but not royalty herself, waited.

"No, I'm very bad with names. I really can't remember if…oh, wait, yes I do. Hello, Ms. Kerr."

"Your Royal Highness," Miriam said, dropping into a flawless curtsy.

"Miriam," Devon said quietly, "Her Royal Highness has need of…the facilities."

Miriam looked at Devon, her light hazel eyes twinkling for a moment, acknowledging the fact that she knew how uncomfortable the captain of the royal guard was in telling her what Kelly Carradigne needed.

"I see. What a dilemma this must pose for you, Captain." She turned to Kelly. "This is, I'm afraid, quite a small airport, ma'am, and there are no private lounges. However, if you were to follow me?"

"I'd be grateful," Kelly said. "I never leave my seat while on an airplane, you understand, so I definitely need to…freshen up."

Devon motioned for another of his men to deal

with the dignitaries who had come not only to see and greet their next queen, but to listen to her speech—which they certainly were not going to hear—and quickly joined Kelly and Miriam as they walked through the small concourse.

"First, Miriam, I'd like you to enter the facilities and ask anyone inside to please leave."

"You're kidding, right? You want her to go scope out the bathroom?" Kelly asked him, shaking her head as she clumsily juggled at least five bouquets in her arms.

"No, ma'am, I'm most definitely not…kidding. Miriam? If you'd please? Once you've asked anyone inside to leave, I'll go in, secure the area."

"Secure the area? It's a *bathroom!* Oh, this is stupid," Kelly said. Then, before Devon could react, she shoved the flowers at him and pushed her way into the public rest room ahead of Miriam.

"I guess she really did have to use the facilities, Captain," Miriam said with a smile, then followed after the next queen of Korosol.

Which left Devon to stand outside the door, holding on to a bunch of cellophane wrapped, slippery posies, glaring at the world through his mirrored sunglasses and cursing his fate.

And then he smiled, just slightly. He really did like this woman. Even when she infuriated him.

Five minutes later, Miriam Kerr having joined them, they were safely in the bulletproof limousine and heading out of the airport, toward the royal palace.

Her Royal Highness and Miriam sat on the plush

burgundy velvet back seat and Devon rode up front, with the chauffeur. He spoke via walkie-talkies to the lead and follow cars, both filled with his handpicked men.

Devon took a deep breath and let it out slowly.

They had about thirty minutes until the motorcade pulled onto the palace grounds, but he finally was back on familiar territory, the streets of Korosol la Vella, and his own highly trained guardsmen were on the job, riding point, and completely trustworthy.

He had time for some small reflection, time to go over these past eighteen hours of travel, yes, but more importantly, time to sort out his feelings for Kelly Carradigne, heir to the throne of Korosol.

She didn't want to be queen. That much was obvious to him. Yet she had agreed, probably out of some sense of duty, or to help her brother out of a tight fix, or even because she believed she owed King Easton something for having financed her scientific research.

Whatever the reason, she had agreed.

And then she'd had the unmitigated gall to turn, overnight, from a shy little mouse to a pain in his neck who seemed intent on driving him crazy.

What was it she had called herself on the airplane? Oh yes, he remembered now. The scraping-the-bottom-of-the-barrel princess.

That wasn't bad, and was pretty much true.

Truer yet, Devon decided, would be yet another title: her royal pain in the highness.

She certainly was proving to be a pain in his—

A knock on the bulletproof glass dividing the front

seat from the passengers got Devon's attention and he depressed the button that lowered the glass.

"Yes, Your Royal Highness?" he asked when he saw her sitting on one of the jump seats, already leaning her forearms on the back of his seat as she all but stuck her face into his. She'd removed her glasses, and he was struck by the unexpected beauty of her eyes now that they were no longer hidden behind the huge, slightly tinted lenses.

Did she know how angry it made him to feel attracted to her?

"I was just wondering, Captain," she said, wearing that mulish expression he believed she must have kept hidden from her doting family for twenty-five years. "Does Korosol have fast-food restaurants? I'm starving."

Devon frowned. "Fast-food restaurants?"

"Yes. You know. Golden arches? Pizza parlors? Sub shops? Drive-through windows and instant service? All the saturated fat and gooey cholesterol you can eat, and at bargain prices. That sort of thing? Does Korosol have that sort of thing?"

"No, ma'am, Korosol does *not* have…that sort of thing. We pride ourselves on our cuisine, which is a mix of French and Spanish, with some fine Italian dishes stirred into the mix. We most certainly do not," he said, dredging up a memory of his visit to San Diego, "speak into the mouths of clowns to place our orders."

Her expression clouded. "Oh, that's too bad. I could really eat a hamburger right now. I barely ate anything on the plane."

"You were served finely roasted quail on the airplane, ma'am."

"A bird," she said, wrinkling her nose. She had the most *mobile* face, he noticed, just as he tried not to notice her huge green eyes, or the way one lock of her blond hair had escaped its decidedly sloppy bun, and curled at her chin. "An itty-bitty little bird. I couldn't eat a bird."

"You eat chicken, ma'am? Possibly turkey as well?" Devon asked, wishing she'd move away from the back of the seat, so that he couldn't see the slight sprinkle of freckles that dusted her nose and cheeks.

"That's different. I don't know how, but chicken and turkey are different. Oh, stop frowning, Captain. Will there be food at the castle do you think? I've adjusted my watch to Korosol time, and I know it's hours until dinner will be ready, but if I could just get a peanut butter and jelly sandwich or something…"

"Ma'am," Devon said, exasperation gritting his teeth. "You are the royal princess, the heir to the throne. Everyone at the royal palace—not the *castle*—is there to serve you. If you want food, you'll get food. If you're chilly, someone will run to fetch you a sweater, or light a fire. If you are bored they will offer different amusements, or even stand on their heads and sing songs to entertain you. Anything. And, as you seem ready to ask, yes, they will even prepare a peanut butter and jelly sandwich for you. Although," he added, smiling evilly, "someone will probably cut off the crusts."

"I'm being obtuse again, aren't I?" Her Royal

Highness said, frowning. "Miriam should be queen. She knows everything correct, everything proper."

"Miss Kerr will, at your pleasure, ma'am, be happy to serve as your lady-in-waiting, and will be delighted to guide you through the learning process as you take on your new responsibilities."

"Yes, so she said," Her Royal Highness agreed, turning to smile at Miriam, who smiled and waved to her from the back seat of the limousine. "She's very nice."

"And perfectly safe, ma'am. A native of Korosol and loyal to the Crown, which means she is loyal to you. I approve of the association."

Those huge green eyes flashed with temper, another emotion he was, sadly, becoming used to seeing. At first, the woman's eyes had been confused. At times, many times, they seemed to be totally detached from the real world, seeing things no one else could see. They rarely seemed to dance with amusement, but they were often heavily lidded as she avoided making direct eye contact with people such as the king himself.

To Devon, to everyone, she had seemed a quiet, shy, bookish scientist, half the time lost in a world of formulas and experiments, and the rest of the time hiding her nose in a book. Why, he'd heard that she often slept at her desk, forgot meals and had more than once been seen wearing two different shoes, so caught up was she in her private world.

But now, now that she'd said yes to becoming the queen, now that she was in Korosol, the dratted woman was showing signs of spirit—if not good clothes sense.

He wondered if building her a scientific laboratory might not be a splendid idea...if it would keep her occupied and without enough free time to discover that she had a temper, and wishes of her own.

Because a monarch, as Devon knew, for all his or her assumed power, had very little opportunity to indulge wishes of his or her own.

"*You* approve of the association, Captain? How...nice for you. What if I had said no, that I don't want Miriam tagging around after me, teaching me, pointing me in all the right directions?"

Devon answered without a moment's hesitation. "Then, ma'am, I would have sent a parade of equally suitable young women past you for you to pick and choose who you wish to attend you. Otherwise, Miss Kerr will be your primary companion and, if you will, tutor, but you will have at least four other ladies-in-waiting at your disposal."

"No. No way," Her Royal Highness said, showing a depressing penchant for American slang. "I didn't join a sorority at college, and I'm not having a sewing circle around me here in Korosol. I'll take Miriam, but that's all."

Devon decided to call her bluff.

"Yes, ma'am. I'm sure King Easton will understand...when you tell him. Shall I arrange an audience with His Royal Highness when he returns?"

Kelly's mouth, which had been slightly open, showing her lovely, even white teeth, closed with a snap. She stared at him, her eyes narrowed. "You think you're so smart, don't you?" she said.

"To employ an American phrase, ma'am, I do have my moments," Devon said, then watched as she moved back, slammed her glasses back onto her head, and practically *dove* toward the back seat.

He depressed another button on the console, raising the glass, and stared through the windshield, looking at the streets as the limousine passed through the city, heading toward the royal palace that was located on the opposite side of the city from the airport.

Now that they were nearing the heart of the Korosol la Vella, Devon saw many of the inhabitants and tourists standing very still on the pavements, watching the three-car motorcade, the central limousine carrying two small royal flags of the House of Carradigne on the front bumpers that announced that one of the royals was inside.

Men and women stood and watched. Children giggled and waved.

The future queen had arrived. Coronation to follow in three weeks, long live the queen, God save the queen.

Devon turned in his seat to see that Kelly Carradigne was now looking out the side windows, first waving to the people on one side of the street, then to those on the other side. She was smiling, but he was certain he could see the panic behind the smile.

In fact, if Miriam Kerr had not told the woman to wave—which he was sure she had done—he would have been willing to believe that the future queen would right now be sitting slumped in her seat, hoping no one could see her.

What a pity that she seemed to have picked him to be the target of the temper, and the willfulness she concealed so well from the rest of the world.

This, as far as the world knew, was an insecure young woman who hid behind her large glasses. A woman who scraped her blond hair back from her face in a severe and, frankly, rather haphazard and sloppy twist held together by an unflattering elastic band. A woman who might do research in gene therapy, but who herself seemed to have been cheated out of the usual female gene for fashion sense.

This was not a woman like the late Princess Diana of Great Britain, who could smile and wave and charm the most hostile audience.

This, alas, was a woman who could be all but tripped over before anyone noticed she was even in the room…when she wasn't tripping over something, because, on top of everything else, the princess was clumsy.

There was no *presence* to the woman. No style, no elegance…no *flair*.

Princess Diana had possessed flair.

Princess Grace of Monaco—another American, and, coincidentally, also with the name of Kelly—had possessed flair.

Princess Kelly, *his* princess Kelly, had all the flair of a…of a…of a peanut butter and jelly sandwich.

Her Royal Highness was definitely not ready for Korosol.

Was Korosol ready for her?

And, selfish as the thought might be, was *he* ready for her? Was he willing to give up thinking about her the way he had before King Easton's announcement had taken her out of his orbit and made her a royal? Unapproachable. Untouchable. Never, ever, to be his, because now she was Korosol.

So he'd done his best to dislike her.

He wanted to believe she'd happily given up her cloistered lifestyle in San Diego to be a princess, a queen. He wanted to believe she saw herself as Cinderella, gone to the ball. He wanted to dismiss her as a woman, a woman he'd been attracted to at first sight. He wanted to believe she was silly and selfish and…and…and, oh God, but she had beautiful eyes…

"Um…sir?"

Devon looked at the chauffeur, a man he'd known for years, as Maurice usually drove King Easton. "Yes, Maurice?"

"Well, sir, not that it's my place, but…is that really the princess?"

"Yes, Maurice, that really is Princess Kelly, Her Royal Highness, and soon to be reigning queen of Korosol. But you knew that."

"Oh, yes, sir, I suppose I did know that. But sir? Does *she* know that?"

Devon bowed his head, hid a wry smile. "Princess Kelly is American, Maurice. This could take some time, but she'll be fine. Miss Kerr will show her how to go on."

"Miss Kerr is a good woman, if young," Maurice, a man of at least sixty, said with a nod. "I used to drive for her father, years ago, when he was a royal advisor. The Kerrs are a good, solid family.''

''I'm glad you approve, Maurice. Tell me, have you been briefed as to the new security measures I've implemented as concerns the royal princess?''

''Yes, Sir Devon, I was given those orders directly from Major Howells. I didn't want to ask, sir, but is there a problem?''

Devon didn't get where he was by telling everything he knew. He would much rather know what everyone else knew. ''What have you heard, Maurice?''

The chauffeur shrugged. ''Nothing much, sir. Just that Prince Markus may have had some sort of…problem. That he might even consider doing something rash. Impulsive. We at the palace are to report any sight of the prince, or any contact. And then there's Winston Rademacher. I've heard that he's dead, sir. No one has said much to me, of course, but I've heard that he was shot, in America, while committing some sort of crime. Prince Markus and he were very close. Is that why the prince has become…rash?''

''That's possible, Maurice,'' Devon agreed, because it was easier than explaining how Prince Markus had ordered the kidnapping of Princess Lucia, at that time the possible heir to the throne.

Maurice didn't need to know that Eleanor Standish, King Easton's secretary, had been taken by mistake, and nearly killed. If it hadn't been for Cade St. John, Duke of Rawleigh, and his act of bravery, Eleanor Standish would be dead.

Instead, Winston Rademacher was dead, and Prince Markus had disappeared into the ether, hurried on his way by King Easton's public announcement that his nephew was not and never would be a candidate for the throne.

"Well, I haven't seen the prince, Sir Devon. We've all been watching, and nobody has seen him. His apartments in the royal palace are empty, except for his clothes, or at least that's what I've heard. Such a shame, sir. His parents killed in that sad accident in Africa, and now the prince having his little problem. I can't say as how I blame King Easton for removing the prince from the line of succession, but it had to be a blow to the boy."

"Yes, we're all heartbroken for him," Devon said without inflection, turning his head to the passenger seat window and rolling his eyes. "But he could be dangerous, Maurice. That was impressed on you, wasn't it? The prince could be a danger to Princess Kelly."

Maurice peeked at the rearview mirror. "That sweet girl? She wouldn't even know how to harm a fly, sir. Anyone could see that."

"It's not her harming anyone else that concerns King Easton, Maurice. So let me repeat. You are to follow the new directives without question. Princess Kelly is to travel only in this limousine—"

"Bulletproof," Maurice said, nodding. "I wondered why King Easton's personal limousine was ordered for her, sir."

"Now you no longer have to wonder, do you, Maurice?" Devon said, adjusting his tie as the chauffeur turned into a wide drive that led to the tall iron gates just then being opened for them. "Just remember that the princess also goes nowhere without me. Do you understand?"

"Yes, sir. But what if she wants to go somewhere without you, sir? She is my future queen. I cannot disobey her and hope to keep my position, sir."

Devon unclipped his seat belt as the limousine drew up in front of the royal palace. "Maurice, I suggest you remember this. You would be wiser to fear my wrath more than that of our royal princess."

"Yes, sir," Maurice said, putting the limousine into Park and grabbing his brimmed cap before leaving the car to open the door for the royal princess.

Devon watched as Princess Kelly exited the back seat, nearly tripping as she looked, openmouthed, at the impressive facade of the royal palace.

A princess? A soon-to-be queen?

So why did she look like she'd gotten lost from her tour group from San Diego?

If he were American instead of Korosolan, and not independently wealthy and only serving at the pleasure of his king, Sir Devon Montcalm knew he'd be inside the throne room right now, demanding a raise...

CHAPTER THREE

"MOM? MOM—HI! YES, YES I can hear you, you don't have to shout."

Kelly collapsed onto the chaise longue—was that what it was called?—and laid her head back against its blue-and-white striped satin cover.

"Oh, Mom, I don't know what I'm doing here," she said, looking around the large, high-ceilinged room. "I mean, I could fly a kite in here, not that I think that would meet with Sir Devon's approval."

Kelly pressed the phone closer to her ear as her mother, Annie, said, "You'll be fine, Kelly. And we'll be flying over for the coronation. When is that, dear? In three weeks? Is that definite now?"

Kelly nodded, then remembered that her mother couldn't see her from San Diego. "That's what I hear. King Easton will formally step down the morning of the coronation, and I'll take the throne an hour later. Oh, and I'm supposed to wear this *gown?*"

"Yes, I've heard about that. An ancestral gown and a fur-trimmed cape long enough that it takes four little girls trailing along behind you to carry it. Your father showed me some photographs of another queen of Korosol, one from the nineteen hundreds. I can't believe you'll actually be wearing the same gown.''

"The same gown, the same royal cape or cloak or whatever it's called, the same diamond and ruby tiara. And not only that. I change clothes a couple of times during the ceremony. Really. Can you believe this?''

"No, darling, I can't, and neither can your father. When Jace turned down the king's request, I thought it was all over, that the king would go back to Korosol, choose someone else. But then, the next thing we knew, you were declared the heir apparent. My mind is still reeling. It's like…like something out of *Cinderella*. You're Cinderella, Kelly.''

"Yeah, Cinderella,'' Kelly muttered, looking around the large chamber that was just one of the rooms in her "apartments,'' as Miriam called her suite of rooms. "Cinderella in Solitary Confinement.''

"What, dear?''

"Oh, nothing, Mom. But we've had this discussion. King Easton provided the funds for my research. Even if he had been acting selfishly, hoping to save himself—which I don't believe—he has done the world of medical research a great service that someday might benefit millions of people. When Jace turned down the crown to marry Victoria, the king was devastated, and I worried how it would affect his condition. I…I couldn't say no.''

"Well, Jace is still worried. He's afraid you've sacrificed yourself for him.''

Kelly looked around the large room one more

time. "Mom, I'm living in a palace. A palace, Mom. I'm getting my own state-of-the-art research lab, all for myself. My own staff of scientists and technicians. And the rest of it? Someone draws my bath, lays out my clothing every morning and evening. I think someone would cut my meat for me if I asked. You always said I needed someone to take care of me, make sure I ate, I slept. Well, now I've got that somebody. Lots of somebodies. Tell Jace to stop worrying, okay?"

"But...but Prince Markus. We're worried he could be dangerous. We've been assured that you're being well protected, but have they found him yet? I know we'd never read anything in the newspapers, because King Easton would just quietly have the prince put under the care of doctors or something, but he promised you'd be safe. Has he been found?"

Kelly considered this for a moment. Her mother was in San Diego, worrying. She was here, under constant guard. She could barely turn around without bumping into somebody walking close behind her, guarding her.

She crossed her fingers, a childhood trait her mother thankfully couldn't see. "Oh, didn't I tell you, Mom? Sure, yeah, they found him. Well, they know where he is," she said, amending her lie slightly.

"Oh, that's a relief."

Kelly smiled, happy to have made her mother happy. "So, see? Everything's just fine. But I can't wait to see you all when you come for the coronation. Think about it, Mom. Your little girl—a queen.

Now admit it, Mom, doesn't that make you want to giggle? Oh, wait—I think I've got to go. It might be time for another of my lessons.''

She put her hand over the receiver and looked at Miriam Kerr, who had just entered the apartment. ''Here we go again, huh? What is it this time, Miriam?''

''Today, Your Royal Highness, you are to learn the rudiments of the waltz,'' Miriam said as she curtsied.

''Mom?'' Kelly made a face. ''Sorry, Mom, but I was right, I have to go. I've been here a week, and all I do is either get fitted for new clothing or take lessons. But you won't recognize me when you get here, I promise. So, just to help you out, I'll tell you now that I'll be the one at the foot of the royal table, using the correct fork. I love you...yes, I know...give my love to everyone...see you soon...bye.''

She slowly replaced the phone, delaying the feeling of having broken contact with what she still considered to be her home. ''Well, the waltz you said, Miriam? I didn't know anyone still did that.''

''Oh, yes, ma'am,'' Miriam said, standing very straight, her shoulders squared, her hands held together in front of her. She had the heel of one foot pressed against the instep of the other, reminding Kelly of a ballet dancer. So graceful, so refined. ''You will be opening the ball after the coronation, ma'am, and that first dance is traditionally a waltz.''

''Well, when in Korosol...'' Kelly said, then sighed as she stood up, tripping over the edge of the carpet and feeling just like the klutz that she was. No ballet dancer was she! "Must I change again? I think I've changed twice so far today. I'm really kind of bored, changing my clothing all the time."

"No, ma'am, another change of clothing is not required at this time, although the ambassador from Greece will be joining you for dinner, so you will of course wish to wear one of your new dresses this evening."

Kelly felt the nervous quavering that was her near constant companion since arriving in Korosol. "The ambassador? He speaks English?"

"Oh, yes. As I've told you, English is generally accepted as the language of diplomacy now that the United States has taken such a large presence on the world stage, following England, another English-speaking empire."

"Okay, good, that's a relief," Kelly said, pressing a hand against her midriff as she took a deep, calming breath. "But this is unusual, right? You told me, Miriam, you even promised me, that all of this party-giving and dinner guests stuff is only until after the coronation. Because I couldn't do this sort of thing every day, I really couldn't. When everything arrives from San Diego, I want to begin setting up my lab."

"Korosol is a very small country, ma'am. For the most part, we are ignored by the world. It is King Easton's planned abdication that has drawn the world's attention. We have many, many dignitaries coming to the country to witness your coronation, but they'll be leaving again once the festivities are

over. Of course there will still be many visitors until
you choose your consort..."

Kelly, who had been busily trying to tuck in her
silk blouse, which always seemed to be coming loose
from the waistband of her skirt, stopped what she
was doing to gape at Miriam. "My what?"

"Your consort, ma'am," Miriam repeated, picking
up a silver-backed brush and smoothing Kelly's hair.
"You cannot have a king, because you are the ruling
monarch. But you will someday have a prince consort. A husband, ma'am," she added when Kelly
frowned.

"Oh, a husband," Kelly said, smiling sheepishly.
"I thought...I thought you meant I was supposed to
take a lover. You know...consort with somebody?
But you only meant a husband. That's much better."

Then she frowned. "No, it's not much better. I
don't want a husband."

Miriam gestured toward the door, and Kelly
started walking. Wouldn't do to be late for her waltz
lesson, now would it? For a royal princess, for a
soon-to-be queen, she sure had to take a lot of orders.

"But, ma'am, you'll most certainly wish to marry.
You do need to ensure the line of succession by
bringing Korosol together with another of royal
blood, and ensuring the line," Miriam said, opening
the door for her.

Kelly hated this, having people chasing after her,
opening doors, pulling out chairs. Anyone would
think she couldn't do things for herself, even walk
and chew gum at the same time. "Children, you
mean? Oh, I don't think so. I'm a scientist. Much as

I'd like a family, because I adore children, I really don't have the time. Especially," she added, smiling, "if I keep having to change my clothes every couple of hours, I won't have time to have children."

They headed for the wide staircase, Miriam walking slightly behind her...another thing Kelly hated. She always felt she had to turn her head to talk to whoever was with her, *see* the person she was speaking with. That invariably led to her walking into a chair in the hallway, or a doorjamb, or knocking over a potted plant.

The entire palace staff must think she had two left feet...or maybe three.

It was embarrassing. But Miriam had explained that everyone was to give her deference, which meant that they walked two or three paces behind her. Everyone, that is, except for others of her same rank...and the only one who fit that bill was King Easton, and he wasn't even in the palace. He was in London, having another small surgical procedure to adjust his internal pacemaker.

Kelly had another question for Miriam, so she stopped, just at the head of the stairs, so that she could turn, face the woman. And, hopefully not fall down the steps because she was looking over her shoulder as she spoke.

"This consort, Miriam? This prince consort? Where would he walk?"

"Behind you, ma'am, unless he was royal, and of the same rank, which is impossible," Miriam said, her cheeks coloring slightly, as if embarrassed by the royal protocol.

Miriam had said *royal*. She'd said it twice.

Sir Devon Montcalm was not royal. Not that she thought...well, maybe she had *thought* it. He wasn't royal, he wasn't a prince. That meant he was probably already ineligible to be a consort...and she'd never be able to think about him walking behind her, being less than her equal, even if he was eligible to be a consort.

Not that she'd thought about Devon in any sort of role. Of course not.

But she dreamed about it.

So much for dreams...

Kelly was upset, very upset. Now even her dreams were gone, and she felt very alone. But she pushed down her feelings and smiled as she said, "Oh, well, that settles it, doesn't it, Miriam? I would never marry a man and then make him walk behind me, any more than I'd let him walk ahead of me."

"Where would he walk, ma'am?" Miriam asked as Kelly turned, began her descent to the black-and-white marble-floored foyer.

"Next to me, Miriam," Kelly said, then realized that when she said the words a mental picture of Sir Devon Montcalm immediately shot into her mind, the two of them walking down this same grand staircase, hand in hand. Equals. Lovers. Friends. Then the vision vanished.

She stumbled, grabbed the railing.

"Ma'am?"

"I'm fine, Miriam. I just had a sudden thought, that's all. So, where do we go for these waltz lessons?"

"The ballroom, ma'am," Miriam said, pointing to her right, so that Kelly preceded her through the foyer, to the long hallway at the rear of the palace.

That was another thing. The palace. It was huge. Really immense. Kelly had been given the tour, twice, but she still took wrong turns. And darn it if everyone behind her didn't also take that wrong turn, just as if they didn't know better.

She wondered what would happen if she inadvertently led them all into a bathroom. Of course, without the royal guard there to open the door, that probably couldn't happen.

Still, the idea did amuse her. There was precious little else that did.

"This way?" Kelly asked, remembering having seen a cavern of a room somewhere off to her right when she'd been shown around the palace.

"Yes, ma'am," Miriam said, deftly stepping ahead of her princess when they approached a wide set of double doors, throwing them open for her. She then stood back, giving another little curtsy, and motioned with a sweep of her arm that Kelly was to precede her into the ballroom.

All that was missing was a fanfare of trumpets.

Kelly stepped inside, marveling yet again at the thirty-foot-high ceiling decorated in a stucco frieze of chubby cherubs holding stucco ribbons attached to stucco bouquets of flowers. And then there were the chandeliers, at least ten of them. And the windows that soared from floor to ceiling.

"It's so *big*," Kelly said, then winced as her words echoed in the almost empty room.

"It's a ballroom, Your Royal Highness," Sir Devon Montcalm said from behind her, so that Kelly nearly jumped straight into the air.

She whirled around, to glare at him, waiting impatiently as he bowed in deference.

"What are you doing here, Captain? Shouldn't you be out somewhere, digging a moat? Boiling pitch in case Prince Markus tries to breach the castle walls?"

Miriam Kerr, bowed her head, biting her lips together—to keep from laughing, Kelly felt sure, which is why she liked the woman so much. She knew what was right and wrong, what was the proper protocol, but she was human enough to appreciate it when Kelly poked at some of the rules and regulations.

"I'm here, ma'am, to tutor you in the waltz," Devon said, bowing once more.

Kelly panicked. There was no other word for it. Her mouth went dry, her heart began to pound and birds were singing in her ears.

She looked at her bodyguard, the captain of the royal guard, her nemesis, the keeper of her maidenly dreams.

He was sinfully handsome, and he knew it, darn him. She was crazy about his military-cut short hair, his amazing hazel eyes. She would have had to have her nose stuck completely through one of her research books not to notice his fine, straight figure; so tall, and with such broad shoulders.

He had been great looking in civvies. But now, in his official uniform? A custom-made uniform, no doubt, that hugged his slim waist, its deep navy blue bringing out the golden flecks in his eyes—flecks that danced and gleamed just like the golden braid on his left shoulder, the discreet sprinkling of medals on his chest.

Sometimes the uniform made the man. This man flattered the uniform.

The man probably had his own fan club of little Korosolan girls who sighed when they saw him, and slept with his photograph under their pillows.

Realizing she'd been silent for much too long, Kelly turned to her lady-in-waiting and croaked, "Miriam?"

"Sir Devon is an accomplished dancer, ma'am, and an obvious choice."

"Obvious to you, maybe," Kelly muttered under her breath as she walked toward the center of the ballroom. She then raised her voice slightly and said, "All right. Crank up the CD player or whatever, and let's get this over with."

"That won't be necessary, ma'am," Devon said, gesturing toward one of the balconies overlooking the ballroom.

Kelly didn't want to look, but she knew she had no other choice. She sighed, then raised her gaze, and sure enough, there was a four-piece band, sitting at the ready in one of the balconies.

All right, not a band. More like a small string quartet, but that was bad enough.

"Miriam," Kelly said, motioning for the woman to join her. "I don't need an audience," she said out of the corner of her mouth, wincing when that echo thing took over again, carrying her words to the ceiling, and then back at her…probably passing by the orchestra on the way.

"I'm sorry, ma'am, I didn't realize—"

"Is there a problem, ma'am?" Devon asked, and Kelly discovered that, although she'd always been a fairly placid person, she would like nothing better at this moment than to see one of the chandeliers break loose and drop—*splat!*—right on the man's head.

After all, the man of her dreams should not be so obtuse, so unaware of her nervousness. Unless he enjoyed it.

"No, of course not," she said quickly. Too quickly, because she stammered out the words. Not at all princesslike. Definitely not queenlike.

But, then, princesses and queens didn't get silly crushes on the captain of the royal guard.

Or maybe they did, come to think of it. Weren't there a zillion scandals about royal kings and queens and their love lives?

Love lives? Oh, yes, certainly, she had a love life. Ha! She didn't even know what a love life was like. She could count her dates on one hand, and have her pinky finger left over. She'd never had a boyfriend. They're been no time for one…and no interest from the males, come to think of it.

That was her problem. She and Devon had been put together, stuck together. She'd never had male attention before, and she didn't know how to handle it. What she had to remember was that the man was doing his job…and that the man didn't like her. Their moments of honesty on the plane last week had proved that to her, and to him.

She'd told him she didn't like him.

He'd as good as said he thought she was a royal gold digger taking advantage of a sick and desperate old man.

They had nothing in common. Nothing.

And he had the most marvelous hazel eyes…

"Ma'am?"

Kelly blinked, realized she'd done it again. Twice in about three minutes, too. She'd gone off into her head, forgetting where she was, who she was with…just withdrawing into her own thoughts.

Some would call her eccentric, and blame her scientific mind. Compare her to Einstein or someone, describe her as the sort of person who falls asleep at her desk, forgets to eat, dresses in whatever's handy and has absolutely no conversation other than her work.

Was she that bad?

Oh, yes. Definitely. She'd always been that bad. Now she was being that bad about Devon Montcalm, as consumed by Devon Montcalm as she'd ever been with her work…and that could be dangerous. He had no right invading her mind, and she had no right letting him in, letting him take up residence.

"I'll just motion for the orchestra to begin," Miriam said, shaking Kelly back to her senses for a third time in as many minutes.

"Good, that's good," Kelly said, smiling brightly. "And then, when Sir Devon is through teaching me the waltz, I can teach him the hokey-pokey. That's the only other dance I know, I'm afraid. I learned it in nursery school, you understand, at the same time I learned my alphabet, and how to read, and began investigating long division. I devised my own calendar in nursery school, using Roman numerals, and showed it to my teacher. I was four, I think. After that, I never saw the fun side of school again.''

''That's so sad,'' Miriam said, looking at Kelly. ''I attended a private school in England, ma'am, but we had very many social activities.''

Kelly shrugged. It hadn't seemed important to her, not being a part of the ''in crowd,'' or going to dances, or having boyfriends. She had her accelerated classes, her college courses. Her books and test tubes and all the rest. She'd never missed what she'd never had.

But it all made what she had now so much more difficult. Interacting with other people was a trial to her. It was, in fact, only Devon Montcalm, and possibly Miriam, whom she felt she could speak to at all, be at all honest with, share at least some of her feelings…her fears.

''Ma'am, if we could begin now?'' Devon asked, holding out his hand to her. ''Unless you wish to have a further silent conversation with yourself…ma'am.''

Kelly gritted her teeth and looked at Devon's outstretched arm. ''Oh, very well.''

''Thank you, ma'am, as I do have other duties.''

''And what would those be, Captain? Peering under beds? Checking the mouse holes? Putting out an

APB for all princes not on the guest list for the coronation?''

Devon looked at her for long moments, then said, ''Shall we dance, ma'am?''

Kelly snapped her mouth shut, knowing she was so nervous she was saying stupid things, being obnoxious. Her own parents, her brother, wouldn't recognize her, wouldn't believe she could say the things she'd been saying to Devon Montcalm from the moment she'd stepped onto that jet and begun her trip into Wonderland, a plain little Alice who felt sometimes too small and sometimes too tall...and always too inept, too clumsy and much too frightened.

''I suppose, Captain.'' And then she did it again, said something sarcastic: ''Are you wearing steel-toed boots?''

What was wrong with her? She couldn't seem to keep her mouth shut!

''I'll need your right hand, ma'am,'' Devon said, still holding his left out to her. And still ignoring the fact that she was being juvenile, and petty, and probably had cheeks as red as fire, burning with embarrassment.

''Oh, yes, of course,'' she said as the sound of violins flowed over her, filled the ballroom. She put out her right hand, and he took it, gently pulled her closer.

But not too close. More than a foot away, actually. But she was a scientist. She knew how far an electrical charge could travel. It was no scientific feat that it traveled now from his hand to hers, arced through the air from his body to hers. Lightning struck with less force.

Could he feel it, too?

"Now, ma'am, your left hand holds up the skirt of your gown. You clutch the material gracefully, just at the point where your hand falls naturally when you lower your arm, then lift the material so that it drapes...flows...also quite naturally. I will place my right hand on the back of your waist, in order to steer you, if I may use that analogy."

He put his hand on the back of her waist, and the only analogy Kelly could come up with had nothing to do with *steering*. Capturing was more the word. Holding with silken bonds. The heat of his palm burned into her skin.

"Holding out the left hand, ma'am?" Devon prompted, so that she blinked rapidly, then raised her left arm as if holding on to the skirts of her ball gown. She probably looked as graceful as a hippo in pink tulle and tights, but Devon didn't seem to realize that.

"Now what?" she asked, wishing she didn't sound so breathless. Hold out your right hand, hold out your left hand. Sure, he'd told her to do that. What he hadn't done was to remind her to *breathe*.

"Now, ma'am, we waltz. Watch my feet, if you will, and then you can just follow me. You'll be going backward at first, ma'am."

"Oh, good, Captain. I can't even go frontward half the time without tripping over something," Kelly muttered as Devon began to move.

He counted as he stepped: "One, two, and slide

together for three, and one, two, slide together for three. Back with the right, back with the left, slide together…and step back with your left, your right, slide together, step back with your right, and so forth. On your toes, ma'am. Go with the music. Very good, ma'am.''

She kept looking at his shoe tops, concentrating. She was a certified genius, a member in good standing of Mensa. She could do this.

She did this.

For nearly ten minutes, they waltzed. She went backward. She learned how to go forward.

''And now, ma'am, that you've mastered the steps, we're going to turn.''

Kelly stopped dead and looked up at him. ''You're kidding, right? *Turn?*''

''Turn, ma'am,'' Devon said, and she saw the ghost of a smile twitching at the corners of his mouth. ''You'll continue moving backward, and then, after the one-two-slide-together-three, you'll step forward with your left foot and make a half turn with the next step, then slide together, get ready to go again. You'll step backward with your right foot for the next part of the turn, then forward with the next, constantly alternating. The effect is that we will be moving round and round as we go down the ballroom. Floating, as it were, ma'am. You can do this.''

''I'd rather recite the Table of Elements backward—in ancient Greek,'' Kelly said earnestly.

But his hand was at her waist, and he began to move once more, so that she had no choice but to follow.

Oh, she could stand very still, and let him dance around her, but she doubted he'd consent to sticking a rose between his teeth...

Kelly giggled. Her logical, scientific brain had gone silly on her, and she couldn't help herself.

Besides, the music was wonderful. Romantic, or at least she was pretty sure that's what most people would call it. Capital R romantic.

She moved backward, having pretty well mastered that part, and then felt Devon's hand press lightly against her waist as he guided her forward, and to the left, in a half turn...and then another...and then another.

She'd got it! Like Eliza Doolittle in *My Fair Lady* learning to pronounce her vowels, she had *got it.*

The long windows became a blur as Kelly and Devon glided by, keeping to the perimeter of the huge room as they twirled and moved and turned.

"I'm...I'm getting dizzy," she told him, daring to look up at him, not watching his shoe tops anymore because she could sense where he would lead her next, just as if they had some silent form of communication only the two of them could hear.

"Look into my eyes, ma'am," Devon said, taking her into yet another spin. "Just focus only on my eyes, and you won't feel dizzy."

"Oh, yes," she said, nodding her head. "There's a simple explanation for that. A focal point. Ice-skaters employ the focal point when they are doing complex spins, for instance. When a person concentrates on one single focal point, then the body believes it is much more at rest than it really is. I believe the scientific term for the phenomenon is—''

"Ma'am," Devon interrupted, pulling her slightly closer, then whispering, "Kelly."

She felt a shiver race down her spine as he used her name. It was the first time anyone in the palace had spoken her name, and she'd been here for an entire week. "Yes?" she asked him, her heart fluttering wildly.

"Shut up, Kelly," he said, then he grinned at her.

"Oh," she answered, feeling the heat rush into her cheeks once again. "I shouldn't be talking about focal points?"

"No, you shouldn't. You should be speaking of the weather, what a fine evening it is, how glad you are that everyone seems to be enjoying themselves. Oh, and turning down marriage proposals. We can't forget that."

Kelly stumbled, stepping on Devon's instep. "Oh, I'm sorry," she said, stepping away from him. "But I've already had this conversation with Miriam. I'm not interested in getting married. I'll be…I'll be like England's Queen Elizabeth the First. The…the Virgin Queen."

Devon smiled. "There's some speculation about that Virgin Queen title. But, Kelly, I think you'd better realize that you're not going to be another Queen Elizabeth. She fought wars, managed a huge kingdom. That's not why you're here."

"Well, no, not wars. I certainly don't want to wage wars. Who would we beat up? Monaco? Rhode Island? Or are we smaller than both of them?"

"And the succession, Kelly? Do you really believe Korosol can go though another trauma such as it has just undergone with King Easton's prolonged search? We need a solid line of succession, and that begins with you."

"In a pig's eye it does!" Kelly said, jamming her fists onto her hips. Her words echoed all over the ballroom. *In a pig's eye...in a pig's eye...it does...does...does...does...*

Kelly bent her head in total embarrassment, covered her ears with her hands.

Devon signaled for the musicians to put down their instruments, then waved them away, so that they left the balcony completely.

Kelly put down her hands and watched them go, taking that moment to tuck in her silk blouse once more, to push a lock of blond hair out of her eyes by tucking it behind her ear. How could she have gotten so messy waltzing?

She watched Miriam head for the doors, then stop, look questioningly at her, and then rather reluctantly continue walking. A few moments later, the double doors closed behind her, the sound of the latches falling into place echoing throughout the ballroom.

Kelly looked at Devon.

The captain looked at her.

They were alone.

And she realized that he wasn't playing "Your Royal Highness," or even "ma'am."

She was Kelly, and he was Devon.

Two people, just two people. Glaring at each other.

Now what did she do?

CHAPTER FOUR

DEVON WATCHED AS Her Royal Highness turned away from him and walked over to one of the windows, to look out across the gardens.

The woman was driving him crazy.

Look at her. Sunlight streamed through the glass, sending silver highlights into her blond hair...a crowning glory she abused by pulling it back into a lackadaisical knot, as if all that her glorious hair meant to her was that she had to do something with it to keep it out of her way.

And that profile. So pure, so perfect. She wore no makeup, not even lipstick. But her eyes were so green, her lips naturally pink...and when she blushed, her exquisite complexion seemed almost too luminous to be real.

To hear her brother, Prince Jace, tell it, his sister had rarely dated, rarely done anything but go to school and to work. She had no social life... Lord knows she possessed very few social skills. She might as well have been a hermit for all of her twenty-five years. She'd never been wined and dined, romanced and danced.

God. Were all the men in America blind?

She wore designer clothing now, and she wore it

with the same sense of "so what?" that she had worn plaid shirts and baggy slacks in San Diego. Clothing was something she had to wear, so she wore it, but it was obvious that she didn't *care* if those clothes were designer made or picked up haphazardly at a local thrift shop.

He cared. He cared that her new clothing had revealed to him that the perfection of her face was mirrored in the perfection of her slim but shapely body. What the plaid shirts and baggy slacks had actually flattered—in his opinion—was now glorified by silk blouses and pure wool skirts and couture dresses.

And she was oblivious to all of it. Oblivious to him, and his private thoughts, his impossible thoughts, his hopeless yearnings. His unending frustration that had been a part of him since first they'd met and spoken to each other.

He'd tried to dislike her. He'd tried very hard to dismiss her. He'd tried thinking of her as someone out for the main chance, grabbing the gold ring, taking advantage of a sick old man.

But that wasn't true, and he knew it. There wasn't a greedy bone in Kelly Carradigne's body, or a thought of malice in her head.

He watched now as her eyelids fluttered slightly, as if she was processing something inside her brain. She shook her head slightly, then sighed.

What was she thinking? Those green eyes, so deep, so full of secrets.

But what sort of secrets? Silly woman thoughts…or a new way to decipher human DNA?

She was a puzzle to him…one he longed to solve even as he knew he'd never be able to solve the mysteries of her. She was a complex woman.

He liked that. He, who had always thought he preferred uncomplicated women.

Did she have the faintest idea how she bothered him? Upset him? Kept him from his sleep at night, filled his days with questions…and then more questions?

That, he doubted. She couldn't know, because he'd been trained never to reveal, never to show his emotions.

Never to *feel*. Just to do, to act, to react.

And, dear God, how he was reacting right now.

He'd known from the beginning, from the first day he'd seen her, that Kelly Carradigne was different. Curiously different. Marvelously different.

Maddeningly different.

But she had to know all of what was required of her. Nobody had mentioned marriage to her in San Diego, probably because everyone assumed that she'd know that she had to marry, ensure the succession.

If she couldn't agree to that, if she wouldn't agree to that, King Easton needed to be informed at once, and other arrangements had to be made…although what those could be, he couldn't know.

He did know that a part of him gloried in the idea that she might step down…because then he could feel free to pursue her, as he never could once she was queen.

No matter what, they needed to talk. Talk openly, talk plainly, talk honestly.

All right, so he'd pretend they were back on the airplane that had brought them to Korosol. He'd be Devon, and she'd be Kelly. Protocol be damned.

He walked across the room, to stand just behind her.

"Kelly?"

She ignored him, continued to lean one shoulder against the wall and stare out through the glass.

"Kelly, please, this is already difficult enough," he said, stepping forward, so that he was now abreast of her, looking straight at her.

"See? See that?" she said suddenly, said accusingly as she pointed at him. "That's what I want. I want someone—everyone—to stand beside me. Not behind me. Not standing behind me, not walking behind me. Not bowing and scraping and…and making me feel as if nobody wants to get too close. Anybody would think I have something…contagious."

Devon shook his head. "All right, Kelly, I'm confused. Enlighten me, please. How did we get from ensuring the succession to royal protocol?"

She blinked furiously. "Miriam…Miriam told me that if I marry, my husband then would be the prince…prince something."

"Prince consort, yes. As is Prince Philip of Great Britain."

She nodded, furiously. "Yes, that's it. I've seen shots of Queen Elizabeth and Prince Philip. He walks a few paces behind her when they're in public. Sort of shambles along, with his hands linked behind his back.''

"Yes, that's correct. She is the monarch, Kelly, and he is her prince consort.''

Kelly shivered, then pushed out her hands, as if pushing away the thought. "No. No, it's impossible. I can't do this,'' she said, then walked away from the window.

Devon followed her, his king's loyal subject, trying to tamp down his elation at the thought she might not take the crown. "But it's only protocol, Kelly. It's the way it's been done for centuries. An outward act of deference and respect to Her Royal Majesty.''

She'd stopped in the middle of the ballroom. "Oh, I'm not *arguing* with it, Devon. I understand it, intellectually. Tradition is tradition. I'm…I guess I'm just too *American* to feel comfortable with it. For *me,* Devon. I can't be comfortable having my own husband walk behind me, or be all the things that would mean. So I won't marry. I can't.''

"That's it? That's your reason?'' Devon gave a short laugh, then scratched a spot behind his left ear. "You're kidding. You are kidding, aren't you?''

She shook her head. "No, I don't think so. I haven't had long to think about this, but I'm positive I couldn't think of my husband as anyone but my equal. And I'd want the world to know that, to see that.''

"Americans,'' Devon breathed, now shaking his own head. "I thought you all admired the royals.''

"Oh, we do, Devon, we do. I've always wanted to travel to England, to see the palace, to hope to somehow get a glimpse of the queen. We're fascinated by royals, as you call them. We admire them. I just...I just don't think I could do what they do.''

"You're a little late with that conclusion, Kelly," Devon said firmly, remembering his duty. "You've accepted the crown of Korosol. You've been named the next queen. All that remains to be done is the coronation. Except for that official ceremony, you are already queen in the eyes of Korosol, in the eyes of the world.''

"I know, Devon, I know." She wrung her hands together, and he felt so sorry for this sad little princess...and for himself, because he was sure of what she'd say next. "I'm not going to abdicate." She looked up at him. "I can't abdicate, can I? I'm not queen yet. But I can't withdraw, either, take it back, or whatever you want to call it. You know what I mean.''

"I know what you mean, Kelly," Devon said, taking her hands in his, because he couldn't bear to watch her twisting her hands together, looking so miserable.

She lifted her chin. "So I'm stuck," she said, summoning a weak smile. "Stuck in a royal palace, being waited on hand and foot. Doesn't that sound insane, when I say it? I mean, there are millions of little girls, all over the world, who go to bed each night, dreaming they could be a princess.''

"Every good thing includes responsibilities," Devon said, squeezing her fingers.

"And I agreed to those responsibilities. In exchange for my own research lab, and to help my brother, to help the king, who helped me so much, I agreed to those responsibilities. That doesn't bother me, Devon. Really. It's…it's the *royal* part that I'm having trouble swallowing.''

''Such as having your eventual prince consort follow behind you, in effect declaring that he is inferior to Your Royal Highness?''

Kelly sighed, nodded furiously. ''Stupid, isn't it? A month ago, if anyone had asked me, I would have said that I would never marry. Now, because of this succession thing, the world is waiting for me to marry. Hey, marry me, walk behind me. Doesn't that sound like fun?'' She made a face.

Devon tried not to smile. ''You could marry a king, I suppose,'' he suggested.

''And are there lots of kings hanging around the world right now, Devon?'' Kelly asked, not looking hopeful. If anything, she looked even more oppressed.

''Not that many, no, and I think they've all been spoken for,'' he answered honestly. ''Sorry.''

''Leaving who, Devon?'' she asked him, still allowing him to keep her hands folded in his.

Devon considered this for a moment, wishing she hadn't asked him. ''Well, off the top of my head, I can think of three princes—younger sons. Although most anyone with a title of some sort and a fairly good lineage would do. The rules haven't officially been relaxed, but simple practicality and a shortage of royals has allowed them to be bent in many occasions.''

"Anyone with a title?" Kelly looked into his face. "You've got a title."

"And even a few drops of royal blood, if we trace the family tree back far enough and squint as we look at it, yes," Devon said, and now he was finding it difficult to hide his amusement. "Korosol is a very small country, overall. Nearly everyone is at least distantly related to everyone else."

"So...so you'd be eligible?"

"Not as eligible or attractive to the populace as the princes who will be knocking on the palace door. To be frank, there would be many who might dislike the idea of the captain of the royal guard having any influence over the queen. It would seem as if you were nothing but a figurehead, and the captain of the guard, our form of military, Kelly, was now running the country. So, although eligible, in one way, I'm quite ineligible in others."

Then Devon grinned evilly. He knew it was evil, and was enjoying himself immensely at her expense. "Why, Kelly? Are you proposing?"

She pulled her hands free. "Don't be ridiculous," she said, turning her back to him. "As if you'd ever walk behind somebody you'd just shared breakfast with, someone you'd just seen brushing her teeth, or...or—"

"Or seen lying in bed beside me, curled in my arms after a night of lovemaking," Devon said, stepping up close behind her, whispering the words close to her ear.

She shivered, wrapped her hands around her upper arms. "Yes...that, too."

"Oh, I don't know. I think I'd consider the compensations. The rest is just tradition, ceremony. It only means something if the people involved let it mean something," Devon heard himself say, turning her by her shoulders, so that they were face-to-face once more.

What was he doing? Was he insane? This couldn't work, this could never work. For all the reasons they'd both stated...and because she was alone in a strange country and saw him as a familiar face she'd first seen in San Diego, the one person who, on occasion at least, treated her like Kelly Carradigne, and not as Her Royal Highness. That was all, nothing more.

Even as he wished for more.

He watched as she bit her lip, as she seemed to mentally digest what he'd said. Then she shook her head. "No. I can't see it. I can't *feel* royal. I'm Kelly Carradigne from San Diego, the girl nobody ever noticed, the girl who was glad nobody ever noticed. I can't be...be put on a pedestal. And I can't allow my *husband* to be the one lifting me up there."

Devon sighed. For a quiet woman, she had a spine of pure steel, and could be more stubborn than his horse, Pegasus, when she didn't want to take the fence he'd put her at while out on a run.

"You'll change your mind," he said, because there was little else he could say. "After all, as I think I've already tried to say, Kelly, anyone you marry will be aware of all the protocol."

"Like you," Kelly said, her tone challenging. "You'd be just fine with it all, would you? And, if you would be so fine with it, how come you've got that little muscle sort of twitching in your cheek?''

His hands tightened on her shoulders and he stepped even closer, turned her slightly. ''Do you know how much I long to shake you, Kelly? Shake you, or kiss—''

He heard the glass break an instant before he felt the pain.

He reacted before the pain in his shoulder became more than a surprise to the rest of him.

Within the space of a heartbeat, he was on the floor, Kelly trapped beneath him, and he was covering her with his body.

''What…what was that?'' Kelly asked, trying to catch the breath he'd most probably knocked out of her. She put up her hands, grabbing his shoulders…at which point he uttered a sharp, succinct curse.

''Stay down. Just stay down.''

She withdrew her hand and looked at it. ''Blood. There's blood on my—Devon, I think you've been *shot!*''

''Yes, that was my first guess, too,'' he said, more than just a little bit aware that he was lying sprawled on top of the future queen of Korosol. ''Don't move. The guards outside will have heard the shot, and they'll be here any moment.''

Silently, he cursed those same guards. No one was supposed to be able to breach the security of the royal palace. Nobody. Not a chef carrying a cake, not a plumber carrying a plunger, not a gardener carrying a rake.

So how in bloody hell did a potential assassin carrying a gun get within a thousand feet of the place?

Kelly began to struggle beneath him...her movements replacing the burning in his shoulder with another burning sensation, much lower on his anatomy, and one he shouldn't be feeling while he was sacrificing his body to save his future queen.

Some sacrifice. If it weren't for the danger, or the hole in his shoulder, he could stay here all day.

"Don't move, Kelly," he told her.

"I have to. You're bleeding all over me," she answered. "Besides, there haven't been any more shots. Whoever did this is long gone. Now, let me up."

"No."

"I said, Captain, let...me...up."

Devon raised his head slightly in surprise, and looked down into her face. She returned his look, her expression determined. Regal. It was an expression he'd seen in the picture gallery portrait of King Easton's deceased sister, the Princess Magdalene, and Kelly's grandmother.

It was all there, not just in the color of her hair and eyes. Those were purely physical resemblances. What he saw, what the world would see if it looked, was the flash and fire of a strong heart and a proud demeanor, one that brooked no arguments, that allowed nothing but her own wishes. No arrogance, but a calm certainty...whether she be wearing the crown, or lying on the floor in the ballroom, half crushed by the captain of the royal guard.

If she had been shot, rather than him, he wouldn't

be surprised if she bled blue. She could fight her destiny, rail against it…as could he when he was being irrational…but it *was* her destiny.

There was no sign of a frightened girl. He was looking at his future queen…whether she knew it or not.

They weren't Kelly and Devon anymore, as they had been on the airplane, as they had been a few minutes ago.

And they probably never would be again.

"Yes, Your Royal Highness," he said shortly, and sat back on his haunches, feeling the pain begin to roll over him in hot waves.

She got to her knees and began opening the buttons on his uniform jacket.

"That…that won't be necessary, ma'am," he said, trying to move away from her.

"You're bleeding, Captain," she said matter-of-factly, pushing the uniform jacket down his arm, exposing his bloody white shirt. She was as gentle as he remembered his mother being with a washrag as she rubbed it over his face—which wasn't very gentle. "It's necessary. Now just sit still, shut up and let me see."

He took her arm as she began unbuttoning his shirt. "Let's at least get out of the line of fire, ma'am. I don't wish to order you about, but I've been shot. I don't want to repeat the experience."

"Oh. Oh, of course," Kelly said, helping him to his feet. He went only into a sort of crouch, bent over at the waist, his good arm around her back so that she, too, was not standing up straight.

He went for the closest cover, which was the short stretch of wall between two of the windows, stopping only as he hit the wall, back first, and then slowly sank onto the floor, out of breath.

"Happy now, Captain? Now let me see," Kelly said, ripping at his shirt once more. She was like a swarm of bees buzzing inside his head, swarming all over him…and he couldn't seem to summon the strength to stop her.

She pulled him slightly away from the wall and inched behind him to examine the now uncovered wound. "So? Will I live?"

"I think so," she said, using his shirt to wipe at the wound. He winced, but he didn't groan. Captains of the royal guard didn't groan. Even if they wanted to.

"It's not your shoulder, by the way," she told him. "It's your upper arm, and there are two holes."

"In and out, good. I wasn't looking forward to having the surgeon digging in me to get the bullet." He looked toward the double doors, which remained closed. "Where the devil is everybody?"

"Giving us our privacy, I'd imagine," Kelly said, folding the bloody shirt and pressing it against the wounds. "You did order everyone to leave, remember?"

"But someone should have heard the—damn it."

"What?"

"I just remembered. I heard glass break. I never heard a shot."

Kelly sat back on her haunches and looked at him.

"Maybe it came from too far away. Someone may have used a rifle and a telescopic sight."

"If someone had used a rifle, ma'am, I wouldn't have an arm right now, or a voice to tell you that it couldn't have been a rifle. I'd be dead."

"Oh," Kelly said, her cheeks pale, even as she continued to hold the folded shirt hard against his wounds. "All right. A silencer. Whoever shot at me used a silencer."

Devon sliced his gaze toward her. Damn, she'd thought of that too soon. "Shot at you?"

Kelly nodded. "You stepped between me and the window just as the shot broke the glass, remember? Somebody was shooting at me. Maybe…maybe there's someone else who believes I wouldn't make a very good queen."

"Besides Prince Markus, you mean?"

"Besides *me,* Captain," Kelly said, then stood up as a set of French doors leading out onto the gardens burst open and four members of the royal guard raced into the ballroom.

"Help me to my feet, please, Kelly," Devon asked quietly, when the men stopped in their tracks, to look at him as he sat there, bare to his waist, being ministered to by Her Royal Highness, who had blood all over her hands and blouse. "They're already shocked spitless. Let's see how big their eyes get when you do that, all right? It is, after all, all this farce needs at the moment to be complete."

"This isn't the time to be silly," Kelly scolded him, then frowned. "Or maybe you've lost too much blood, and you can't help being silly."

"That's probably it," Devon said, wincing as he pushed himself to his feet, Kelly's arm around his waist. "Lieutenant Bateson, your arm, if you please," he said to the closest guard, who then rushed to assist him.

"One of the gardeners said he heard glass breaking, Captain," Lieutenant Bateson said as he supported Devon, who was beginning to see two of everything…which couldn't be good.

"Bullet," he said succinctly.

"Yes, Captain. We didn't know that at first. But when the gardener reported the noise, we made a check of the perimeter, then of the palace itself. Corporal Stevenson finally spied the broken window, sir. I'm sorry we were delayed, but we didn't know."

"Silencer," Devon said as they all walked toward the doorway, Kelly in the lead, wiping her bloody hands on what was probably a three-hundred-dollar skirt.

Miriam Kerr met them in the hallway, standing up from the chair she'd been seated in, and put down her almost ever-present needlework. "Your Royal Highness?"

"The Captain has been shot, Miriam. Is there a royal physician in residence? Does Korosol have 911? We need an ambulance."

Miriam looked past her, to Devon, who tried to gather his wits.

"No ambulance, Miriam," he said quickly. "I wouldn't mind a doctor, but no ambulance. And no word of what just happened leaves the palace. In fact, it didn't happen. Did it, Lieutenant Bateson?"

"No, sir," the lieutenant said, heading toward the foyer, and the stairs.

"That's far enough," Kelly said, stopping at the bottom of the wide staircase. "Carry him from here, if you please."

"The bloody blazes they will," Devon said before his brain remembered that he'd concluded that Kelly and Devon were gone now, and they were once more Her Royal Highness and the captain of the royal guard. "That is to say, that won't be necessary, ma'am. I can manage the stairs under my own steam."

"Lieutenant Bateson? I may be wrong, but I do believe I gave you an order." Then she added, "Please?" and Devon, lousy as he was beginning to feel, laughed shortly.

"Yes, Your Royal Highness," the lieutenant said, coming to attention even as he supported his captain's weight, and the next thing Devon knew, two of the guards had made a chair of their arms, and he was being ignominiously carried up the winding staircase.

"Miriam," he heard Kelly saying from somewhere in the distance, "the physician, if you please. A surgeon, preferably, because I believe the captain will require stitches. Inform him that he is to come prepared to cleanse a deep wound, and to stay here at the palace until his services are no longer needed. Now, where do we put him?"

"I…I don't know, ma'am," Miriam said.

"In that case, I do. Lieutenant? Have your men install the captain in the first chamber you come to.

I don't care who it belongs to, just put him on the bed. Miriam? Please, I asked you to phone for a surgeon. Oh, and please have someone bring me some boiled water, some clean white cloths—rip up some sheets if necessary. And two aspirin. I think I have a headache."

Devon smiled, realizing that Kelly was rolling over everyone like a steamroller. This quiet woman who swore she didn't have it in her to be queen.

Queen? Hell, she could rule the world.

Moments later, he was lying in a wide bed hung with red velvet curtains. "The Red Bedroom?" he managed to say as Kelly shooed everyone away and dumped a pillow out of its case, using the pillowcase to apply pressure against his wounds once more. "Ma'am, these apartments are always reserved for visiting royalty."

"So?" she asked, blowing at a strand of hair that had broken loose from her rubber band. "I hereby dub you king of San Diego, Captain. Does that make you happy?"

"You're nothing like you pretend to be," he said, looking up at her as she repositioned the folded pillowcase beneath his arm, then untied his shoes.

"How do I pretend to be?" she asked him, throwing one shoe on the floor after the other.

"Meek. Mild. Scared of her own shadow."

"Yes, that sounds like me," Kelly told him, pulling the covers up over his body.

"So what happened?" he asked, wishing the sensations in his arm would go back to the low throb he'd felt earlier, and not this hot, burning pain.

"Somebody shot at me, Captain," Kelly said, stepping back from the bed. "Somebody shot at me, and hit you. I'm *mad,* Captain. Do you ever get mad?"

"On occasion," he said, trying to smile.

"Well, I never have. At least, never this mad. Are you comfortable? I can get you another pillow." She looked toward the door. "Where is that doctor? I should have had someone call for an ambulance."

"No, you shouldn't have. Can you imagine what would happen if it got out that the captain of the royal guard had been shot while protecting the future queen? Not that I was protecting you at the time."

"No, you weren't, were you." Kelly bit her bottom lip between her teeth, and color raced into her cheeks. Suddenly, she was the shy woman again. "You were going to...that is, you *said* that you might...are you sure you're all right?" she ended quickly.

"Having never been shot before, I have nothing to compare this feeling with, ma'am, but I'm fairly certain that I'll be fine by tomorrow. I've just lost some blood, that's all. Everything still works, see?" He lifted his arm and flexed his fingers. "The bullet couldn't have hit the bone."

"It hit something," Kelly said, taking the pillowcase away, refolding it so that she had a clean side to press against the wounds. "You're really bleeding. Not pumping blood, because that would mean the bullet hit an artery, but you're definitely losing quite a bit of blood. I'm going to put a tourniquet on you. I know how, I think. Ten minutes on, then released for a little bit, then back on, alternating until the surgeon gets here. You're just losing too much blood.''

''Maybe that explains all the stars floating up there,'' Devon said, looking up at the canopy, amazed to see not only stars, but a dark sky. A very dark sky, that slowly ate the stars, so that there was nothing but darkness...

CHAPTER FIVE

KELLY DEVOTED ALL OF HER concentration to picking up the cup of tea without spilling any.

That, she instantly learned as hot tea sloshed onto her hand, was the ultimate exercise in futility. Giving it up, she shakily returned the bone china cup to its matching saucer, then wiped her wet hand on the fine linen napkin in her lap.

"Maybe later, Miriam," she said, smiling wanly at her lady-in-waiting, who had been clucking and fussing over her so much for the past hour that Kelly wouldn't have been surprised if the woman laid an egg.

"Perhaps I should have the doctor come see you, ma'am," Miriam said, wringing her hands together in front of her. "You have had quite a shock. A sedative perhaps?"

Kelly wrinkled her nose. "No, I don't need a nerve pill, or any pill. I've had a bath, I've gotten dressed and I've had some tea. Well, I've tried to have some tea. Now that you've gotten me to do three things I hadn't wanted to do, I need to go see Dev—the captain."

"He's resting, ma'am," Miriam told her, not actually moving to throw herself against the door, arms spread wide to keep Her Royal Highness inside the apartments, but looking as if she might just be considering such a move.

"I didn't think he was out on the palace driveway, shooting hoops with Lieutenant Bateson," Kelly snapped, then shook her head slightly. "Oh, Miriam, I'm sorry. I shouldn't have said that. I…I don't know what's come over me, really I don't. If my mother were here, she'd say 'shame on you, Kelly,' and make me apologize. I did apologize, didn't I?"

"Yes, ma'am, and thank you, I'm sure. The sedative, ma'am?"

Kelly folded her napkin, replaced it on the tray, and slapped at her knees before rising to her feet. "I'm not that sorry," she said, grinning. "No, I want to see Captain Montcalm. I know we've got electricity and running water and a private jet here in Korosol, but I need to satisfy myself that your doctors don't still use leeches."

When Miriam frowned, she added, "I'm joking again, Miriam. I've never joked often, so I'm probably not doing it quite right. Just bear with me, all right? Oh, and excuse me while I go down the hall and see the captain."

"Yes, ma'am. I'll attend you."

Kelly stopped, blinked. "You'll what me?"

"Attend you, ma'am. I should have been attending you in the ballroom, but Sir Devon seemed most insistent." She lifted her shoulders, let them fall as she sighed. "This is all my fault."

"Really," Kelly said, her hackles rising again. She was pretty sure they were her hackles, although they'd never really risen up and knocked on the door of her temper before today. "And how is any of what happened your fault, Miriam?"

"I…I don't know, ma'am, not exactly. But King Easton will certainly think so, when he learns that I left you unattended."

"I'm not a candle that might catch the curtains on fire, Miriam. I don't need to be *attended*. Besides, someone shot at me while I practiced waltzing with the captain. I know I'm new to all of this, but I'm fairly certain the waltz is for *two*, not three. You wouldn't have been anywhere near me when the bullet came through the window. King Easton is an intelligent man. He won't blame you. And, lastly, as far as the world is concerned, you *were* there. All right?"

"Yes, ma'am," Miriam said, dropping into a graceful curtsy. "Thank you, ma'am."

"Hey, think nothing of it," Kelly said, feeling a little drunk with power. Or maybe just a story or two short of the top of a tower of hysteria left over from touching Devon's shoulder, her fingers coming away wet with his blood. "Tomorrow, I may decree that there will be no classes in Korosol the day of the coronation."

"There is no school on the day of the coronation, ma'am," Miriam informed her as she followed Kelly down the wide hallway to the Red Bedroom. "Or two days preceding it, because of all the festivities."

"Darn," Kelly said, turning to look at her lady-in-waiting. "Well, think up something I can decree, okay? I've got to practice. Darn it!" She stopped dead, looked at the chair she'd just walked into, stubbing her toe. ''Miriam, if I'm going to be looking back at you when I'm talking to you, you have to be looking ahead of me, making sure I don't bump into things.''

''Yes, ma'am,'' Miriam said, desperately trying to control the smile that danced around the corners of her mouth. ''I'll remember, ma'am.''

''Good. Now, if you'll excuse me?'' she asked as the guard standing outside the Red Bedroom came to attention, his eyes nervously shifting to Miriam.

''Open the door, please,'' Kelly said, sighing. This really was tedious. She wasn't allowed to open her own doors, but the guards were still unsure as to whether or not she was to be allowed to go where she wanted to go…which meant opening the occasional door.

Still trying to tamp down the adrenaline rush that had overtaken her in the ballroom, Kelly resisted turning to Miriam to hold out her hand and say, ''Sit. Stay.''

Instead, she just quickly walked into the Red Bedroom and just as quickly closed the door herself.

''Devon?'' she whispered, slowly walking into the room, stepping carefully in the dimness, as if someone might have strewn marbles all over the floor. ''*Psst*—Devon? It's me. Are you awake?''

''I am now,'' she heard him grumble wearily, and followed the sound of his voice to the large, tester bed.

No wonder she hadn't seen the bed at first. Someone had put down the red velvet draperies surround-

ing the huge thing, then drawn all the matching draperies on the windows.

"You might as well be holed up in a cave," she
said, detouring away from the bed as she went from
window to window, throwing open the drapes so that
the afternoon sunlight poured into the room. "There,
that's much better. Now for the rest of them."

She walked back to the bed and reached up to
yank on the heavy draperies, giving them a mighty
pull so that one side slid back, all the way to the foot
of the bed, and she could see Devon lying there on
the pillows.

"If this were Nevada," she said, grinning at him,
"I'd think you were in a bordello."

"A bordello? You shouldn't say words like that,
Your Royal Highness. You shouldn't even know
them."

Kelly busied herself pulling back the remainder of
the heavy draperies. It kept her from looking directly
at Devon, who looked so defenseless, lying there beneath the covers, his chest bare, his left shoulder and
upper arm wrapped in white bandages.

"How do you feel?" she asked at last, perching
herself on the side of the bed.

"Ma'am, you shouldn't," Devon said, and began
struggling to sit up.

"Where are you going, Captain? Better yet—
where do you *think* you're going?" Kelly asked him
as he almost got into a sitting position, then fell back
against the mounded pillows once more.

"I shouldn't be lying down while you're here,

ma'am. Not that you should be here. Where's Miriam, ma'am?''

"Pacing up and down and wringing her hands in the hallway, I suppose," Kelly said, then sighed. "And we're alone, Devon. Call me Kelly."

"I...no, ma'am. I can't."

Kelly felt the first niggling notion that something had changed, changed drastically, since he'd announced that he wanted to shake her...or kiss her.

"What's going on?" she asked after a moment, wondering if she should get down from her perch on the mattress. Pull up a chair, maybe. Or leave the room. Leave the country.

"Nothing is going on, ma'am," Devon said, seemingly addressing a spot just above her left ear. "I have been shot in my arm, rather than my head, but it still has served to bring me to my senses. What happened...nearly happened in the ballroom cannot be repeated."

She looked at him.

He looked...adorable.

He looked a thousand miles away.

"What happened? I don't understand. I thought we were...we were..."

"I am to guard you, ma'am," Devon said, and his voice didn't come to her from a thousand miles away. It was more like a million miles away. "I failed this morning, failed in my duty, and now I'm out of commission for at least a few days, which doesn't matter because I'm sure King Easton will have me replaced in any event."

"But...but you were shot," Kelly said, trying to

understand. "How does that end up being your fault?"

He closed his eyes, sighed. "Lieutenant Bateson did some reconnoitering outside, and found where the attempted assassin had been standing when he fired. Inside the gates, ma'am. I set up security, and the man got through it. That's my fault."

"Yes, but if it was Prince Markus, he probably knows the palace grounds from his childhood. Maybe, maybe there was a secret entrance, or something? The palace is old enough to have had secret passages built into it, right?"

"Anything's possible, ma'am," Devon said, shifting slightly on the bed.

"Yes, it is," Kelly said as another thought hit her, chilled her. "The king isn't going to replace you, is he, Devon? You're going to ask for other duty."

He looked at her this time.

"It would be better, yes, ma'am."

"Because you wanted to shake me?"

"Because I wanted to kiss you," he said quietly.

"Oh." Kelly felt hot color running into her cheeks.

He reached out with his uninjured arm, took her hand in his. "Just this one more moment, and that's all, Kelly," he said, and his words may have been spoken softly, but she heard them as a threat. "I don't know how it happened, or precisely when, Kelly, but I have become the greatest liability you could have as long as Prince Markus remains a threat."

Kelly shook her head slowly. "I don't understand you. Why?"

"Because this is personal for me now, Kelly. My feelings for you are personal. I was and am prepared to guard Your Royal Highness, Your Majesty when the time comes. I am not prepared to guard Kelly Carradigne, because when I'm with her all I can think of is her. You fill my mind, and I do stupid things."

"What sort of stupid things?" Kelly asked, her heart pounding hurtfully in her chest. Was this love? How would she know? She'd never been in love, not even close.

He smiled, but it wasn't a happy smile. "I watch you standing at a window and can think only of how the sun lights up your hair, rather than the fact that you're standing, exposed, to anyone with a rifle and a reason."

"Oh," Kelly said again, bowing her head, avoiding his eyes. "I...I didn't realize."

"It wasn't for you to realize, ma'am," Devon said, and she could hear that he was tiring. The doctor may have given him a painkiller, and that could be making him drowsy. "I've put Major Howells in charge, in any case, because I'm going to be convalescing for a few days. I can make plans from here—even have the blueprints of the palace brought to me to check for that secret passage you'd like to believe exists. I can go over the security for the coronation and the festivities leading up to it. But I cannot be in your presence and be the captain of the guard at the same time. I can't put you in that sort of jeopardy, ma'am.''

''Kelly,'' she said. ''I can't put you in that sort of jeopardy, *Kelly*.''

He closed his eyes. ''I'm sorry, ma'am. I'm very, very sorry.''

''Yes, you are,'' Kelly said, getting up from the bed.

She had something…something almost in her hand…almost where she could see it, touch it. And she wasn't going to let it go because of Devon's sense of duty or whatever it was that was making *her* want to shake *him*.

''And you're a quitter, too. I don't think anyone has ever complimented me, all but told me he has a…has a crush on me, and then *quit* on me. It has been quite a day, hasn't it, Captain, and it's not yet supper time.''

Now Devon did get to a sitting position. He probably would have gotten out of the bed entirely, but Kelly was pretty sure someone had taken his clothing. ''I'm no prince, Kelly,'' he said, ''not by birth or by manner. I'm the captain of the royal guard, a soldier, and that's something I do very well. Something I used to do very well.''

''So you say, as you're quitting,'' Kelly told him, walking toward the door. Then she stopped, turned to look at him. ''I have that reception with the Greek ambassador or someone this evening, Miriam tells me, but I'll be back tomorrow morning, right after breakfast. Do you play chess, Captain?''

He pressed a hand against his forehead. ''What?''

She was fighting, and she didn't know if she was fighting fair, as she'd never fought before. But she also knew she wasn't going to lose...not without first waging that fight.

"I said, do you play chess, Captain? I do. I find it helps concentrate the mind, and it's good practice for anyone who needs to plan more than one move at a time."

"Yes. Yes, I play chess. I...I was captain of the chess team at school."

Kelly smiled at him. "Always the captain, Captain. Well, I've been warned. And so have you. We'll play a game of chess tomorrow morning, Captain. If you win, you can hide in here with your charts and blueprints and spreadsheets and security plans. And if I win, you'll continue to be my escort, the moment you're well enough to follow three paces behind me again, watching my hair in the sunlight."

"Kelly..." Devon gritted out, throwing back the covers to his waist.

"That's Your Royal Highness, Captain, until you figure out once and for all who we really both are." She smiled. "And I thought *I* was confused."

She got out of the room while her wobbly knees could still carry her, and leaned her back against the door.

"Your Royal Highness?" Miriam asked, rising from a nearby chair. "Is everything all right?"

"No, Miriam, it's not. But I think maybe it's going to be," Kelly said, heading back to her apartments. "Did you know, Miriam, that there's a saying in America? When someone does something that feels so right, or is someplace that feels so right, they might say 'I was *born* to do this.' Well, I'm saying it now, Miriam, for the first time in my life, unbelievable as it would have seemed to me a few hours ago. Miriam, I was *born* to do this!''

And then she ruined it all by bumping into the same chair she'd hit on her way down the hallway.

Ah, well, even a princess who has just come into her own, as both a woman and as a princess, could still have the occasional small mishap...

THE MANTEL CLOCK CHIMED out the hour of noon as Kelly sat back in her chair, watching Devon watch the chessboard.

They'd been at it since eight, and he had one move left.

He knew it. She knew it.

He sat across the table from her, a table brought into the room by one of the guards, a table with a chessboard actually built into the design of the top of it.

The chess pieces were wooden, painted and quite intricately carved. They had to be at least three hundred years old and priceless.

Her stained and bent chessboard at home doubled as a small tray to put on her lap to eat dinner from as she worked on her experiment notes, and the chess pieces were plastic. She'd bought the entire set at a flea market during college, for seventy-five cents.

It was a long, long way from San Diego to Korosol.

Devon rubbed at his chin with his right hand, his

left arm secured in a sling of navy silk that matched his uniform. Very natty looking, she thought, using her "princess vocabulary" for the fun of it.

He was so handsome. So very handsome.

She longed to hit him on his hard, handsome head, repeatedly, until he either shook her...or kissed her.

"Oh, come on, Captain, we both know you only have one possible move," she said at last. "Of course, that would expose your queen. I can understand your reluctance to expose your queen."

He looked across the board, glaring at her. "You're enjoying this, aren't you...ma'am."

"I'm not bored," she agreed brightly, raising her eyebrows at him. "I am going to be late for some appointment Miriam has scheduled, however. I think I'm supposed to be getting my hair cut."

Devon moved so quickly he almost toppled the small table. "No!" he said, then quickly coughed into his hand, controlling himself. "That is, ma'am, do you really think that's wise? Cutting your hair? Perhaps if you were just to have it...styled in some way?"

So this was power, Kelly thought, her heart singing. Not the power of a princess, or a queen. It was the power of being a woman. She'd felt it for the first time yesterday, having ignored its existence for all of her twenty-five years, and she liked the feeling.

Not that she'd abuse such a power...but until Devon figured out that he wanted her, really wanted her? Well, then he'd have to forget about his supposed station in life, and hers...and come and *get* her!

After all, she'd already figured out the rest of it, the parts that had bothered her, not that she was ready to share that with him. But figure it out she had. After all, she was a genius, wasn't she? She wanted him, he wanted her. And then comes love…

"I shouldn't get my hair cut, Captain?" she asked him, watching as he moved the piece they'd both known had to be moved. She'd sacrificed her rook, true, but sometimes sacrifices were necessary in order to gain the ultimate prize.

"It's not my place, ma'am," he said, and she could tell he'd rather be chewing shards of broken glass than saying the words.

"I believe you've already commented, with looks if not words, that you don't approve of my rubber bands."

"It's not my—"

"Oh, for crying out loud, Devon!" she interrupted, then giggled. "Whoops. And I was doing so well at this acting the princess thing, too. Let me try again, okay?"

She sat up straighter, squared her shoulders. "Tell me, Captain, if I had been Queen Elizabeth the First, do you think I'd have been the sort of queen that regularly called out *off with his head?*"

"Let's just say I'm glad I'm not Sir Walter Raleigh, ma'am," he answered, his smile turning to a frown as she moved her piece and said "Check."

"Interesting bit of history, Captain," Kelly said, because she'd spent part of last evening speed-reading about Queen Elizabeth the First in a book she'd found in the royal library. "Raleigh's widow carried his head around in a hatbox, everywhere she went, for years and years. She must have been a real hit at parties, don't you think?''

She watched as Devon tried not to smile, tried not to laugh, and failed miserably.

Satisfied, she sat back and crossed her arms in front of her, waiting for him to make his next move. His last move. From the moment he'd made his first move with his knight, employing the renowned Reti Opening, she'd known how to beat him. He was good, very good, but she hadn't planned on losing.

He moved, she leaned forward, made her move. "Checkmate, Captain.''

And then she stood up, brushing her hands down the sides of her skirt. Her palms were slightly damp, and she was nervous as all get-out, but she wasn't going to let him know that.

"My congratulations, ma'am. You win.''

"Thank you, I know. I'll expect you at the dinner table tonight, Captain. And tomorrow, after the surgeon checks you, I think I'd like to go for a drive. I haven't seen much of Korosol, now have I? I've looked at some maps, and I think a drive to Serenedid would be quite nice. I'd like to see the Mediterranean.''

"Kelly, I—''

"Ah, ah, Captain,'' she said, poised to take her exit…which was how she'd like to think about it, rather than to say she was on the point of fleeing before she lost her nerve. "I won, you lost.''

"This can't work…ma'am,'' Devon said, rising from his seat. "King Easton will expect you to marry a prince. Someone with an impeccable lineage. My mother was a commoner.''

Kelly lifted her chin. ''Is that right? Funny. So is mine, and I'm going to be queen. Go take a nap, Captain, you're looking a little pale.''

DEVON TURNED FROM THE window at the sound of the door opening to the Red Bedroom, and immediately bowed. ''Your Majesty,'' he said, then walked toward King Easton. ''I hadn't been told of your return, sir.''

King Easton, a man nearing eighty and yet looking decades younger for all his illness, shifted a cane from his right hand to his left as he pulled out the chair Kelly had sat on earlier and seated himself.

''I have this captain of the royal guard, Captain, who has told me that announcing my every move to all and sundry might not be prudent until Prince Markus has been…contained.''

''Yes, sir, that's true. But…''

''Your orders were followed to the letter, Captain, and I'm here, safe and sound. Well,'' he added, smiling ruefully, ''safe at least. I was very worried when I heard about the shooting, Devon. You are quite dear to my heart, you know. Do they give you many pills, Captain? I'm awash in pills.''

''No, sir, I've been fine without them, thank you, sir,'' Devon said, watching his king as the man set up the chessboard. ''I would be back at my duties now, if anyone would allow it. As it is, sir, I return to duty tomorrow.''

''Guarding my heir, yes, I know. You're doing a

splendid job, Captain, although I might suggest you consider ruining the line of that equally splendid uniform with a bulletproof vest? My grandson seems to have well and truly lost his mind, to try to assassinate the future queen when there is no gain for him in the exercise.''

''We can't know for certain that Prince Markus is responsible, sir,'' Devon pointed out, not because he questioned that conclusion, but because the king looked so sad.

''We also can't know for certain that he murdered my son and his wife—murdered or caused to be murdered his own parents, by God. But we can be certain he attempted to kidnap my granddaughter, Lucia, in New York. Is assassination of a future queen such a large step for a patricide, a matricide, a kidnapper?''

King Easton placed the last piece in place. ''Sometimes, Captain, I want to live forever. And sometimes, I believe I've already lived too long.''

''Sir, I—''

''My grandniece tells me you saved her life yesterday, Captain. She was quite graphic in her description of how you threw your body into the line of the bullet. Not quite as graphic as Miriam was in describing how my niece metamorphosed from shy little caterpillar to magnificent monarch butterfly, but in all, I'm rather sorry I wasn't here to see it all.''

''Her Royal Highness took complete charge after the shooting, sir. Of the situation, and of me. She is a grand choice for queen.''

''Yes, she is, isn't she, Captain? You don't swim upstream against the world all during your formative years, battling to feed your genius while coping with an adolescence that is far from normal—imagine, Captain, graduating at the top of your college class at the age of seventeen—without gaining quite a bit of interior fortitude. Guts, I believe my American relatives would term it.''

''Yes, sir.''

''And then to take on the still male-dominated world of scientific research? A woman, still very young, standing toe to toe with the great minds of science, and daring to put forth her own ideas, her own opinions. That also takes…guts, Captain. The pity was that she didn't realize just how brave she is, what a marvel she is.''

King Easton looked at his captain of the royal guard. ''Until yesterday, Captain. I believe things changed for my grandniece yesterday. Quite dramatically. I think she knows who she is now, I think she knows what I saw when I looked at her, spoke with her, in San Diego. All these months of searching for the perfect heir, and there she was, hiding behind those glasses she doesn't need, thinking herself to be a shy and perhaps even timid woman.''

''She…she hasn't worn the glasses since arriving in Korosol, sir.''

''No, she wouldn't, would she? She's not hiding anymore. And, to hear Miriam tell it, she now seems not only to know what she wants, but is prepared to go after it, full force. Good luck to you, Captain, but I think you're waging a losing battle, against both your pride and your heart.''

''Sir?'' Devon said, sitting down as the king motioned for him to take the seat on the other side of the table.

"Oh, Captain, don't disappoint me. I know you believe you'd be betraying me by taking what you want when you think—wrongly, Captain—that you know what *I* want, for my grandniece and for Korosol. I saw a lot of things in San Diego before I finally shocked everyone and chose dear little Princess Kelly as my successor. One of them was the way you looked at my grandniece."

"Sir?" Devon couldn't believe what he was hearing. What had the king seen, and what did he want? Could he, Devon, believe that the king, his king, had seen the hunger in his eyes when he looked at Kelly? Could he, Devon, believe that the king, his king, *wanted* him to be Prince Consort, help to rule Korosol? Had actually *planned* for it?

"Pick your battles, Captain, pick them well. But a truly wise man never even attempts those he knows he is destined to lose."

"Yes, sir," Devon said, straightening his spine.

The king smiled as he leaned forward to advance his pawn. "Not that I'd consider a life spent with my grandniece a battle, or a loss—for you, for her, or for my beloved Korosol. Your move, Captain."

CHAPTER SIX

KING EASTON'S BULLETPROOF limousine left the palace grounds at precisely nine the next morning, accompanied by two other long, sleek black cars holding members of the royal guard.

Inside the limousine, the blond female nodded and waved to the guards at the gates, and her uniformed companion sat ramrod straight on the seat beside her.

Miriam Kerr sat in the jump seat, her window rolled down, so that her face was visible.

Twenty minutes later, a small station wagon also left the palace grounds, through the service entrance, carrying the driver—clad in work clothes—and his companion, also dressed in gray overalls and a peaked cap. On the side front doors of the station wagon were the painted words *Korosol Lighting and Fixtures*.

Kelly kept her head very still, but her eyes were dancing beneath the peaked cap as she looked left and right, taking in the scenery. "Now what?" she asked, feeling a little like James Bond, and a lot like one of the Three Stooges.

"Now we drive, ma'am," Devon said, and she sneaked a quick look at him. He looked good in the cap, good in the gray overalls. Fantastic in the black sunglasses he'd exchanged for his guard-issue mirrored ones. And he handled the driving neatly, using the knob attached to the steering wheel in order to drive one-handed.

"We drive here, we drive there," he told her, taking a turn with little effort, "and we watch the rearview mirror. Correction, I watch the rearview mirror. You just sit there, Your Royal Highness, and try to look a little more masculine and a lot less beautiful."

"You're just saying that because you hope I'll get so flustered I'll shut up and leave you alone," Kelly said, trying to fight the blush that was invading her cheeks.

She watched as Devon kept snatching looks in the rearview mirror as they turned left at the first intersection, right at the next one.

"Anything? Is anyone following us?"

"Not so far, ma'am, no," he said, stopping to allow an orderly line of schoolgirls in white blouses and plaid skirts to move through a crosswalk. "Some of your loyal subjects, ma'am," he said, nodding his head toward them.

"Oh, how cute. Is this their school? Yes, I can see the sign," Kelly said, smiling. She looked at the school building, then at the double row of large gray stone buildings lining the block. All so ancient, so beautiful. There was such a history here, and she knew so little of it. "I wonder if I could borrow one of their history books."

"You'll learn, ma'am," Devon said, smiling at her. "And not all of Korosol looks like this. Wait until we get to Serenedid. There the buildings are more Spanish in style. Lots of stucco, and red tile roofs. For a small country, we are quite diverse.''

Kelly was just getting used to driving along in the station wagon when Devon turned the vehicle into a building—well, he almost turned straight into a building. At the last moment, an automatic metal garage door slid upward, and then just as quickly closed behind them.

''Now, why don't I think this is the road to Serenedid?'' Kelly said, looking around the large, dimly lit garage.

''We change cars here, ma'am,'' Devon said, already unbuckling his seat belt. ''The limousine will be here at any moment, unless it was followed.''

Kelly nodded, pretty sure she'd seen a movie where someone had made a switch like this. She unbuckled her seat belt and waited for one of the royal guards to assist her from the vehicle, then unzipped her overalls and stepped out of them.

She smoothed down her pale yellow silk blouse and steel-blue skirt, then readjusted her ball cap that she'd put on her head earlier, pulling her ponytail through the opening in the back of it. ''There. That's better.''

''Yes, Your Royal Highness,'' the guard said, folding the overalls over his arm. ''My apologies, Your Royal Highness, for the inconvenience.''

''Oh, that's all right. It was sort of fun to—''

She turned at the sound of the metal door lifting once more, to see the long black limousine glide into the garage.

''Excuse me, ma'am,'' the guard said, following

Devon over to the limousine, to speak with the driver.

Kelly stood with her hands linked together, rocking on her heels as she looked up at the high ceiling crisscrossed with large metal pipes, then at the rows of stalls marked for cars, all of them empty.

"Where are we, Captain?" she asked when Devon rejoined her.

"In the garages beneath the ministry building, ma'am," Devon said, leading her to the limousine. "I've been assured the limousine wasn't followed, so we should be safe now. Good work, Lieutenant Winters," he said as he opened the back door of the limousine and the tall, slim blond woman stepped out onto the cement.

"Thank you, sir," the lieutenant said, then curtsied to Kelly. "Your Royal Highness."

"Yes, thank you, Lieutenant," Kelly said, finding it difficult to believe that Devon thought this beautiful woman was anything even close to resembling her. "If the limousine had been attacked, you would have put yourself in danger for me."

"My duty and my pleasure, ma'am," the lieutenant said as she was joined by the other passenger from the back seat, Lieutenant Bateson. Both headed for the station wagon, and Kelly stepped inside the limousine, to say hello to Miriam while Devon spoke with the driver.

"Are you all right after your adventure, Miriam?" she asked after sliding across the seat. She was getting better at that, too. Sliding across seats. Her skirt only hiked halfway up her thighs this time.

"Fine, ma'am," Miriam said, sighing. "It was...rather exciting, actually. But nothing happened. We just drove about the city, as if sightseeing, and then came here. Am I to accompany you and Sir Devon to Serenedid, ma'am?"

Kelly bit her lips between her teeth for a second, then shook her head. "Do you mind?"

"No, ma'am, I don't mind. Lieutenant Bateson has agreed to wait for me, and return me to the palace. He's...quite nice, ma'am."

"And cute, too," Kelly said, realizing that although it was just a snippet, she and Miriam were indulging in a little "girl talk." She'd never really done that before, which had never seemed strange to her before. But now she wanted to confide in someone, giggle with another woman, do that "talk about boys" stuff she'd never done as a teenager. "Miriam? Do you think Sir Devon...likes me?"

"I think, ma'am, that he wishes he could lock you up in a velvet cage until Prince Markus is found. I think, ma'am, that you're upsetting him very much. And, yes, ma'am, I think he likes you very much."

Kelly sighed. "Thank you, Miriam."

"You're welcome, ma'am. Have a wonderful day. Serenedid is a lovely city, and the day is warm enough to enjoy a walk on the beach, if Sir Devon can arrange it."

"And even if he can't," Kelly said under her breath after Miriam had left the limousine. "After all, how many times does a girl from San Diego get to dip her toes in the romantic Mediterranean Sea?"

"You were saying something, ma'am?" Devon asked as he joined her on the long bench seat.

"Talking to myself, Captain," she said, taking a pair of dark sunglasses from her purse and putting them on. "Are we going now?"

"Yes, ma'am. We should be in Serenedid in less than an hour."

Kelly snuggled against the soft cushions, feeling very satisfied. "And, on the way, you'll tell me about everything we see, won't you, Captain?"

"Every sheep and goat, ma'am," Devon said, and Kelly heard the amusement in his voice.

DEVON FELL MORE IN LOVE with each mile that passed, as he watched Kelly watch the world go by...watch *her* world, her country, go by.

Everything interested her. Everything excited her. She asked more questions than a room full of students, and listened to each and every answer. Listened, absorbed, committed to memory. He could tell, because she would then ask questions of his answers...her thirst for knowledge astounding.

She had no thoughts of a possible kidnapping, a possible assassination attempt. Or, if she did, she'd pushed them to the back of her mind so that there was room to gather up all the sights and sounds and smells—yes, somehow she'd talked him into opening the windows—of Korosol.

Thank God she wore a seat belt; otherwise, he would have to hold on to the back of her blouse, to be sure she wouldn't jump out of the limousine when they stopped to let a flock of sheep cross the road.

He did stop the limousine beside a roadside stand to buy her a large bouquet of fall flowers, which she all but shoved her face into, to catch the scent.

The entire drive to Serenedid, Devon decided, was an awakening for her.

Like a child. Like a kitten. Like a woman who had powers she'd not begun to understand, or use.

But, oh, she was learning!

"Oh, look, Devon," she said—for she had "decreed" that they were to be Devon and Kelly for the day. "Is that Serenedid? I see rooftops. Red ones."

Devon nodded. "Yes, we're nearly there. Serenedid is a major tourism center for us. As I said, tourism is our most important industry here in Korosol."

Kelly leaned out the window as the winding highway wended down a series of curves, all the while heading down, into the city of Serenedid. "I can see why. It's beautiful. Oh, look, over there—on the cliffs. Isn't that a fabulous house!"

Devon smiled. She was pointing at a large, sprawling white stucco house with miles of red tile roof, tall cypress trees and a winding staircase that went from the cliffs down to a snow-white beach. "You like it? It's yours."

She turned away from the window, to goggle at him. "Very funny, Devon. I know I'm going to be queen, but that doesn't mean I can point at what I like and have it magically be made mine. That must be from some other fairy tale."

"No, Kelly, I'm serious," he told her. "What you're looking at is the royal residence here in Serenedid. There's a royal residence in each of our major cities. Serenedid, Aladair, Esperana, Avion. Oh, and Montavi, which is located right on Lake Montavi. I think you'll like that one, although the lake might seem small after the Mediterranean Sea.''

Halfway through his recital of names, Kelly had sat back against the soft seat, overwhelmed by it all. ''Royal residences? In each of the larger cities? You know, Devon, when I think about all of this—and believe me, there are times when I really, really don't want to—I think I must have stepped into a fairy tale. I don't deserve all of this.''

''It's not all a gift, Kelly,'' Devon said, giving in to the impulse that had him taking her hand in his, giving it a comforting squeeze. ''Being queen of Korosol may have its perks, as you Americans might call it, but the crown comes with its share of responsibilities.''

''I know,'' she said, nodding her head, then blinked at him. ''What responsibilities? Honestly, Devon, I don't know. We're not a major power, certainly. We don't have huge banks with numbered accounts, we don't have a strategic seaport—do we? I mean, what *is* Korosol?''

He squeezed her hand again. ''It's home, Kelly. Your home.''

''Okay,'' she said, her voice small. ''Tell me about my home. Please.''

Devon depressed the button that lowered the glass between the rear of the limousine and the driver's seat and asked Maurice to please proceed to the royal residence. Lunch awaited them there, and the beach, and probably more of Kelly's questions, once he told her a little bit more about Korosol.

"All right, Kelly," he said, raising the glass once more. "I've already ordered the royal librarian to prepare a packet of information for you, which will be at the palace by tomorrow, as you do need to do some studying, don't you? But, in the meantime, I can give you some information."

"Begin at the beginning, please," Kelly said, removing her hand from his grasp. Clearly she was going into "student mode," and he'd better be prepared, because she was not going to be satisfied with generalities. Not with her scientific mind.

"All right. The beginning was over eight hundred years ago, when Korosol was carved out of portions of France and Spain and the first king was named. For a small country, we're quite diverse. We've got mountains, the Larellas, as well as the beaches we're seeing now. Our main source of revenue is the tourist trade, although we do export flowers, wool and other sheep products, and the wines of Aladair are gaining popularity throughout Europe."

"Interesting," Kelly said, wringing her hands in her lap. "But where do I come in? Am I one of the tourist attractions?"

Devon laughed. "To be honest? Yes, you are. The royal counsel and our parliament do most of the actual day-to-day running of the country, but you're still very important, Kelly."

"Riding around in an open carriage, smiling and waving at people?"

"I'd be lying if I said no, but there's much more

to it than that, Kelly. You are the head of the government, of the kingdom. What you say, what you think, carries a great amount of weight with it. For instance, King Easton devoted himself to improving the roadways and clean water delivery systems all across Korosol, and has set up extensive programs to benefit both the sheep industry and the wineries in Aladair. I'm sure you'll want to concentrate on your own projects, once you become more familiar with the country, with its needs.''

Kelly bit her lips between her teeth for a few moments, then smiled. ''What about hospitals? Could I tour them? I'd like to do that, I think. See how well they're run, if they're set up for elder care, hospice care. A pediatric intensive care would be wonderful. Oh, and education. How extensive is the science curriculum in Korosol schools? Are the labs well equipped? Are the teachers well trained? Are there up-to-date computers? Oh, and—''

''We're here, Kelly,'' Devon said as Maurice pulled the limousine up to the door of the royal residence. ''And that's probably a good thing, because I think you've just, in the space of five seconds, outlined enough projects to keep you busy for the next fifty years.''

''I did, didn't I? I'm sorry, Devon, really. It's just that…well, suddenly this is very exciting. Not the waving, and the being a public figure. But to improve the lives of the people? To educate? It…well, it makes all the rest of it bearable.''

''Bearable?'' Now Devon threw back his head and laughed. ''Do you know, Kelly, how *frightening* you can be at times? You don't want to play, you want to work. I think your New York cousins saw the possibility of assuming the throne to be an adventure, and possibly a burden. But you see it as a job, and the perks are being able to work hard to help others. The drawbacks are that you'll have to dress in beautiful clothes, live in a palace, preside at banquets and wave to the people.''

"You're making fun of me," Kelly said as Maurice opened the door.

"No, Kelly, I'm not," Devon said, holding on to her arm to keep her from leaving the limousine. "I'm amazed by you, impressed with you, and so damn grateful you said yes when King Easton asked you to assume the throne. Korosol will be the better for it. I will be better for it. So thank you, Kelly. Thank you.''

He watched as her cheeks turned a becoming pink. "Your thanks aren't what I want, Devon," she said quietly. "There, I've said it. I've said it, and now you'll have to decide what you're going to do about it.''

Then she turned away, exited the limousine, and began asking Maurice questions about the royal residence as she walked toward the carved mahogany double doors, as if she'd forgotten Devon existed.

"Thrown down the gauntlet, haven't you, my lovely princess, my beautiful queen?" he muttered to himself as he climbed out of the limousine and followed after her. "Little do you know how ready I am to surrender.''

THEY ATE LUNCH ON THE patio, which was a fairly mundane description for the wide expanse of flagstone that ran the length of the rear of the royal residence, and was ringed by a low brick wall painted white and decorated with every flower and potted tree imaginable.

Kelly carefully spooned consommé, then thoroughly enjoyed a salad of field greens and plum tomatoes, finishing with a club sandwich so tall she had to break it apart and eat it with knife and fork. When the brownie topped with vanilla bean ice cream and crowned with real hot fudge was placed before her she decided that being a queen could very definitely be fattening.

As she downed the last of the brownie, resisting the desire to lick the fork, Devon asked her if she'd like to go down on the beach.

"I think you know the answer to that, Devon," she said, starting to push back her chair even as a young man in black slacks and a white coat came up behind her to pull it out for her. "Thank you," she said, blushing. "I have to remember that I'm not supposed to be able to do that for myself," she said to Devon as they walked over to the edge of the patio and the flight of flagstone steps that led down to the wooden staircase to the beach.

"Yes, you are going to have to remember that," Devon said, walking about three paces behind her. "Serving you is a sign of respect, and you show your respect for your subjects by allowing them to serve you. Table."

Kelly, who had turned to listen to Devon—and had

kept on walking—quickly halted, glared at the low wrought iron table, and moved to her right before walking on. "I hate this part the most," she said, reaching the steps.

"Steps?" Devon asked, but he was smiling, and she knew why he was smiling.

"No, not steps," she said, then sighed. "Do you know how many black and blue marks I have on my shins from walking into things in the palace? Miriam says something, I turn to look at her, and *bam!* I walk into something."

"Perhaps if you didn't turn to look at Miriam when she speaks?"

"That's impolite," Kelly said, looking back at Devon as she said it, and darn near missing the top step.

He reached for her, grabbing her arm just as she began to topple forward. "Whoa! No more talking and walking at the same time, Kelly. You nearly fell."

Kelly took several deep breaths as she looked down the steep flight of flagstone steps, imagining herself tumbling down them, headfirst. "Well," she said as she tried to regulate her breathing, "that's it. That's really it. I've got to make a decree, or a law, or a—something. I don't want people walking behind me."

"I don't know how you'll do that."

"Neither do I," Kelly said, holding on to the wrought iron bannister as she navigated the steps to the wooden landing poised directly on the side of the cliff. "But unless I can figure it out, Korosol better get ready to crown somebody else, because this queen is going to be in traction. I mean, I've always been sort of clumsy, preoccupied, but since I don't seem able to break myself of turning to look at whoever is talking to me, I can't think of anything else to do but that decree…or law, or whatever.''

''You could decree that nobody talks to you while you're walking?'' Devon said, and Kelly didn't have to turn around to know he was smiling. Laughing at her.

''No, that wouldn't work,'' she said, starting down the wooden steps that twisted and turned several times to help break the flights, for it had to be at least one hundred feet to the beach. If he could laugh, so could she. ''Maybe I'll commission a necklace with a rearview mirror attached to it. That could work.''

''You could set a trend,'' Devon said, joining her at the bottom of the steps, the two of them now on the soft, warm, white sand. ''Later, if it catches on, you could add a horn, possibly some sort of early-warning system?''

Kelly put her hand on his arm as she slipped off her shoes, placed them on the bottom step. ''You mean, like some sort of sonar, that would bounce back signals, warning me as I approached a chair, or a potted plant? There. That's me. Now you take off your shoes. Oh, and roll up your slacks, because we're going in the water.''

''I don't think—''

''Devon, I'm standing in front of the Mediterranean Sea. I'm going into the water. Now turn your back, because I have to take off these panty hose.''

''Yes, ma'am,'' Devon said, turning his back, then sitting down on the sand and taking off his own shoes and socks. He obediently rolled up his pants legs.

''And don't call me ma'am,'' Kelly said, heading past him and moving across the beach—dancing across the beach—toward the blue, blue water. ''I'm not a princess today,'' she called back to him. ''I'm a tourist.''

Devon got to his feet and followed after her. ''Then perhaps you'll want a straw hat with a stuffed sheep figure on the brim? Or maybe a snow globe with a miniature rendition of the royal palace in it? No, I've got it. For you, and only you, Kelly, a sand bucket and shovel. Could you build a DNA model with them, do you think?''

''Probably,'' Kelly said, grinning. ''I was always pretty good with a sand bucket and shovel. When I was seven, I think, I built a pretty accurate depiction of the human heart on the beach at San Diego, as a matter of fact. My mother was appalled. Jace was building a sand castle, and she couldn't understand why I wouldn't want to build one too. Poor Mom. She wanted a little girl to dress in frilly dresses and she got a kid who built anatomically correct hearts out of sand and seashells. But she got over it. Oh, how warm!''

Kelly had stepped into the water that glided against the shore, rather than crashing against it in waves. She looked down, and the water was so clear she could see her feet and ankles beneath its surface.

She turned to smile at Devon, and saw that he wasn't joining her. What he was doing was looking at her, and his expression was so intense...so personal. She could feel the tension between them, feel it growing, blocking out the sound of the seabirds circling above them, blocking out even the sudden pounding of her heart.

So she splashed him.

She turned toward him, stepped back into slightly deeper water, and kicked out her right leg, splashing him from head to toe.

"No princess today?" he asked, wiping at his face with the sleeve of his white dress shirt. "No future queen?"

"Nope," she said, backing up a little farther, backing to her left, putting some distance between them. "And you're not even wearing your sling today, so you can't claim injury. Or, at least, not much."

"That's a pity, because I was just going to ask you to be gentle with me, an injured man."

"It would take more than a simple in-and-out bullet wound to bring down the captain of the royal guard, I'm sure."

"Yes, it would," Devon said, advancing toward her through the shin-deep water. "Although I will definitely claim I was delirious at the time if anyone asks me how I ever dared to do this—" he said, and then he kicked out his foot, splashing *her* from head to toe.

Kelly sputtered, shook her head, then turned and ran off through the shallow water, knowing Devon was right behind her.

This was what she needed. A few moments without having to worry about playing the royal princess, the royal heir. A few minutes of silly fun, of laughter, of carefree *joy* in being alive, of being young, of being in a fairy-tale land that featured white sand, blue water and a handsome man chasing her...

No, she hadn't got that quite right. She realized that the moment Devon put his hand on her shoulder and turned her around to face him. She didn't need just a moment of fun. She needed Devon with her, his hands on her, his body close to hers, his mouth...his mouth...

They just stood there. His hand on her shoulder, standing so close that she could feel his breath on her forehead, see the sprinkling of golden hairs in the small vee of his opened shirt collar.

He was dripping water. She was dripping water.

His shirt was plastered to his broad chest, and she could see the small bandage on his upper arm that had replaced the larger bandage of two days ago.

She didn't look down at herself, but she knew her blouse—that thin yellow silk—was also plastered to her chest. She knew because Devon was looking at her strangely, as if he was taking in the fact that, yes, she was real. She was a woman. She was a woman who wanted...who needed...who had hopes and dreams that had nothing to do with Korosol, but everything to do with him, with Devon.

"For a woman who swears she has rarely dated, had a very limited social life and experience, you certainly do know how to flirt. How to tease."

"Am I...am I flirting?" Kelly tried to swallow,

but her mouth was too dry. So her heart stayed firmly lodged in her throat.

"Um…and teasing. And so damn beautiful…"

Kelly's eyelids fluttered closed as Devon lowered his head to hers, pressed his mouth against her lips.

She just stood there, her arms at her sides, trying to take in all the myriad emotions that had moved in and taken control of her body. She wanted to laugh, to shout. She wanted to cry. She wanted to die, right now, because nothing in life, after this, could possibly compare.

Devon stepped closer, slanted his lips against hers, teased her with the tip of her tongue, and she realized that, no, she didn't want to die, because now it was all even better, more intense.

Devon's uninjured arm slipped around her, pulling her closer. She could taste the salt on his lips, smell the sea in his hair, on his skin.

The warm water of the Mediterranean lapped gently against their legs as they stood there, locked in each other's arms, holding on to each other, holding on to the moment, glorying in the moment.

Now she knew. She'd thought, she'd wondered. She'd hoped.

But now she knew.

An hypotenuse. A theory. Followed by experimentation. Ending in discovery.

This, she knew, was love.

Eureka!

CHAPTER SEVEN

DEVON MOTIONED FOR THE palace guard to open the door, then took a deep breath, squared his shoulders, and entered the king's private office.

King Easton was standing at the window behind his large, gilt-edged desk, his back to the room.

Devon approached the desk, remained at attention, his uniform molded to his body, his uniform hat tucked under his arm. He wore white cotton gloves, his shoes were spit shined, his gold braid gleamed on his left shoulder.

He felt like the rawest of recruits.

"I'm disappointed, Captain," King Easton said, still with his back turned, still looking out the window.

"Yes, Your Majesty. I have failed you. I have failed Korosol."

King Easton turned around, his hands still clasped behind his back. "Failed me? No, Captain, you've failed my grandniece."

Devon lowered his head. "Yes sir."

The king sat down behind his desk and picked up a newspaper. Put it down, picked up another. Then another. "You and my grandniece are above the fold in every newspaper in Europe, Captain, and several in America. One of the English papers ran a four-page photo essay.''

Devon looked at the newspapers on the desktop. He'd already seen them, but seeing them again still held the same shock quality.

He and Kelly standing locked together in the surf, kissing.

He and Kelly sitting on the sand, holding each other…and kissing.

He and Kelly walking together across the white sand, their arms around each other's waists, her head pressed against his shoulder.

Kelly putting on her panty hose…

How could he have been so stupid?

''I…I was so sure we hadn't been followed. But there's no excuse, sir. Instead of a telephoto lens, that could have been a rifle trained on Her Royal Highness.''

''Yes, Captain, that thought had occurred to me. What had not occurred to me was that my captain of the royal guard would so compromise my grand-niece's reputation.''

''You'll have my resignation this afternoon, sir,'' Devon said, his gaze still on the newspapers, especially one headline: Panty Hose Princess And Play Pal.

''I don't want your resignation, Captain. I want you to fix this.''

''Sir?''

''You heard me, Captain. I want this fixed. Can you tell me how you'll fix it?''

''Surely, sir, you don't still want me to—''

"I don't? Tell me, Captain, why wouldn't I want today what I wanted two days ago?"

"I've made a mistake, sir, a damaging mistake and a potentially fatal one. I don't deserve—"

"This isn't a reward, Captain. Nor is it a punishment. I want my grandniece to be happy. I want Korosol to thrive. A union between the two of you satisfies both my desires. I just don't need you satisfying *your* desires on the beach in Serenedid. Do you understand me, Captain?"

"Yes, sir. I, um, do you know if Princess Kelly has seen these newspapers yet, sir?"

"My grandniece is to be queen of Korosol, Captain. I do not baby-sit her. But," he added with a ghost of a smile, "as her brother—a very angry man, Captain—is arriving from the airport at any moment, I would guess that she will soon know, if she doesn't already. I believe my grandniece is in the solarium, doing a preliminary photography sitting for her official royal portrait."

"Thank you, sir," Devon said, then waited for permission to retire.

"Yes, yes, thank you, sir," King Easton said, shaking his head. "Oh, relax, Captain. I was young once, you know, several centuries ago. Love can do many things, including clouding the judgment from time to time."

"Yes, sir," Devon said, relaxing just a little.

"Here," the king said, rummaging through the newspapers until he unearthed an English tabloid. He paged through it until he found one particular photograph, then laid the newspaper on the desk and pointed to the photograph. "You see this smile on my grandniece's face, Captain? Do you see the look in your own eyes? They say a picture is worth a thousand words. This one speaks volumes to me, Captain. Look. Amazing what a telephoto lens can capture, isn't it?"

Devon looked at the photograph. Although somewhat grainy, the color photo showed Kelly smiling up at him, the wind blowing at her sun-kissed hair, her smile wide and dazzling. He was looking down at her, his face solemn, his eyes showing an emotion that hovered between devotion and desire.

"I like that my grandniece looks like this, Captain. Even more, frankly, I like that you look at her the way you do. And I thank God you're a man of honor, even when your heart is so obviously involved. These photographs, when you get to the heart of it, are of two young, beautiful people in love, and nothing more. In fact, they're quite tame, compared to some I've seen of royals from England and the like."

"Yes, sir, thank you, sir," Devon said, relaxing his shoulders.

"Don't think I'm patting you on the back, Captain. You've got a problem."

"Sir?"

"Ah, the young," King Easton said, almost as if talking to himself. "Captain, think. I know that's difficult, when one is hot with the first flush of love, but think. You already have my permission to ask for my grandniece's hand. But you also have these," he said, waving his arm over the newspapers on the desk. "And now your dilemma. How do you prove to my grandniece that you love her, when an intelligent young woman might think that you were only doing your duty? Proposing to save her reputation and not embarrass Korosol any further? And my grandniece is an intelligent young woman.''

Devon closed his eyes, his stomach suddenly cold, his whole body reacting to his king's words. ''She won't believe I love her,'' he said, mostly to himself, although it was obvious his king heard him.

''Precisely, Captain.'' King Easton came out from behind the desk, to place his hand on Devon's shoulder. ''The course of true love never did run smooth, or so some poet said. Good luck...son.''

Devon nodded, unable to find his voice, then bowed to his king and left the room.

KELLY SAT ON THE low-backed chair, turned slightly to her right, her back straight, her hands folded in her lap, looking out over the gardens.

Princess Magdalene, her grandmother, had been posed the same way, in this same solarium, wearing this same lovely ivory silk gown, this same tiara, this same royal purple sash over one shoulder, clipped at the waist with a diamond, ruby and gold brooch.

The portrait was in the solarium, set on a large tripod, and Kelly had marveled at it when she'd entered the room, then commented to the artist that there was no need to sit for a new portrait—they could just run this one through a photocopier. She and Magdalene were that much alike.

No wonder King Easton had chosen her when at last he'd met her, seen her in person. He must be suffering some delusion that she was his dead sister come back to life.

Still, no matter his initial reason, Kelly now believed her great-uncle had made the correct choice, that *she* had made the correct choice.

She belonged here, as she'd never belonged anywhere before in her life. She *fit*. Not perfectly, that was for sure, but she did fit. This place, this palace, this land—they were her destiny.

Just as Devon Montcalm was her destiny.

Kelly closed her eyes and smiled as she thought about everything that had happened yesterday, in Serenedid.

So this was love.

Warm kisses, even hot kisses. Longing looks. A feeling of completeness she'd never known.

And a yearning, to complete what they'd begun on the beach at Serenedid...

"Your Royal Highness," Miriam said, and Kelly opened her eyes, blinked. There was Miriam, right in front of her, dropping into a formal curtsy.

"I'm sorry, Miriam," Kelly said, relaxing her stiff shoulders. "My mind was about a million miles away. I wasn't supposed to change my expression. I'll open my eyes, I promise, although I am getting sort of tired. I didn't know that sitting still took so much work."

"The artist is gone, ma'am," Miriam pointed out, and Kelly looked around the room, to see that the photographic equipment, and the artist, really were gone. A million miles away? Perhaps a billion.

"Oh, I didn't notice," Kelly said, getting up,

stretching. "I'm so glad all I had to do was pose for photographs, Miriam, and that the artist will work from them. I can't imagine sitting here day after day, until he painted the portrait—and yet another one, once I am queen. Now I'd better get out of this gown. It's so old, and so beautiful. I'm afraid I'll ruin it."

"Yes, ma'am," Miriam said, then added, "but you might want to wait. We've been alerted that your brother, Prince Jace, will shortly be arriving at the front gates. I've asked that he be shown in here, if that's all right with you, ma'am?"

"Jace? Jace is here?" Kelly looked down at her gown, then at Miriam. "Well, you'd better introduce us, Miriam, because my brother will never recognize me like this. Are my parents and sister-in-law with him?"

"No, ma'am. They'll be delayed another week, I understand, but Prince Jace was traveling in Europe, on business, and he chartered a jet early this morning, to fly here from Paris."

"Really? Jace chartered a jet? That doesn't sound like him." She turned as the door opened, thinking to see her brother, but it was Devon who entered the room.

What would she say? Did she smile? She knew she was already blushing. They'd been so easy with each other yesterday. On the beach, in the limousine on the ride back to the royal palace.

But now it was another day, and she was suddenly nervous. Now, here, she was the royal princess. How was she supposed to react, with Miriam in the room?

She'd have to take her cues from Devon…sort of

learning on the job, she supposed. Besides, she could always ask Miriam to leave the room, she thought, hiding a quick smile.

"Your Royal Highness," Devon said, bowing in front of her. "If I might have a word, ma'am? Privately?"

"I'll...I'll just go alert the housekeeper to have rooms prepared for Prince Jace, ma'am," Miriam said, rushing away.

"That was odd," Kelly said, watching Miriam go. "She didn't even ask permission, not that I'll ever get used to people asking my permission to leave a room. Is she upset about something?"

"Possibly," Devon said, motioning for her to sit down once more. "Kelly...we have to talk."

Kelly sat down, her knees almost buckling at Devon's tone. "Talk? All right."

She watched as he took a deep breath, his shoulders rising and falling as he seemed to mentally gather himself for whatever he would say next.

"Kelly...about yesterday...I...well, there's no easy way to say this. It turns out there were paparazzi on the cliffs, possibly one in that small yacht we saw off the beach."

"Paparazzi? Oh, wait. You mean photographers? The sort that followed Princess Diana and Princess Sarah all over the world?"

"Yes, that's exactly what I mean. We...we were headlines this morning, Kelly. Here, all over Europe, and in America as well. We've also been on the television, I understand. Everything we did on that beach was captured on film."

Kelly sort of rolled her eyes, trying to remember everything that had happened on that beach. That wasn't difficult, because she'd been reliving the whole day again and again in her mind, in her dreams last night.

"Was King Easton terribly upset?"

Her question seemed to take Devon by surprise. "You're worried about the king's reaction? What about your own reaction, Kelly? How do you feel about it?"

She shrugged. "I don't care if you don't," she said, laughing nervously. "Oh, I *care,* of course I care. I don't like the idea of being spied on. But," and now her smile was wide and genuine, "I'll bet tourism revenues go way up in the next few months. Who knows, perhaps we could put on shows, every day at three and six?"

"That's not funny."

"I know, I know," Kelly said, standing up once more, putting her hands on Devon's forearms. "I think I'm just trying to digest this. I mean, I know that Jace had it happen to him. No, not pictures, but the scandal newspapers were going to go after him. And in New York? The same thing happened there, didn't it?"

"Krissy Katwell, yes," Devon said, his skin drawn rather tightly over his cheekbones. "I had, well, let's say I had to discourage her while in New York, when she was being fed snippets of gossip from Prince Markus and his associate."

Kelly thought about this one for a few moments. "So Prince Markus was behind all of the gossip, too?

Of course. That makes perfect sense. He was out to discredit any other possible heir. But now he knows he will never be named the heir, so why is he still doing all of this?''

Devon shrugged. ''King Easton believes he's mentally ill, pushed beyond his limits. That explains the shot taken at you, ma'am, but not the photographs. I think the two things are separate.''

''This Krissy Katwell again?''

''Possibly. I'm leaving here shortly and going over to the passport office, to see if she has entered the country.''

''And if she has?''

''Then, ma'am, she'll be leaving it again. Very quickly.''

Kelly nodded, then got back to what was really important to her. The pictures might be embarrassing, but she was much too sane a person to allow outside influences to dictate her mood, or her actions. ''All right, that sounds good. Now tell me, why you're so standoffish today? We're alone, remember, Devon? Or am I wrong, and yesterday was some sort of aberration, never to be repeated?''

He took a step closer. ''We're being official here, ma'am. This conversation is between Her Royal Highness and the captain of the royal guard. However, if you want the truth—I want to kiss you so desperately that I'm thinking of kidnapping you myself, just so that we can be alone. Does that answer your question…ma'am?''

Kelly nodded, unable to think of anything else to

say except "then kiss me, you fool," and that probably wouldn't be a good move.

"Is it kidnapping if the victim goes willingly?"
she asked instead. "And there's something else. Isn't
there?"

"Oh, the devil with being official." Devon took
her hands in his, looked deeply into her eyes. "Kelly,
would you…would you think I might ask you to
marry me because I thought that it was the only way
to salvage anything from the scandal these photographs are raising all over the world?"

"Say that again…differently. Plainly, please."

"His Majesty knows I want to marry you, Kelly,
and he's given his permission. But how do I get you
to believe I'm not just following orders? How do I
get you to believe that I want to marry you…for you,
not for Korosol."

Kelly took a deep, shaky breath. "You…I don't
know, Devon. I suppose you could…could tell me
that you love me…"

"I love you, Kelly," he said, his voice low, and
rather husky. "I really, truly love you, and it would
make me the happiest man in the world if you
would—"

"There you are, you bastard!"

Kelly looked past Devon, to see her brother Jace
advancing on them, murder in his eyes. "Jace?
What's wrong? What are you— Omigod!"

Devon was on the floor, Jace having delivered one
heck of a punch to his jaw. Now her brother stood
over Devon, his fists still bunched, saying, "What in
hell do you think you were doing, opening up my

sister to those damn scandal tabloids? You were supposed to *protect* her, not *maul* her in public. I saw the papers this morning and flew here, just so I could punch you in the mouth. Damn it, stand up, Montcalm, so I can knock you down again.''

"That sounds good to me,'' Devon said, rubbing at his jaw. "That first one was free, sir, because you and I both earned it. But you only get one free.''

"Oh, for pity's sake, stop it, the both of you. Stay right there, Devon,'' Kelly ordered, stepping between her brother and the man she loved. "Jace, I don't believe this. The man was proposing to me. He was *proposing*—and I was saying yes. Then you come in, acting the big brother, and knock him down? I could have your head chopped off, you know. I'm going to be queen, so I can do that. Except I'd rather give you a big hug and thank you for being so sweet and concerned. Right after you help Devon up, that is.''

Jace looked at his sister, then down at Devon, who was getting to his feet, one hand rubbing at his jaw. "Married? You're going to be married?'' He narrowed his eyes. "Why?''

"You know, Prince Jace,'' Devon said, his tone dangerous, "I think it's now my turn to knock you down. Why? How can you know your sister, and ask why?''

So Jace looked at Kelly, and she sort of grinned at him, waved to him.

"You…you look great, kid,'' he said, smiling at last.

"Yes, Prince Jace, she does,'' Devon said, slipping one arm around Kelly's waist. "But that's not it. You really have to meet our future queen, Prince Jace, get to know her. I don't think you know her at all. I think you love her, that her entire family loves her, but she's not who you've always thought she was. Oh, she is all of that, but she's also so much more. And now, sir, if you don't mind, I was proposing to your sister?"

Kelly buried her face against Devon's shoulder, giggling, as Jace opened his mouth to say something—who knew what—then closed it again, turned on his heel, and left the room.

"My jaw hurts," Devon said. "Your brother really packs a good punch, Kelly."

"He really hurt you? You saw him coming, Devon, and you didn't move, didn't protect yourself. Why did you do that?"

"Because I deserved a good punch in the face? That could be it, Kelly. Those photographs never should have happened. I did warn you that I can think of nobody but you when we're together, remember? I wasn't doing my job."

"In that case, Sir Devon, you're fired," Kelly said, touching her fingers to his reddened jaw. "But I believe you might have been applying for the position of prince consort before we were interrupted?"

"Prince consort," he repeated, gathering her close. "And if I vow to love and cherish you for all the days of our lives, will you vow to *consort* with me?" he asked her.

"As often as possible," Kelly said, just before he kissed her.

DEVON STOOD AT THE window of the large apartment, ignoring the view of another fine Korosolan morning, his interest otherwise occupied as he watched Kelly slowly rousing as the sun crept across the wide bed, to light her face, her glorious, wonderful face.

She was so precious to him. His life, his love.

And they had their entire lives before them, once they got through this day, this wonderful, dangerous day.

Kelly had been right and wrong about secret passages explaining how Prince Markus had gotten into the palace grounds. There were no secret passages that led outside the walls, although a close examination of the blueprints drawn up by some industrious soul a century earlier did show that there were a few boarded-up passages no longer in use.

So she'd been wrong about secret passages, but not about there being a "secret" way for Prince Markus to enter the grounds, and Devon had found that way.

The sewers.

A personal inspection had shown him how it could be done, how Prince Markus could have entered the storm drain half a mile away, then half walk, half crawl through the pipes until they ended just below the palace gardens. A determined man, Prince Markus. Devon had found evidence of footsteps in the muck, a flashlight and several handprints on the muddy walls.

The sewers had been secured with iron grates over each entrance, but that did not mean that Prince Markus would not find some other way to get inside the abbey on the palace grounds, to interrupt today's coronation…to try, once more, to assassinate Kelly, or the king—who knew what the man was thinking. And, with today's firepower, one man with a gun could do a lot of damage.

So he had kept Kelly involved with preparations for the coronation. Fittings for gowns, lessons in protocol, rehearsals of the ceremonies and coronation itself.

And then there were the guests, who had been arriving daily for the past week. Kelly spent considerable time with her parents, and getting to know her cousins from other parts of America.

And Devon had welcomed his father, and his father's bride, the Princess Lucia, back from America. How good it had been to see him, after so many years spent not understanding each other, at times barely tolerating each other. But they were friends now, in addition to being father and son, and Princess Lucia was pregnant. Amazing. He was going to have a brother.

While he had welcomed his father, he had also said farewell to Krissy Katwell, who he'd personally escorted to the airport and seen onto a plane leaving the country. It had taken him two days to find her, as her passport had been issued under her real name, Bertha Rumple. Did she really think Krissy Katwell to be an improvement?

What a tenacious woman! Her stories in the American papers had led to a possible book deal, or so she'd said, so that she was here to cover the coronation, and to dig up as much dirt as she could. She already had two possible titles for her book, she'd told him. Either *Kelly in Korosol,* or *Killer in Korosol*—and she didn't seem to care which scenario played out.

A detestable woman.

He remembered her last words to him: "You can't throw me out of the country. Haven't you ever heard about the freedom of the press?"

And his last words to her: "Have you ever heard of the dungeons of Korosol?"

She'd gone then, white-faced, probably to write a very nasty book.

He'd told Kelly, and she hadn't cared. How wonderful, to have a woman so happy in her own skin, that the sniveling scorpions of this world couldn't touch her.

Could the world get any better? Could life get any better?

Once this day was over, without incident, and once Prince Markus was found…no, it couldn't.

Kelly stretched, like a cat, and a slow smile curved her full mouth as she relived a dream, perhaps, or just enjoyed the way the silken sheets caressed her bare body.

He watched as she reached out one hand, toward the side of the bed he'd occupied last night, and every night for the past week. Her eyelids fluttered open. "Devon?"

"Over here, darling," he said, leaving the window and rejoining her in the bed. "Good morning, Your Royal Highness. Sleep well?"

"Sleep?" she asked, pushing her hands through her hair. "What's that? I don't think I sleep anymore."

"You were doing a good job of it a few minutes ago. You may even have snored."

She sat up in the bed, the sheets tangled at her waist...and gave him a quick hit on the arm. "I do *not* snore." Then she frowned. "Do I?"

Devon smiled, shook his head, then reached for her. "No, darling, you don't. But you do purr. I like it when you purr."

"Oh really?" she said as he lowered her onto the pillows, followed her down. "You growl. I *love* it when you growl."

He looked at her, at her blond hair spread on the pillow, at the tracing of freckles across her nose and cheeks, at those marvelous green eyes that had swallowed his heart, his soul.

"I want to make love to you every minute of every day. Do you think your subjects would mind if your prince consort-to-be never let their queen out of bed?"

"They might today, darling," Kelly said as he began kissing her neck, her upper chest...her breasts. "I think the coronation is today, unless I've just lost all track of time?"

"Oh, that. Well, maybe we can postpone it," Devon said, nibbling her soft skin even as he slipped one hand down her body, finding what he sought, being welcomed by her sweet sigh as she shifted slightly beneath him.

"Coronation canceled because Her Royal Highness is otherwise engaged?'' Kelly's hands were also busy; stroking his sides, her fingernails lightly scraping against his skin, sending shivers through his body. ''It might work.''

''I love you. I love how American you are, while at the same time you are the head and heart of Korosol. And, after today, I have a feeling Korosol will never be quite the same,'' he said, lifting his head slightly, to smile at her silliness. And then he kissed her, and her arms came up to hold him close against her, and he shifted his body between her legs.

From the moment they'd met, he'd known. From the moment they'd danced, he'd dreamed.

Now he held her, now he loved her, and now they would be together, forever.

His love, his soon-to-be wife, his queen…

KELLY SAT ON THE THRONE that had been brought to the abbey from the palace, looking out over the crowded pews.

She was here, she was about to be named Queen Kelly of Korosol.

And it was right. It was her destiny.

She smiled at Devon, who was standing at attention behind King Easton's chair, resplendent in his guards' uniform. So handsome, so loving, and the best part of this fairy tale that had taken a shy girl from her research lab to the throne of this beautiful country.

Kelly swallowed hard as the archbishop approached, carrying the crown that had so lately resided on King Easton's head—former King Easton's head. It was hers now.

She'd been in the abbey for two hours. She'd done the sacramental pledge to God that she would rule fairly, with a good heart.

She'd sat and accepted the homage of every prince, every noble in Korosol—goodness, there were so many!—as they pledged their "fealty" to her.

And now it was time. She sat there, trying not to cry, because the solemnity of the ceremony had stirred her heart deeply, holding the scepter of Korosol in her right hand, a golden orb topped with a squared cross in the other. The train of her cape lay draped down the five steps leading up to the throne, the embroidered gold and silver thread depicting all the medieval symbols of the Orders of Chivalry on the lush red silk, from thistles, to wildflowers, to oak leaves.

It was a fairy tale. It was something out of a storybook.

It was her destiny.

The archbishop raised the crown high above his head and Kelly bowed hers, waiting for the weight of her lifelong office to descend on her, crown her even as it bound her to Korosol and its people.

She welcomed that weight.

The archbishop's voice droned on in prayer, then suddenly cut off. Kelly raised her head to look at him, and he had the strangest expression on his face as he stared past her, toward the rear of the altar.

"What's—" Kelly asked, turning on the throne, trying to see around its high, gilt back.

The next thing she knew, Devon was vaulting past her, knocking down the archbishop, pushing her to the floor, and then running again, running…

Kelly stood up, not without difficulty, thanks to the long train on the royal cape, just in time to see Devon charging out a side door.

"What's happening?" she asked as King Easton came over, took her hand.

"My grandson," the former king said, sighing. "The archbishop saw him, and that alerted Devon. He…he had a pistol. Archbishop?" he then said, as that man was helped to his feet. "You have a duty yet to finish?"

"Now?" Kelly shook her head. "Not now. Devon could be in danger. I have to—"

"You have to assume your duties, my dear child," the former king told her quietly. "Devon will be fine."

Kelly bit her lip, looking out over the pews, to all the people who stood there, looking at her, looking *to* her.

"Yes, Your Majesty," she said, then took a deep breath and sat down once more, bowed her head.

DEVON WALKED INTO THE room with Major Howells and Lieutenant Bateson at his sides, not knowing what to expect. Would everyone be there? All the royal princesses and their mates? Prince Jace? His own father?

But the room was empty, save for the former king and Kelly, the newly crowned queen of Korosol.

He wanted to rush over to Kelly, to hold her, to tell her how much he loved her, how frightened he had been for her when he'd looked into the dimness behind the altar to see Prince Markus there, taking aim with his pistol.

But the major and the lieutenant were with him, and he was here as the captain of the royal guard, reporting to his queen.

"Your Majesty," he said, and all three guards bowed.

"Sir Devon," Kelly said, and he could see how white her knuckles were as she held on to the arms of the chair.

"I am sorry to inform Your Highnesses that Prince Markus is dead. He commandeered one of the gardeners' trucks as he tried to flee, but the truck crashed into the gates that had been ordered closed."

What he did not say was that he was all but certain that Prince Markus had rammed the gates on purpose, not to escape, but to die.

"I see," Kelly said. "Thank you, Captain. You may…you may dismiss your men, with Korosol's thanks."

The major and lieutenant bowed and departed, even as Devon stood there, staring at his queen. His love. His life.

"Well, I see that I have been rendered invisible," King Easton said, getting to his feet. "The ball begins in two hours, children. I believe the first waltz is yours?"

Kelly nodded, not taking her gaze from Devon.

Once the door closed, leaving them alone, he rushed to her, took her in his arms.

"I missed the coronation," he said, kissing her hair.

"That's all right," she said, burrowing against him. "We'll watch the tape once a year, with our children…"

EPILOGUE

KING EASTON TOOK THE child from his nurse and walked with the three-week-old Prince Alexander under the warm Korosolan sunshine.

"Your mother, the queen, is mucking about in her laboratory, you know," he told the sleeping infant as he sat down on a chair set in the shade of an ancient tree in the gardens. "And your father is meeting with somebody he said wishes to sell his wares here—and from a building that will have golden arches on it, which is amazing, isn't it?"

King Easton sighed, then smiled. "What a world you've come to, little Alex. Your mother is blending the old with the new, Korosol with America—California, no less. But do you know? I think you're going to like it here."

The baby stirred slightly in the former king's arms, trying to shove a fist in his little mouth. He opened his eyes, all at once, and they were his mother's green eyes.

"Ah, you're waking up. Wonderful. Because, you know, I've been meaning to tell you a story. Your mother and father already know it, which is why they chose to name you Alexander, but I think the story bears repeating. It's the story of one of our greatest kings. Almost a fairy tale, little Alex. So, while we sit here, the past and the new beginning of Korosol, let me tell you the story. Let's see, we'll begin this way. Alex, young prince, once upon a time..."

A KING WITHOUT A COUNTRY

Carolyn Davidson

Writing about a king was enjoyable. Living with one might be another matter altogether. The love of my life is an ordinary man, but one with strong ideals, one who has willingly made sacrifices and has committed himself to his wife and family. He has provided for their welfare, sharing himself and his bountiful love with an ever-widening circle. Although deserving of a crown and a title worthy of royalty, he is known to all who love him as just "Mr. Ed."
What a guy!

PROLOGUE

Korosol—1839

"A PILLOW OVER HIS FACE will suffice." Prince Jon's eyes glittered with malicious intent as his royal advisor paled.

"I can't do that." Quince visibly shuddered as he backed from the bed where the infant lay. The babe was newborn, the son of a king. Fair-haired, his eyes unfocused, he looked upward, and yawned widely as if to scorn the threat of imminent death.

"Would you deny your monarch?" the prince asked, his voice a silken menace to the underling who served him.

"You are not yet king," Quince reminded him.

"And I never will be, so long as this child lives." He turned toward the door, his final threat uttered from the threshold. "The boy stands between me and the throne. If you value your position in Korosol, you will obey the command of your future king."

Quince looked down at the infant as the door closed, its sound like that of a nail being driven into his coffin. What he did next would determine his fate, and to that end, he lifted the babe into his arms and left the room by a secret stairway beside the bed.

Locating a baby who had not survived birth was not difficult in an area where the poor multiplied rapidly and often died young. Quince's minions scoured the city, finding such an infant within hours. The young, impoverished, first-time mother was sent on her way, sworn to secrecy and well paid for the use of her time during the next months.

The woman's dead infant was presented to the queen, and wails of anguish were heard throughout the halls of the palace. She mourned less than a week before she succumbed to childbed fever, and by that time the babe was on his way to America with his wet nurse. Placed on the steps of an orphanage, a strange medallion tucked within his blankets, the infant boy was taken in and given space in a vacant bed.

Even at the age of five weeks, he possessed masculine beauty, his eyes swiftly turning emerald green, his hair thick and lustrous, as golden as a field of wheat. He wore the medallion that was his only claim to identity, its beaten-silver surface bearing an intricately wrought crown beside an image of fleur-de-lis, a bird of prey pictured beneath. It was said he shunned those who cared for him, was insolent and arrogant as he grew to be a youth. His counterparts teasing him, yet admiring his leadership, called him *King.*

Staunchly, he vowed to be as much a predator as the falcon, and held fast to a determination that bade him be worthy of the crown and the name his fellow orphans gave him. Wherever he should go, he swore he would excel. In whatever circumstances he found himself, he resolved to earn the respect inherent in his name...*King*.

CHAPTER ONE

The Dakota Territory—1872

HOSPITALITY IN THE TOWN of Creed came wrapped in a bullet, it seemed. His mouth twisted with pain accompanied by an ironic smile as Alex Carr lurched from his saddle and fell heavily to the ground. For the second time in his life he'd been shot, and his mind searched for reasons. At least the part of his mind that wasn't occupied with staying conscious.

The town had seemed receptive to change, yet perhaps some dissenting gunman—some foe of progress—was out to nail the messenger.

Damn. If they don't want the railroad coming through, they could have just said so. He groaned as his wounded shoulder struck solid ground and then he rolled to his back. The stars twinkled above and the moon shone brightly, as if mocking his predicament with a display of beauty he'd barely noticed earlier.

The noise from the saloon in town carried on the midnight air, crisp and cold as if winter would not yet release its hold on the flatlands of Dakota. He'd only just left the warmth and stale scent of whiskey behind, his single drink roiling in his stomach as he considered his circumstances.

Whoever had shot him might yet be lingering in the shadows beside the road where he lay, watching to see if he still breathed. Lowering his lashes, he concentrated on the subtle sounds of the night, the whisper of some small rodent through the weeds not far from his head, the soft hoot of an owl from a nearby tree.

No jingle of harness or creak of saddle leather broke the stillness, and after an endless five minutes, he staggered to his feet, thankful for the horse who obeyed the dictates of dangling reins. His vision blurred by the pain of his wound, he grasped the reins and lifted himself into the cradle of his saddle. He leaned heavily on the pommel, keeping his horse to a walk, unable to bear the uneven jolt of a trot beneath him.

His nostrils caught the unmistakable scent of blood as its warmth flowed from his wound, soaking into the shirt he wore. Shelter was the first consideration, he decided; and, if luck was with him, maybe a warmhearted soul capable of applying a bandage until he could seek out a doctor.

"A barn will do just fine," he muttered beneath his breath, peering into the darkness ahead for a shape that would fit the bill. "And maybe a friendly farmer." His head swam and his eyes blurred as he spoke aloud, determination holding him in the saddle. A light caught his eye and he blinked, then focused on the glowing lantern that moved slowly toward the outline of a small building.

The man carrying the lantern might not be as friendly as he hoped, he thought in a moment of cynicism, and his good hand groped for the revolver he carried tucked into his belt. It fit precisely in his palm, the butt warm from his body heat. His horse turned readily toward the buildings clustered within easy reach, lured perhaps, Alex decided, by the scent of hay.

The lantern was lifted high as he approached, and he recognized the skirted form of a woman holding it. Her body was a dark shadow behind its glow, but the face revealed held a purity of line that put him in mind of what an angel might look like, had he believed in such a thing.

Maybe there is a heaven after all, he thought…just before he slid from the saddle to the ground. Sensing the darkness gathering around him, he clutched his gun, and groaned aloud.

A hand plucked it from his grip as he sprawled at the woman's feet, and a soft voice welcomed him.

"Were you going to shoot me or ask for help?" she asked quietly, not expecting an answer. The man at her feet gazed up through narrowed eyes, and her lantern reflected in those glittering emerald orbs for just a second. Then his heavy lids closed and his body relaxed against the ground.

Rebecca Hale looked down at the tall, rangy stranger and sighed. "Hope you don't mind being dragged through the dirt." She slid her hands beneath his shoulders and dug in her heels, lifting him with calloused fingers gripping his armpits. Blood stained his clothing from an area high on his shoulder, and she winced at the unconscious groan he uttered as she lifted him.

"Sorry, stranger," she said, the words harshly voiced from between her teeth as she dragged him the first few feet in the trek to her house. Moving his inert body an inch at a time, she backed to the porch, lugging him up the steps, then lowering him to the wooden surface while she caught her breath.

Another eight feet would put him squarely in the center of her kitchen floor. She propped open the screened door with her fanny as she bent to lift him again. The taut spring caused the door to snap against his arm and he inhaled sharply.

"Hope you're still out like a light," she told him, finally lowering him next to the round table in the middle of the small room. A hanging kerosene lantern provided enough light to make out his features, and she knelt beside him. One hand touched his brow, and she bent low, searching his face. It was a harsh blend of features, a strong jaw and broad forehead framing a straight blade of a nose and a generous mouth.

Handsome was not the word to describe her unexpected guest. Perhaps "rugged" or "hard-edged" was more to the point. His hair was the darkest gold and a bit long, as though visiting a barber was not high on his list of priorities. His brows were darker than his hair, a startling contrast that lent him a rakish look, she decided. Wide shoulders strained the fabric of his shirt, where blood stained the garment a bright red.

She scanned his form quickly. He seemed lean and

raw-boned, and so far as she could tell, bore no other wounds. One was enough, she thought ruefully, especially when it bled as profusely as did this neat little example of mayhem.

She viewed him with a measure of hesitation. Living alone made her suspicious. Having male visitors at any time of day was cause for concern, given her reputation in the town and the isolation of her farm. Yet, this man appeared to offer no threat of danger, not in the shape he was in. And unless she did something to relieve the bleeding, he wouldn't be a danger to anyone.

"Never saw you before," she said quietly, her voice soothing. "But then I don't see many men hanging around here. And the ones I manage to lay eyes on aren't worth spit." Her hands were deft as she drew a small pair of scissors from her pocket and cut away at the stained fabric of his shirt. Blood oozed slowly from a hole beneath his collarbone and she wiped it away with a piece of his shirtsleeve.

Against his throat a leather thong was threaded through a bit of silver, and from it hung a medallion. The glisten of blue enamel edging caught her eye, and Rebecca touched her index finger to the regal emblem of a crown inlaid against a silver background. Formed in intricate detail, it covered a third of the piece. Beside it three dainty shapes held an equal share of the medallion. Beneath them a bird of prey, perhaps a falcon, she thought, looked off to his right with a menacing eye.

She shivered, tracing over the symbols on the ornate, yet delicately wrought, piece of jewelry, wondering that a rude piece of leather should dangle so dear a treasure from its length.

And then her eye was drawn back to the wound her visitor bore. "You're lucky that bullet didn't hit an artery," she told him matter-of-factly, speaking as if her unconscious guest were awake and aware of his circumstances. Used to her solitude, accustomed to speaking her thoughts aloud, Rebecca murmured softly, coaxing his aid as she turned him a bit, hefting his weight with a grunt of effort. Then she peered behind his shoulder to seek out an exit hole.

Her teeth touched her lower lip and she inhaled deeply. Smooth skin, its surface marred by a faint, dark bulge, met her gaze. "Looks like I'll be digging for a bullet," she said with a sigh, lowering his shoulder again to the floor. "Guess I'd better scout up the whiskey."

She rose, intent on moving toward the pantry where her supplies were kept, and was held immobile as a large hand grasped her ankle with a firm grip. The fingers tightened, jerking her leg from beneath her, and she sprawled beside the man on the floor, crying out, the air rushing from her lungs as he rolled to cover her with his weight.

"Who are you?" The query was rasped against her ear as his head fell to rest against her shoulder.

She was quiet, holding herself still beneath him, unable to speak as she attempted to inhale. His own breathing was harsh, his weight pressing against her breasts, one heavy thigh holding her legs prisoner.

"Damn it. Where am *I?"* His voice harsh, his heavy frame pressing her against the unyielding sur-

face of the floor, he whispered the question, and she caught the faint scent of whiskey on the syllables. He shifted a bit and she inhaled quickly, her mind sorting out the aroma of soap on his skin, the smell of horse and evening air on his clothing. Except for the trace of whiskey on his breath, she found nothing distasteful in the blend of man and animal that met her nostrils.

"You're in my kitchen. I'm Rebecca Hale." That her voice trembled was not to be helped. She considered herself fortunate to be breathing, and she squirmed in an attempt to free herself from beneath his weight. "If you're not planning to bleed to death on my kitchen floor, I'd suggest you let me up so I can help you."

Lifting his head, he squinted and blinked, as if he would focus on her face.

"How'd I get in here?" His words were as bleary as his narrowed eyes.

"If you'll let me up, I'll answer all your questions, mister," she said quietly. "Right now you're bleeding all over me, making a mess of my shirt, and I don't think you can afford to lose any more blood."

"I was shot," he said, and his eyelids closed as if he tried to recall that moment.

"You sure were. Right below your collarbone, and you're not long for this world if I don't get some pressure on that wound."

He nodded, a minute movement of his head, and rolled back from her to lie flat on his back beside her. "You a doctor?" he asked, and the query was couched in doubt. His eyes opened a bit as she rose to her knees beside him, and again, she was struck by the brilliance of green irises that rimmed his enlarged pupils.

"No," she answered, tearing his shirtsleeve with a sharp tug of both hands. "I'm a midwife, but I've tended wounded men more than once in my time." She bent low, pressing her fingers against the sides of the wound with careful touches, watching as the blood flowed brightly.

His lips tightened, and she offered the only anesthesia available. "Want some whiskey before I start?"

He shook his head. "Just do what you have to." His words slurred as he spoke, and she recognized the toll his movements had taken on the limited amount of strength left in the man.

"All right, whatever you say." She stood and went to the pantry, retrieving a satchel from the top shelf and scooping up several clean towels. The water in the teakettle was hot, and she poured her wash basin half-full and placed it on the floor beside him. "I'll have to wash away the blood and take a good look at you first," she told him, dipping a towel and wringing it out.

It was hot against his skin and her movements were quick, cleaning the area, soaking up the bright blood that oozed from the bullet hole. "I think I'll have to go in from the back to get it out," she told him. "It's not close enough to the front surface of your shoulder to feel."

"Have at it," he muttered. "Want me to roll over for you?"

"I'll help you turn," she said. "And then scrub up before I begin." With careful movements, she turned him over, noting again the suspiciously dark area high on his shoulder. She folded a clean towel so that several thicknesses were placed beneath his chest to protect the open wound from the floor. His weight alone, pressing against the thick pad, should control the bleeding somewhat. Rolling her long sleeves above her elbows, she washed in the sink, using copious amounts of soap, cleansing her arms, then scouring her fingers and nails.

She owned but a single scalpel, and she lifted it from its case and opened the whiskey bottle she kept in her bag with a quick twist. "Sure you don't want a swallow of this whiskey?" she asked as she poured a dribble of the liquid over the blade.

His grunt was reply enough, she decided, and her murmur was agreeable. "Suit yourself, mister. Just don't jerk when this blade touches your skin." Her hand was steady as she drew a short line where the blue bulge revealed the slug he'd taken. His skin pebbled with gooseflesh as she cut, and an indrawn breath revealed his pain.

Just beneath the surface, the dark bit of metal lay revealed, and she grasped it with her thumb and index finger and sighed with relief. It had gone smoothly, better than she'd expected, and she uttered a short word of thanksgiving as she dropped the spent bullet into the pan.

"I've got it out," she told him. "Now I'll get you cleaned up."

"Yeah." It was a single word, muttered beneath

his breath, and she felt his shoulder relax beneath her hands as he took a deep breath.

"This is going to burn," she warned him, tilting the bottle as she allowed the whiskey to cleanse the wound.

"Hell's bells!" His jerk was spasmodic and his voice was raw with pain as he groaned the words. And then his body was limp beneath her touch as he lost consciousness.

"Just as well," Rebecca said, leaving him where he lay as she rose and put together a drawing poultice from bread and milk. With but a single layer of cotton between his raw flesh and the soggy mass, she placed it over his wound, then covered the whole of it with a thick pad of sheeting and a square of fabric.

Swiftly, she stripped him from his shirt and used a roll of bandage torn from old sheets to bind the padding in place. Of necessity, one arm was held captive against his side, the other left free, with the bandage secured beneath his armpit. Leaning back on her heels, she inspected the security of her binding.

It would hold so long as he didn't attempt to lift his arm, and if he was in as much pain with each movement as she surmised, he'd be happy to behave himself and let it heal. She bent to him again. "Come on, let me help you up," she coaxed. Her hands touched his golden skin, brushing against the damp hair on his neckline, and then she turned him to his side.

"You're going to have to help me here, mister." She wiped his face with a clean towel and slid her arm beneath him. "Can you hear me?" she asked quietly. "Put your good arm around my neck and I'll lift you."

"Fat chance," he muttered, barely moving his lips as he whispered the taunt. "I weigh over two hundred pounds."

"I'm strong," she said. "If you'll help a bit, I can get you off the floor."

"All right." He took a deep breath and winced, then pushed with the flat of his palm against the floor, sitting upright at her feet. "Give me a hand and I'll be on my feet."

It was a struggle, but together, they managed to get him through the doorway and across the narrow hall into her bedroom. He staggered and leaned heavily against her, and Rebecca braced her feet lest they tumble to the floor. "Careful," she warned him. "We don't want that wound to start bleeding again."

His answer was unintelligible, a sound rather than words she could understand, yet the meaning was clear. He had no intention of falling and taking her with him. The bed was before them and she turned with him, lowering him to the mattress and then helped him lie flat against the sheet.

"I'll take off your trousers," she said, giving him no choice in the matter. She'd be doggoned if she'd allow him to crawl beneath her clean sheet with dusty pants on. "Boots first," she decided, tugging at them in turn. It took longer than she'd expected. He was tall, probably well over six feet, and even though he tried to assist, lifting his hips at her command, by the time the task was accomplished she was perspiring and he was ashen.

His drawers did not conceal the blatantly masculine lines of his lower body and the knit fabric clung faithfully to each muscle and bulge. He was tough, well-muscled, and possessed a body honed by long hours of work. Her grin was wry as she straightened from her task. He was the best-looking male specimen she'd ever seen around Creed, and certainly the only man to see the inside of her bedroom, and she hadn't the least notion who he was.

His eyes flickered open as if he sensed her gaze and he scanned the room quickly, then fastened on her face as she spoke. "What's your name? I'd like to know what to call you, mister."

"Alex Carr."

"Alex? Or shall it be Mr. Carr?" She frowned, recalling a sign in town with a bid to recruit men for work. "Are you the fella from the railroad?"

He nodded, his gaze wary. And well it might be. Emotions were running high in the quiet Dakota town. The rail bed must be laid for the coming line of track that would pass through Creed within the next months. There had been murmurs from several townsfolk who distrusted the idea of having strangers invade their quiet community and others who disliked the idea of the progress inherent in such an endeavor.

And this man was the instigator of the whole project, if the rumors were true.

"That's me," he said agreeably. Too long for her bed, he shifted with care until his feet hung over the side of the mattress. "By this time next year, you'll hear that train whistle three times a week."

"Do you think someone shot you because of your work?" she asked, a sharp pang of fear settling in her chest as she considered her predicament. Perhaps his assailant might have followed him here. She'd left the door wide open and Alex's horse standing in the yard, a blatant message announcing to any passerby that she had a visitor.

His head moved a bit, a negative gesture. "Can't say. Could have been a stray bullet." And then he grimaced. "Not likely, is it?"

"You'll be safe here," she assured him. "Once I get the house closed up, anyway. I have a shotgun by the door. And your revolver in my pocket."

"My gun." His voice deepened. "Give it to me," he said harshly, opening his fingers and waiting, as if his words were enough to bend her to his will.

And it seemed they were. She hesitated but a moment, then drew the gun from the depths of her skirt pocket. "I suspect you'll feel better with it close at hand, won't you?" Even before his short nod, she placed it in his palm, watching as his grip tightened, as if he gained peace of mind from the weapon's presence.

"Rebecca?" Her name was a question and she looked up at his face. "Thank you," he said. "I'll take a swallow of that whiskey now, if you don't mind."

"All right. I'd say you probably need it." She left the room and returned to the kitchen, retrieving the bottle of spirits from the bottom of her bag before stowing the leather satchel on the pantry shelf. The wash pan was dumped and rinsed, and the towels put to soak in cold water before she returned to the side of her bed with the whiskey.

"Here's the bottle. Drink what you want," she said, lifting his head with her forearm, supporting it while she offered the opened bottle.

He accepted it, sniffed the opening, and tipped it to his lips. She watched as his throat moved and he swallowed twice. "Thanks," he said harshly, and she took the bottle from his grip, lowering his head to the pillow.

"I'll go take care of your horse and then lock up the house," she told him. He nodded in reply and she went to the open back door, looking into the darkness for the mare he'd ridden. His mount stood patiently, reins touching the ground, halfway between house and barn, and as Rebecca watched, the animal whickered softly. Lighting a lantern, she stepped from the house and down from the porch.

"You need some feed and a stall for the night, don't you?" she murmured, approaching the mare. Grasping the reins, she led the acquiescent creature into the barn and exchanged bridle for halter before she made ready a stall. Hay in the manger and a measure of oats in the bucket would do the trick, Rebecca decided, and she led the mare into the stall. Water stood in a bucket on the floor, and the animal dipped her head for a long drink.

In moments, the saddle was upended in the aisleway, the saddle blanket draped over a sawhorse, and Rebecca picked up her lantern. In the next stall, her own gelding was shifting, obviously aware that his domicile had been invaded. He lifted his head and sounded a welcome or warning, and Rebecca laughed aloud.

"You can get acquainted tomorrow," she told him. "I'll put you out in the pasture together." Within moments, she'd closed up the barn door and made her way back to the house. There she tended to the door, then turned to the stove, banking the fire until morning. After filling a large tumbler with water from the pump, she blew out the lantern and placed it on the table till morning.

Alex Carr appeared to be sleeping, his hand limp against the sheet, the gun he held balanced across his palm. His face was turned away, the line of his throat vulnerable, the pulse beating beneath his ear. Opening the wardrobe, she snatched her nightgown and warm wrapper from the hook and held them across her arm, then turned back to face the bed, as if she were somehow drawn to the man who sprawled across her mattress.

Her gaze lingered on him. He was different, she decided, not just a stranger, but a breed apart from the men she knew. None of them had ever appealed to her, those farmers and townsmen who frequently looked at her as if peering beneath her clothing to see the womanly attributes she hid so well. Even the eligible men who'd attempted to court her had left empty-handed, her stark refusals of their offers gaining her a reputation in the territory.

She was a woman alone and aware that she was likely to remain that way. With one step closer to the bed, she flexed her fingers and then struck aside the unfamiliar urge to touch him, to run her palm across that smooth flesh where the white bandage contrasted sharply with tanned skin.

It would not do, she decided firmly. She'd long since decided that attraction to a man was the downfall of many women, and she would not allow that particular failing to become a part of her life.

With a silent shake of her head, she retired to a shadowed corner of the room, then changed from her clothing into the gown she held. She'd grown adept over the years at stripping beneath the billowing fabric of a nightgown, and she did so now, finally stepping from the circle of dress and petticoat before slipping her arms into the long sleeves of her gown.

She was buttoning it, looking down at the long line of plain, white fastenings as she returned to the bedside, and a movement from the bed caught her attention. He'd turned back to watch her, and she was caught in the midst of placing buttons and their corresponding holes together. Her fingers stilled on the final button and she dropped her hands to her sides, aware of the altogether intimate picture she offered. Long, russet-colored hair hung in waves down her back and across her shoulders to drape her breasts with a tangle of curls. For the first time in her life she was alone in her bedroom with a man—a stranger, at that.

His mouth was curved a bit, his eyes at half mast, and he whispered words she could barely hear. She leaned forward just a bit, reading the movement of his lips.

"You're a sight for sore eyes, ma'am." He grimaced as he shifted his position and she glared at him, stunned by the offhanded compliment he offered.

Her chin lifted and her mouth was taut with derision. "Sweet talk doesn't impress me, Mr. Carr. I'm not interested in your opinion of me."

It seemed he was not put off by her harsh stance, and as she watched, his free hand lifted and his fingers gestured at the bandage he wore. "Maybe getting shot was less of a misfortune than I thought." His lips quirked at one corner, his brilliant eyes dark now with the pain of his injury. He was in no condition to be flirtatious; yet he persisted, and she was torn between amusement and irritation at the arrogance of the man.

It would not do to be taken in by his smooth talk and elegant masculine beauty, she decided firmly. She could not afford to let him get beneath her skin with his coaxing words and elegance of face and form. And so her words were blunt.

"You're only here on sufferance," she said. "Once you're out of danger, you'll be out the door."

"Don't bet on that, sweetheart," he murmured. And then his eyes closed and he was asleep once more. Or perhaps unconscious. She cared little which it was right now, only reached for her wrapper and stuck her arms into the sleeves as she bundled it around her.

"*Men.*" The single syllable was a sound of disgust. *Men.* Half the human population shared too many of the same aggravating tendencies and were pretty much alike, no matter how varied in size, shape and color they might be.

And, she decided firmly, Alex Carr hadn't done much during the last few minutes to elevate himself above the rest of the members of his sex.

CHAPTER TWO

THE VISITOR WAS UNEXPECTED, arriving soon after Rebecca arose. Ted Duncan's fist banged against the door impatiently as his horse stood at the hitching rail, and Rebecca was in no hurry to answer the summons. Ted didn't rank highly on her list, and the presence of a man under her roof might be difficult to explain should her admirer discover Alex Carr making himself at home here.

Hoping for silence from the barn as Ted's horse lifted his head and neighed loudly, Rebecca held her breath, fearful that the horses behind those double doors might answer the challenge. Ted's fist pounded harder the second time, impatience sounding with each thump against the door, and Ted added to the clamor by calling her name.

"Rebecca. Answer the door. I need to talk to you."

If he thought to endear himself to her with his highhanded actions, he had another think coming, she decided, taking her time as she slid back the bolt and swung the heavy door open. She blocked the opening, holding the screened door shut with one hand, and tried her best to look pleasant.

"What do you want?"

"There's several of us scouting for a fella who may have gotten himself shot last night. Have you seen anybody out this way?" He peered past her through the screen as he spoke, and she looked over her shoulder, following the direction of his gaze.

"Who would I be looking for?" she asked. "Do I know this person?"

"Not likely," he said shortly. "He's that railroad scout who's been rustlin' up men to work on the rail bed. His kind just come in and take over, whether the town wants such a thing to happen or not."

"I've heard a lot of folks who are real excited about the idea of a train passing through Creed." Rebecca couldn't help but jar him a bit, contradicting his opinion and making him take notice that they were not on the same line in this story.

"Well, the ones who know about such things are dead set against it," Ted said staunchly. "You womenfolk don't understand the ins and outs of the thing."

"Really?" Anger mounted, but she subdued it, unwilling to continue this conversation any longer than necessary. "Well, I don't know anything about your friend. You'll have to look elsewhere."

"Do we have company, sweetheart?" From behind her, Alex's voice was low, filled with an early-morning husky tone that made a chill run the length of her spine.

"Thought you didn't know anything about the man," Ted said accusingly, grasping the door handle and tugging it futilely in an attempt to open the screen.

"Oh?" She turned her head and sought Alex's gaze. "Is *this* the man you're looking for?"

Alex grinned, the movement of his lips lifting one corner of his mouth, but his eyes were dark with pain as he leaned against a kitchen chair. "You didn't say it was Alex Carr you wanted," Rebecca said lightly.

"I said it was a stranger and the fella was probably wounded, didn't I?" Ted asked, giving up on the door handle as Rebecca held firmly to the knob on the inside. His gaze accused her as he pointed at the bandage and binding Alex wore.

"Oh, that little nick," she said, waving her other hand in a dismissive movement. "I thought you were talking about a seriously injured rascal of some sort. This is just...Alex."

"Just Alex." The two words were spoken in a measured tone as Ted's index finger pushed his hat back. He loosed an exasperated sigh. "How well do you know *Alex?*" he asked bluntly.

"Well enough to make his breakfast," Rebecca answered.

"I'm hungry, sweetheart," Alex said, prodding her verbally as he sat down in the chair that had been holding him erect for the past few minutes.

Rebecca shrugged and began closing the heavy door. "You can see I'm busy, Ted. Sorry I couldn't help you more."

"Wait just a durned minute here, Becky," Ted said, his tone a threat. "You can't just close the door on me that way."

"Don't call me *Becky,*" she said quietly. "And I

can close the door any way I please, Mr. Duncan. This is my house, if you recall.''

He sputtered, attempting to peer past her even as the door shut with a thump in his face. Rebecca turned to lean against the solid panel.

"Why didn't you just stay in the bedroom until he left?''

"Thought you might need help,'' Alex said. He leaned his elbows on the tabletop and inhaled deeply. "Now I'm wondering if I don't need a bit myself.''

"You should have stayed in bed. You have no business being up and around.'' She looked at him, glancing to where his trousers hung open. "How did you get dressed?''

"I didn't, as you've already noticed,'' he said with a smile. "Got my pants pulled up one-handed, and then found I couldn't do them up in front. I guess I need you to help me with them.''

"If you'd stayed in bed you wouldn't have a problem.'' She knew she sounded grumpy, but right now she didn't care. She had two men causing trouble, and she feared the one in front of her would give her more hassle than the one climbing on his horse out in her yard. Neither was much help when it came to her peace of mind.

Alex Carr had the ability to arouse feelings she'd never had to examine before in her life. As for Ted Duncan, he'd have it all over town by noon that she had a man sleeping in her house. That the man was wounded was of little matter. His presence at the farm would set tongues to wagging for miles around.

And when he was gone from here, she would still be bearing the brunt of the gossip inherent in this mess.

"As long as you're up and around, I'll take a look at your shoulder," she said shortly, aware that her voice was clipped and cool.

He looked up at her quickly. "Now, I surely hate to put you to any trouble, ma'am," he said, his eyes narrowing as he spoke. "I'll pay you well for your services when I leave."

She halted the movement of her hand, resting her palm against the bare skin of his shoulder. "Don't insult me, Mr. Carr. I didn't ask for payment."

The shoulder lifted beneath her hand and he winced at the movement. "Nonetheless, I'll leave gold behind. The railroad pays its debts."

She worked at the bandage and unwound it with care. The padding was damp, the poultice seeming to have done its job well. Rebecca lifted it and inspected the raw flesh beneath. "I'll make another poultice," she decided aloud. "Once more should do it. I don't think you have a fever, but I don't want to take the chance of infection developing."

"Whatever you say," he told her, bending his head as she worked. Perhaps to hide his expression, she thought, aware that her touching the wound was painful.

"I'll wash it with carbolic soap this time," she told him. "I don't think I need to cleanse it with whiskey."

"Well, that's a relief," he said, a half laugh betraying him. "I'm trying to be brave here, ma'am."

She smiled. The man could withstand anything she

threw in his direction, she'd warrant. He exuded strength and courage, both qualities seeming to be inbred. How she knew that was beyond her. But somehow, the sure and certain knowledge of his bone-deep worth was apparent, and she felt safe and secure with him beneath her roof. She washed the wound, both front and back, with care and then placed another poultice on his back, padding it well and applying the bandage anew.

"You're all set for now," she said quietly, noting the pale cast of his skin as he looked up at her. Even with that, he was an appealing man, and instinctively, she fought the attraction of masculine beauty.

"I have to go out and feed the stock and milk my cow before I fix your breakfast," she said. They could have waited for a half hour, but Alex was making her feel things she wasn't comfortable with, and distance between them might be the best thing for her right now.

"I'll wait right here, Rebecca. I'm not going anywhere." Indeed, he looked like he wasn't in fit shape to move from the chair he'd claimed, his brow furrowing as he spoke, a line of perspiration appearing above his lip.

She relented. "Let me help you back to bed," she said with a sigh. "I don't think it's wise for you to be on your feet any more today."

He hesitated, glancing toward the kitchen window, and she surmised his thoughts. "Ted is gone. He found out what he came to discover and he's gone. I'll be fine."

Alex nodded, reluctantly she thought, and placed

his palms flat on the table's surface, boosting himself
from the chair. She moved quickly to place her
shoulder beneath his armpit and slid her arm around
his waist, grasping a handful of his trousers' waistband to hold them up as they walked. His other arm
was still held in place by the bandage. At least he
hadn't attempted to move it, and she was thankful
for that. Having the wound bleed again was not in
the man's best interests.

In fact, bed was where he belonged, and to that
end, she steered him across the floor and into the
room where he'd spent the night.

"Where did you sleep?" he asked as she helped
him settle on the edge of the mattress. His trousers
settled around his bare feet, and she kept her gaze
well above the line of muscled thighs and calves that
filled out the knit fabric of his drawers.

"On that chair," she told him, nodding in the direction of an overstuffed chair she'd dragged from
the parlor well after midnight.

"I feel guilty, taking your bed," he said.

"How guilty do you feel?" she asked with a skeptical note invading her words. "I didn't notice you
offering to trade places."

"I didn't wake up until I heard all the bangin' and
hollerin' out in the kitchen a few minutes ago."

"Well, put your head on that pillow and stay put
while I do the chores and cook something for you to
eat. I'll put the coffee on before I go out." She bent
to lift his legs to the mattress, then pulled the sheet
and quilt over him. "I'll be back in half an hour
or so."

Snatching her shawl from the hook by the back door, she hastened across the yard and opened the barn door. A whinny greeted her from the new occupant, another from the second stall echoing the first. She'd turn them both out into the pasture and let them fend for themselves. The grass was green and halfway to her knees, and the two acres her father had fenced for his horses several years ago would abundantly assuage their hunger.

The cow waited patiently as Rebecca settled the horses, shooing them out the back door and through the narrow passage to the pasture gate. She closed it behind them and watched as they tossed their heads and chased back and forth a bit. Within minutes, both heads were bent to the lush grass, and Rebecca turned back to her chores. The milk pail awaited her on a shelf near the cow's stanchion, covered with a clean cloth to insure that no dirt sullied its surface before she filled it.

The brown-and-white Guernsey mooed long and loud as Rebecca settled on the three-legged stool and reached for the swollen teats. "Did you think I'd forgotten you, sweetheart?" she asked the bovine creature, leaning her forehead against the coarse hair on the cow's shank. And then she winced as she recalled Alex's voice calling her by that same title. He'd said it not only once, but several times, in fact, and she wrinkled her nose at the thought. The man was nervy, and arrogant, and a few other things, too.

But mostly, he was handsome. And clean-cut. And possessed of green eyes that made her want to see them sparkle with that bit of humor he managed to display, even when he was struggling to conceal the pain of his wound. His hair was thick, waving to his collar, and she'd stifled the urge to touch it last night. Her snort of laughter was grim. She'd touched enough other places on his muscular body to keep her thoughts in an uproar for the next month of Sundays.

She'd noted another scar, one that marred the pale skin on his hip, almost identical to the fresh injury on his shoulder. He'd been wounded before, and that in itself told her that the man was at risk, with an apparent bent for trouble. If Ted Duncan and his clutch of friends were after him, Alex Carr might not live long enough for her to find out any more about him than she already knew.

She lifted the milk pail and headed for the porch, where she left the bucket while she tended the chickens. Feeding the hens and gathering the daily bounty of eggs was next on her agenda and, after that, fixing breakfast. Then when the cream had risen nicely, she would churn butter this afternoon.

"Rebecca?" Alex's voice came from the bedroom as she closed the outer door behind herself ten minutes later. He sounded impatient, and she tossed her shawl over the hook and slid from her shoes. Stocking-footed, she made her way to the bedroom.

"What is it?" she asked, standing in the doorway.

"I just wanted to be sure you were all right. Your gentleman friend didn't hang around, did he?"

The man should look ridiculous, she thought, sprawled across her bed, his feet poking from beneath the quilt. Instead, he'd made himself at home, both pillows propped beneath his head, his arm still secured against his chest, managing to appear in control of this whole situation, even while abed and wounded.

"He's not my friend," she told him, exasperated by his assumption. "And yes, I'm just fine. Are you ready for eggs and bacon? Or will toast do as well?"

"How about eggs and toast?" he offered. "I'm not sure how much I can get down. I've about decided I don't feel quite up to snuff, yet."

If she hadn't helped him into the bedroom earlier, and been privy to his weakened condition, she might have doubted his assessment. As it was, she looked beyond his smile, noting the pallor beneath his skin. "I could have told you that to start with," she said sharply. "You'd have saved yourself a lot of trouble if you'd stayed in bed earlier. Now, that whole gang of men knows exactly where you are. If they're serious about getting rid of you, they'll know right where to come to find you."

"I don't think their kind does their work in broad daylight," Alex said quietly. "They shoot from ambush, usually. Besides, unless I miss my guess, Ted doesn't want to get on your bad side. He'll wait till I'm on my feet, maybe wait for me to leave here, before he sets out to finish me off."

"He's already on my bad side," she said, turning back to the kitchen. And wasn't that the truth. Ted's eye was more on her farm than she liked to admit, for that knowledge was not conducive to bolstering her ego. Four hundred acres was a tidy bit of property, and if he persuaded her to marry him, Ted Duncan stood to walk into a ready-made living.

She hadn't toiled from morning till night over the past three years to hand it over to Ted or any other man, Rebecca thought dourly. She had an agreement with a neighboring farmer to cut the hay and fill her haymow with half of it. Another neighbor ran his cattle on two hundred of her acres and paid her cash money for the privilege.

Both arrangements were to her advantage, allowing her freedom from worry when it came to feeding her stock and paying her account at the general store. Her chickens brought in enough egg money to fill the coffee crock and put flour and sugar in the pantry. The garden she planted provided vegetables aplenty to do her for the long winter months.

Rebecca had learned well from her mother how to put food on her table. And from her father, she'd gained the knowledge needed to run the farm. Planting and sowing the fields was beyond her capabilities, but gardening was a pleasure she cherished. Survival was the basis of her life it seemed. Though she might never find happiness with a man to share her days and nights, she could make it on her own.

She scooped scrambled eggs onto a plate and added a slice of bread, toasted in the oven and spread generously with the last of the butter and a layer of jam. A large cup of coffee completed the offering, and she carried her tray to the bedroom, placing it on the bedside table.

"Let me help you sit up," she offered, lending her strength to his, lifting him to sit against the headboard. He leaned forward and she propped the pillows behind him, her nose almost touching the splendid waves that lay in rumpled splendor on his head. Even at a disadvantage, half-clad and weakened from his ordeal, he possessed a strength that made her think of him as a remnant from another time and place.

Perhaps a regal air about him, as though he were from another world. She smiled at her own foolishness and placed the tray on his lap. "Shall I help you?" she asked, watching as he picked up the coffee cup and sipped appreciatively.

His eyes closed for a moment as he savored the taste, and then he placed the cup back on the tray and picked up the fork she'd provided. "No, I'll be fine," he said. "The coffee's good." The eggs were fresh from the henhouse, fluffy and golden, and Rebecca watched as he ate. The toast was from yesterday's baking, and he licked a bit of jam from his upper lip, then looked up at her.

"You're a fine woman, Rebecca Hale. I can't thank you enough for tending to me."

She shrugged, settling on the straight chair beside the bed. "My mother taught me to be hospitable and my uncle gave me lessons in healing."

"Your uncle?" He lifted a brow in question. "He was a doctor?"

She nodded. "Had a practice in town until he died last year. Now I'm about all the folks around here have to depend on."

"You get a lot of calls?" he asked, lifting the coffee cup to his lips.

She shrugged idly. "Enough to keep meat on my table. Folks pay in foodstuffs usually, and they know I don't have animals to slaughter. I get the occasional ham or quarter of beef when my patients do their butchering."

"Would you do better living in town? It would be handier, I'd think, than having folks trot clear out here when they need you."

"That's their problem," Rebecca answered. "This is my place, and I'll probably live and die here."

Alex leaned his head back, cushioning it against the pillow she'd propped there. "Haven't you ever wanted to travel, see the world?" he asked idly.

She shook her head. "Leaving Creed would please me, I suppose. The town doesn't have much to offer, but some of the folks hereabouts are good people. And I don't really have a lot of choice, do I?" She spread her hands in a gesture of acceptance, and her words reinforced the movement. "A woman can't do much on her own. I'm very aware of that fact."

Alex watched her, noting the shimmer of sunlight through the window as it lit fires in the auburn depths of her hair. Her eyes were soft, resembling brown velvet, he decided, and then smiled at his fanciful thought. The woman would think him daffy, should he reveal his notions about her. She had indeed seemed to resemble an angel last night, and now he viewed her and found her to be a more than tempting package. Feminine, and yet reeking independence from every pore, she appealed to him mightily.

He'd been without the comfort of a woman's body for longer than was healthy for a man. Perhaps that fact alone made her more appealing, he thought, idly measuring her against the women he'd been acquainted with in the past. Not true, he decided as she stirred in the chair and rose to take the tray from his lap.

Rebecca Hale was a woman set apart. Lovely in both face and form, if the curves beneath her layers of clothing were as full and shapely as he suspected.

But her purest attraction lay in the abilities she possessed, both in the art of mending and healing broken bodies and in expressing the intelligent, sensible ideas that formed her life. If he could settle down here, make a life on this farm and possess the essence of feminine beauty she exuded, he'd be content. At that thought, he almost jolted upright. Where had that fanciful vision come from?

It was not to be, he thought, recognizing a dream when he saw one up close. A dream he could never live in this life. He was a man hired by the railroad, the spearhead that drove through ignorance and prejudice to make the steel rails a reality across the northern part of the country. His time in Creed, in the Dakota Territory for that matter, was limited. He'd do well to back off from his attraction to Rebecca Hale and focus on the job he'd come to perform.

She walked from the bedroom, and he forced his gaze to be critical as he watched her move away. A farm woman, gifted with a subdued beauty perhaps, but a simple creature stuck in a backward town, nonetheless. And then he smiled as he recognized the foolishness of that thought.

Simple? Not by a long shot. Complex was more to the point. And attractive, to boot.

Carefully, he scooted down against the pillows and closed his eyes. A couple of days and he'd be on his way, the woman forgotten. He'd pay her well for her hospitality, reaching into his store of gold coins for a generous stipend. His position was secure with his employer. They would not begrudge Rebecca a healthy reward for her care of him and his wound.

An image of russet hair danced behind his closed eyelids, and brown eyes flashed with beguiling promises. He opened his eyes and surveyed the ceiling. Foolishness. Utter foolishness to be intrigued by a woman he would walk away from in mere days.

THE REST OF THE DAY passed slowly, Alex allowing himself the healing power of sleep during both morning and afternoon. Dinner was soup, simple and nourishing, and he ate it propped against the pillows once more. He heard Rebecca's comings and goings as she went from kitchen to outdoors and back.

The unmistakable sound of a dasher being plunged into cream as she worked a churn piqued his interest. He recalled the cook at the orphanage working at the task, and remembered one afternoon when she'd invited him to complete the churning while she took bread from the big oven and worked around him.

He'd gloried in her words of praise, and now he wondered if she hadn't called upon his services in order to make him feel a sense of importance. Or to keep him out of trouble. He'd been handy with his fists in those early days, earning the respect of his mates in the rigid atmosphere of an orphanage. Smiling, he recalled their taunts, words of derision that had turned to admiration as they tagged him with the name *King*.

"Are you asleep?" Rebecca's low voice blended with his memories, and his eyelids were slow to open as he felt her presence beside the bed. She touched him then, one cool hand pressing his forehead and he murmured words that caused her hand to still its movement.

"I'm no angel," she said, a smile tinging her voice. "You're dreaming, Alex Carr. And much as I hate to interrupt your reverie, I need to replace your dressing and tend to that wound."

"All right," he said agreeably, struggling to sit upright, the better to expose his wound to her care. "You're right, you know. I was dreaming. About churning butter when I was a child."

"I just finished with that job," she said, bending to unwrap the long bandage from his body. "You must have heard the sound in your sleep."

"Got any buttermilk?" he asked, looking up at her. He thought her eyes softened as she replied.

"There's always buttermilk left when the churning's done." She peered down at the exposed wound. "It looks better. The red edges are pink now. I think the poultice helped."

"The cook used to shave raw potatoes to draw a wound," he said, remembering another bit about the woman who'd been kind to him.

"Your cook?" she asked. "You came from a home with servants?"

His short burst of laughter was harsh. "Not so's you could notice. I was raised in an orphanage. Got left there when I was just a little bit of a thing. If they hadn't had access to a wet nurse, I'd probably have died."

Her hands stilled their movement. "An orphanage? How did that happen?"

"Who knows? I doubt they even bothered to look for the person who left me. There were lots of children wandering the streets. I was one of the lucky ones, I suppose. I had a warm place to sleep and food to fill my belly. Until I left to make my way in the world."

"How did they come up with a name for you?" she asked idly, her hands moving slowly as she bandaged him.

"Whoever left me there wrote 'Alexander Carr' on a bit of paper, and I suppose they assumed that was name enough." he told her. "That and this thing I wear were all I had in the world." He bent his head and lifted his free hand to touch the silver pendant. His fingers wrapped around it possessively, and she whispered his name.

"Alex?"

Looking up into brown eyes that spoke of sadness, he attempted a smile. "Don't get weepy on me, Rebecca. I'm a grown man and those days are gone forever. I don't much care where I came from, only where I've been in the last twenty years."

She touched the back of his hand and he relented, releasing the medallion from his grip. Her fingers lifted it, and she tilted it to catch the light from the window. "It's beautiful," she told him. "The blue enamel hasn't a single chip in it. How did you ever keep it so perfect?" Her index finger traced the raised figure of the bird of prey. "Is it a hawk?" she asked. "Or a falcon, perhaps?"

"I don't know. I suspect a falcon. I've read that royalty raised them and indulged in the sport of hawking."

Her glance upward was swift, her eyes widening. "Do you think the crown is significant of your background?"

He grinned. "Doubtful. Although the others used to tease me in the orphanage after they realized what images were on the surface. They called me *King*. It used to make me madder than— Well, it made me angry, but then I kinda liked it, made me feel important, and boys in that situation need all the importance they can get."

He looked down at the pendant, then back into her eyes. "Myself, I think it was a pretty thing that appealed to whoever dumped me. Maybe someone wanted me to feel good about myself and left the thing with me to add an air of mystery to my beginnings. Where the name came from I'll never know."

She smiled archly. "Maybe you're sprung from royalty, Alex Carr."

He grinned at her. "We'll never know, will we?"

Rebecca dropped the pendant against his chest and stood beside the bed. "Why don't you sleep now?" she said quietly. "I'm going to finish my chores before I begin supper. Do you think you can eat a bit later?"

Alex considered the idea. "Probably. I need to build my strength."

"All right," Rebecca said. "Sleep now, and I'll be in soon."

But sleep escaped him, probably because he'd dozed for hours all day long. He listened as she went out the back door, heard the slam as the taut spring latched the screened door, and he rose from the bed and made his way to the window. He needed to gain his strength. Should there be repercussions from the men who sought him out, he didn't want Rebecca in the midst of the fray.

He watched her from the bedroom window, catching sight of her as she opened the chicken yard gate and shook a pan of feed in one hand. The birds gathered from their daylong wanderings and bustled past her into the fenced yard. She turned, as if she sought stragglers, and then closed the gate, crossing to scatter the feed on the ground. A bucket of water filled a basin, and her task was complete.

He felt somewhat a voyeur, watching her without her knowledge, and then she looked up and met his gaze through the open window. Their eyes meshed for long moments before she turned away and let herself out the gate. Her movements were slow and measured, her head bent as if her mind dwelt on serious matters. And well she might be concerned about events that had taken place and might yet occur, he thought grimly.

He feared he had brought trouble to Rebecca Hale's farm, and when the day came that he should leave here, he would not willingly cause sorrow to be added to the burden she bore. She moved from his line of vision and he walked back toward the bed. The pain in his shoulder was dull—constant, but bearable. Another couple of days and he'd be ready to ride.

The back screened door slammed, announcing her presence, and he looked up expectantly, chagrined as he recognized his eagerness. She appeared in the doorway and her expression was enigmatic, her eyes touching his face and moving on to the pale bandage standing out sharply against the tanned skin beneath it.

"Can you pull on your trousers?" she asked. "Or do I need to help you?"

"I'll manage," he said. It would not do to have her hands fumbling with his garments. Already, he felt the beginnings of an arousal stirring in his nether parts. He might do well to cut short this recuperation process. It would be to Rebecca's advantage if he left tomorrow.

CHAPTER THREE

BY MORNING, A HEAVY RAIN had begun and sheets of water sluiced past the windows, caught by the gusting wind and blowing against the west side of the house. Rebecca reluctantly donned her waterproof cape, a homemade, oilcloth affair passed down from her father. It draped over her from head to midcalf, with only her father's tall boots exposed beneath.

She felt awkward in the footwear, shuffling through the driving rain toward the barn. Yet it would be a waste of money to buy boots to fit her smaller feet, when her father's still had so much wear left. The residue of thrift drummed into her by her proud, frugal parents would not allow such a purchase, and she grumbled each time she tugged the boots in place.

The animals were vocal in their greetings, the cow lowing loudly at the lateness of the hour. Alex had tried to dissuade Rebecca from doing chores until the rain should let up somewhat, but his coaxing ran out when the roof vibrated even more from the downpour. Waiting was not an option after breakfast was out of the way, and the heavy clouds hung lower than ever over the drenched barnyard and outbuildings.

She'd plodded through the water, falling too heavily to soak into the ground, and now the interior of the barn was welcoming. A lantern on the wall was lit quickly and she checked the horses' stalls for feed. A sheaf of hay split between them provided breakfast, and she turned to her cow.

Within fifteen minutes she was finished, the milk pail half-full and the cow contentedly chewing her cud. There would be no turning them into the pasture today, Rebecca decided. And the chickens would hole up inside the henhouse, requiring her to feed them there. She left the barn and carried the milk pail to the house, setting it inside the back door.

A basin of feed was settled on the floor of the coop and the hens gathered around it, noisily fighting for a spot. Rebecca filled the water dish and left them to their squabble, gathering eggs while the Plymouth Rock hens ate breakfast. One stalwart cluck refused to move, apparently having decided it was time to hatch a clutch of eggs, and Rebecca eyed her judiciously.

"You'd might as well make it worth your while," she told the hen, sliding several more still-warm eggs beneath the noisy creature. Dodging the sharp beak, she backed away and slid through the door into the yard, her gathering of eggs held within her apron, beneath the enveloping oilcloth she wore.

"I thought you were lost out there," Alex said from the kitchen doorway. He leaned one forearm against the frame and smiled at her. "I'd have done the dishes for you, but it doesn't work with only one available hand."

She sent him a scornful glance. "It's easy enough to offer when you're out of commission, Mr. Carr." Lifting the oilcloth over her head, she hung it next to the door, watching the raindrops stain the floor.

"What a mess," she muttered, striding to the pantry where she found towels in the dirty clothes basket. She dropped them beneath the dripping garment and turned back to the stove. The coffeepot held enough for several cups and she nodded at Alex.

"Want another cup?"

He straightened from his nonchalant stance and walked to the table. "I hope you noticed I managed to get my trousers fastened. Not easy to do, one-handed, but I didn't want to offend your sensibilities, ma'am."

His eyes glittered in the lamplight as he settled in a chair. Green as emeralds, she decided. As if she'd ever seen the gems themselves. Her mouth twisted wryly. Only read about them in books, but she'd be willing to bet more than one woman had fallen hard for the glittering glances the man offered.

"You don't offend me, Mr. Carr," she said lightly. Deftly, she poured coffee and placed the cup before him. "Sugar?" she offered, snatching a spoon from the jar that shared the center of her table with the butter dish and a covered bowl of jam.

"No, just straight from the pot," he said, warming his hands on the cup. He shot her a grin. "Are you going to join me?"

She shrugged. "Might as well. I can't do much planting in the garden with this downpour, but it'll make the soil easier to work once it passes over."

"How much garden do you plant?" he asked. "I noticed a fenced area beside the house. I'll bet you fight with the rabbits for the vegetables, don't you?"

Rebecca nodded. "Once in a while deer jump the fence, but not often. I've shot more than one that thought he'd have a feast out there."

His brow lifted disbelievingly. "You shot a deer? And then what?"

Her gaze was level. "What do you suppose? I gutted it and hung it in the shed for a couple of days before I skinned it out and cut it up. Usually give some to my neighbors, and in exchange, they share their kill with me. I've got jars of canned venison in the pantry."

He nodded slowly. "I suppose you have to do it all, don't you, living alone here."

"I learned from my father," she said quietly. "My parents had me late in life, long after they'd given up on raising a family. And when they died neither of them was much more than sixty years old."

"That's not a bad age," Alex said. "Although I'd hope to last a few years longer than that."

"I wish they had," Rebecca told him. "They weren't sickly. Pa was taken suddenly with a bad heart, and after he died my mother just gave up. I buried them both several years ago."

"You've never wanted to get married, have a family of your own?"

She shook her head. "There aren't many decent candidates hereabouts. Several of them have come courting, but my mother used to tell me I was persnickety. She was probably right. I prefer the word *choosy.''* She smiled at him, looking up quickly to catch him with a calculating look on his face.

''What?'' she asked, sitting up straight in her chair.

''Just wondering what you would consider a *decent* candidate.''

She felt flustered by his close attention, and spurned the quick reply that sat behind her closed lips. *Someone like you.* And wouldn't he skedaddle out of here like the hounds of hell were behind him, biting at his heels, should she voice those words aloud?

Yet, it was true. In her years of sorting through the available men in Creed and the outlying parts, she'd never seen anyone to match the man who watched her. And if she had, she decided, bending her head, drawing her gaze from his…if she had, she'd have snatched him up, quick as a wink.

Alex pressed her for an answer. ''What sort of man appeals to you, Rebecca?''

She felt a flush begin beneath the collar of her dress and rise to color her cheeks. Thankful for the shadows provided by the hanging lamp overhead, she shrugged, unwilling to look up, lest he see her blush and surmise its cause.

''I don't know,'' she countered. ''Probably a man who would pitch in and help me with the farm, one who would provide me with a family.'' She inhaled deeply. ''A man who would be kind and understanding, I suppose.''

''Don't forget love,'' he said quietly. ''Attraction is a big part of that, maybe. But the men and women

I've come across who seem to be enjoying life are usually involved in a marriage where love plays a part.''

''I'm not sure I believe in such a thing,'' she told him. ''My folks had a good marriage, but they rarely touched or displayed any affection.''

''Not even with you?'' Surprise touched each syllable he spoke. ''Your mother didn't fuss over you?''

She felt a laugh bubble within. ''Hardly. She was wrapped up in survival, in gardening and cooking and keeping us and our surroundings clean. I was expected to share the load once I was big enough to lend a hand.''

''Hasn't anyone ever…haven't you ever been hugged and kissed, sweetheart?'' His voice was softer now and she couldn't resist a peek at his face, certain she would find a bit of humor there, perhaps a wide grin even, as if he offered to fill the lack.

But no glimmer of whimsy touched those lips, no smile curved their corners into the grin she'd expected to see. Instead, his eyelids half concealed a glittering appraisal; his mouth was firm, offering no clue to his thoughts.

''No.'' She spoke the single word flatly, as if to repel his queries, putting an end to the conversation they'd begun. A conversation she was ready to put aside permanently. It was no business of his whether or not she'd existed her whole life without being held in a welcome embrace.

Once, Ted had grasped her closely after a dance in town and she'd fought her way free of his greedy hands, cuffing him stoutly until he released her. His eye had shown symptoms of bruising for several days, and she heard the story in the general store that he'd had a tussle with a hired hand. She'd laughed quietly all the way home.

Alex stood abruptly and circled the table. "Stand up, Rebecca," he said firmly, grasping the back of her chair and then, when she made no move to obey his words, his fingers spread wide across her shoulder. "Please," he said softly. "I hope you know I won't hurt you."

A soft chuckle escaped Alex's lips, and she tilted her head to peer up at him, her mouth set in a stubborn line. "I couldn't hurt you if I tried," he said. "I'm operating with one hand here, sweetheart."

"What do you want?" she asked, eyeing him with suspicion.

"Only to put my arm around you."

"Why?" Her heart began a steady, heavy beat that drew her attention, and she felt a lump rise in her throat. The thought of being held next to that muscular chest was almost frightening, she decided. And yet, the idea beckoned her with tendrils of longing.

"Rebecca." He spoke her name quietly, shaking his head slowly. "Are you always this suspicious? Or is it just me you don't trust?"

"I'm not," she blurted. "I have no reason not to trust you." And so saying, she scooted her chair back and rose, turning to find herself smack-dab against his long, rangy frame. He was warm, and his scent was of the soap she'd used to wash him and the fresh air from her bed linens. His arm circled her waist and tugged her gently, closer to the width of his chest, her face tucking into his throat. Her nose inhaled more of the male aroma he wore, and she felt a chill speed the length of her spine.

His mouth touched her temple, then grazed her forehead as he bent his head, his lips following the line of her jaw. She found, in losing the small comfort of nuzzling against his skin she'd gained greater pleasure, that of myriad small kisses as he nudged her head back, allowing the vulnerable curve of her throat to be exposed to his caresses. And then he brushed her mouth with his, carefully, a touch as gentle as the brush of butterfly wings against her lips.

It was warm, just a bit damp, this kiss he offered. And if she should push him away, he would move back. She knew it with a certainty that allowed her to remain quiet in his embrace. He would not hurt her. Alex Carr had promised her safety, and though he might be willing to seek more than a kiss, should she offer, he would not grasp what she withheld.

And so she allowed his touch, sorted through the whispers of warning that whirled in her mind as he touched her, oh so gently, his mouth easing from hers then returning anew. It was a kiss such as she'd never imagined. She'd seen mothers embrace their children, smacking their lips against cheek or forehead with brief bursts of enthusiasm, usually in the general store or beneath the trees in the town square.

However, she'd never seen a man and woman embrace, unless she were to count the occasions in town when couples touched lightly in courtly dances or whirled in squares while Pop Jensen called the movements over the sounds of his fiddle.

Now she was held against a man's body, with only one arm, with his other forearm pressed against her breasts by necessity, held there by the bandage she herself had put in place. And again his mouth sought hers, his lips barely open as he pressed them with careful movements against her own. She lost her breath, gasping for air and finding only that which escaped his lips.

Looking down at her as she shivered in his arms, his eyes darkened, shining with a seductive glow. "Did that hurt?" he asked.

"No." The single word was uttered on an indrawn breath and she cleared her throat and repeated it, forcing a small laugh. "No, of course it didn't hurt."

"Did you like it?" he asked, drawing back as if he would hold her gaze.

"I...I don't know." She watched as his eyebrow lifted at her words.

"Shall I repeat it? Give you another chance to consider the idea?" His smile was sweet, a strange word, she thought, to describe the movement of his lips, the crinkling at the corners of his eyes as he spoke the invitation.

"I don't—don't really think that's wise." She managed to whisper the words, watched as his smile broadened, and held her breath, struck with dismay as he slowly released her from his embrace.

"All right." He nodded once and moved away, only inches, but far enough to set her free from the spell he'd woven with such ease.

The man was a charmer, and she'd fallen into his web. "Don't do that again," she told him harshly.

"You didn't like it?"

She thought she detected a note of hurt in his query and was obliged by common courtesy to deny his words. "It isn't that," she said quickly. "I just don't think it's wise, or even decent, come to think of it. A woman has no business being free with herself unless she's certain of a man's intentions."

"Is that what your mother told you?" he asked, tilting his head as if the notion amused him.

"Yes." Firm and certain, she spoke the single word of reply. And then elaborated on her stand. "I'm not a loose woman, Alex."

"I'd say not, if that was your first experience with the art of kissing."

Rebecca laughed. "I didn't know there was an art to it. Although…" She looked up into his face, elated by the rush of excitement his touch created within her. "Although, now that I think about it, I'm sure you've had practice."

"A bit," he admitted. "But probably not as much of it as you might imagine."

"I wouldn't know," she said. "I've heard about men and their shenanigans, things my mother warned me against, but—"

"But you never gave anyone a chance to get close enough to give you a taste of *shenanigans,* did you?"

She shook her head. And then brushed past him.

"Afraid of me, Rebecca?" he asked quietly, turning to watch her as she busied herself at the sink.

She poured a dollop of soap into the dishpan and turned to the stove, dipping her smaller saucepan into the reservoir and carrying water to mix with the liquid soap. The quart jar that held her odds and ends and bits of bar soap sat beneath the sink, behind the curtain her mother had made to hide the bucket of scrap and cleaning utensils. A cup of water added to it every couple of weeks kept the soap liquid, a gelatinous solution used for dishes and washing of hands at the sink.

She plunged her hands into the hot water, adding the few dishes from breakfast, and made a production of washing them, setting them aside to rinse. Alex was behind her, his breath warm against her neck as he bent to peer over her shoulder. "I'd dry those if I had two hands available. I'm not at my best one-handed."

If you were any handier with that one hand, I'd be in deep trouble. The thought raced through Rebecca's mind and she shook her head quickly. "This will only take a few minutes. Why don't you sit down at the table?"

He laughed, a soft sound that ruffled the strands of hair that had escaped her braid. "Now *that* I can do."

His body warmth was gone from behind her, and she felt bereft for just a moment at its loss. *Foolishness.* Pure foolishness to allow herself to be swallowed up by the whispers and touches of a scalawag like Alex Carr. A man who would be gone, on his way within days, leaving her to make do with the dull, lusterless life she lived.

"Tell me about yourself," he said, sliding a chair from the table, sitting down gingerly, aware of the pain that radiated from his shoulder. Holding Rebecca had put a strain on the wound. But it had been worth it, worth the dull ache that throbbed from collarbone to elbow and back. Just the soft, plush weight of her breasts against his forearm had been enough to put him in a state of readiness, and he'd been hard put not to hold her against his pulsing arousal. Only the fact that she would have bolted had subdued his instinctive response.

Now he repeated his words, aware that she had not responded. "Rebecca? Tell me about yourself, your life here."

"There's not much to tell," she said after a moment. "I keep my livestock tended and garden throughout the summer and fall. I sell my eggs at the general store, and go to church in town on Sunday. I read whenever I can find something worth looking at, usually books I manage to order once in a while from the city. Sometimes a newspaper makes its way here, but by the time I get my hands on it, it's about in tatters."

"Do you have lady friends?" he asked, and was not surprised when she shook her head.

"No, not really. I like the minister's wife. She's been kind to me since my mother died. And the lady at the general store always speaks nicely."

"How about the people you went to school with when you were young?"

Rebecca looked over her shoulder at him, her mouth pursed. "I lost touch with them years ago. We never had much time to neighbor. My folks weren't real friendly."

"Didn't your mother want you to marry and have

a family of your own?'' His heart ached for the girl who had missed so much of what life had to offer, and the urge rose within him to embrace her once more. Only the fear that she would push him away deterred him from the few steps it would take to approach her at the sink and enclose her waist with his good arm.

"I don't know." She turned in a half circle, holding a plate in her hand, the water and suds dripping from it to the floor. "We never talked about my leaving here. And I never had any reason to want to go. Not till—" Her lips compressed suddenly as she shot a quick look at him, and a red stain washed her cheeks.

"Not till now?"

"Do you enjoy embarrassing me?" She turned quickly, and her foot slid on the small puddle of suds. Grasping at air, she dropped the plate and clutched at the drainboard. At her feet, the heavy china shattered, chips scattering hither and yon. She muttered a word beneath her breath, and then cried aloud, "Just look what you made me do!"

Stepping over the clutter of broken pieces, she groped inside the pantry doorway and emerged with a broom and dustpan. A few short strokes of the cornstraw and she'd swept up the mess.

"Let me hold the pan." Alex took it from her other hand and squatted in front of her, holding it at an angle while she swept. "It's my fault," he said, apologizing nicely. "I didn't mean to upset you."

"I think you did," she retorted. "I'm a woman unused to being around men, especially men such as you, and you've managed to set my whole life on end in the past days.''

''A man such as me?'' What did that phrase say for the men she'd met? The male creatures who had entered her life and been shooed from her presence.

''You know what I'm saying,'' she told him staunchly. ''You're city born and bred, and you've a way with you. You're elegant and polished and you know all the right words to say to a woman.''

''I've a way with me? You think I'm elegant and polished?'' His voice touched the words quietly and, as he watched her from his position at her feet, her eyes filled with unbidden tears.

''Yes.'' The lone syllable was a soft hiss in the stillness, and he rose, awkwardly off balance with his arm tucked neatly across his chest. The dustpan in his free hand was lifted from his grasp, and she held aside the curtain beneath the sink to deposit the pieces into the trash basket.

''My elegance, as you put it, comes from my association with a man I met during the war,'' he said quietly. ''I lived in his home for a time afterward, recovering from a wound I'd been dealt just before the end of the fighting. He taught me much about the ins and outs of society. And then offered me a job with his railroad.''

She wiped at the tears that continued to flow and he felt helplessness envelope him. A woman obviously not given to tears, she was shedding a copious amount of them.

''What can I say to make you stop crying?'' he asked, breaking off his story to attend her distress.

Stiff and abrupt, his words caused her to sniff discreetly, even as her fingers searched the depth of her pockets for a nonexistent handkerchief.

"I'm not crying," she denied, brushing quickly at the tears that had escaped to stain her cheeks.

He drew a handkerchief from his pocket, one he'd not used, fortunately, and pressed it into her palm. "Please, take this."

"No." She shook her head. "If I do, I'll have to wash it before I return it to you, and I don't want you here that long."

His chuckle caught him off guard, but he could not resist the laugh that bubbled up in his throat at her petulant words. Her mouth pouted, the lower lip pushed forward, and he thought she resembled a small child, thwarted and unhappy.

"I mean it," she said. "Don't laugh at me."

"I'm not. Well, I'm not laughing at *you*," he added quickly, "only at the look on your face." His arm circled her waist, and she stumbled as he caught her up in a clumsy embrace. He held her close, bending to press his cheek against her hair. "You are a most appealing woman, Rebecca Hale. I'd give much for the gift of time spent with you."

"You've spent time with me," she murmured.

"Not enough. Not nearly enough."

SHE'D ALMOST PUT HIM from her mind, she decided. Kneading bread dough and ironing everything she could lay her hands on had done much to fill the afternoon hours. Hours during which she'd sent Alex into the parlor, waving at her scant collection of books, telling him to stay out of her way while she did her chores.

That he'd obeyed her edict was a mark in his favor, she decided, testing the sole of her flat iron with a damp finger. It spit nicely, and she ran it over the collar of her Sunday dress. The yards of fabric she'd sewn into the skirt took forever to press, and they hung almost to the floor from the ironing board she'd set up near the stove. A woman could solve a lot of problems while she ran an iron back and forth, she'd found.

In fact, housework gave her a lot of time to think. Between the mindless tasks of washing dishes and clothes and the summertime chores of shelling peas and snapping beans, she'd managed, over the years, to keep her life pretty much on an even keel. Now, with the addition of Alex to her household, even temporarily, she had new problems to solve, new issues to consider.

If all men were as attractive as Alex, she'd have married long ago. If she could expect the same sort of excitement at the hands of Ted Duncan, he'd be installed in her home in jig time. But he still wouldn't be Alex. That thought stopped the movement of her hands, and she looked up and out the kitchen window. Only the smell of scorched cotton brought her mind back to the business at hand, and she uttered a snarl of despair as she looked down at the collar she'd seared.

Fortunately, the brown mark was on the underside and she could wear it without exposing her ineptness, but *she'd* know it was there, and that was enough to cause her lips to press together in a pout, the lower one protruding a bit.

"What did you do?" Alex asked from the doorway. He hovered there as if he doubted his welcome in the kitchen, and well he might. She'd just about gotten shed of his image putting her mind in turmoil, and here he was back again.

"Burned my collar." She deposited the flat iron on the stove and shook the dress, smoothing the collar, checking it from the back to be sure the mark would not show.

"Are you finished with the ironing now?" he asked.

"This is the end of it," she told him, picking up the stack of clothing on the table and readying it for storage in her bedroom.

He stepped aside as she approached the doorway, and she brushed past him. "I'll look at your shoulder in a minute," she said, wishing it might be the final time she would lay her hands on his skin...even as she acknowledged the thought as a lie. Her heart ached already, anticipating the loss of his presence, once she told him he was healed enough to leave her house and be on his way.

He'd had time to remove his shirt, having only to slip it from one arm in readiness. He sat at the table, his green eyes appraising her as she stepped toward him.

"Can you turn just a bit?" she asked, her reach long as she tried to unwind the length of torn sheeting that wrapped around his broad shoulder and beneath his other arm. She lifted his medallion from where it nestled against the golden hair on his chest and her fingers clasped it, her gaze moving to where her thumb rubbed across the crown.

"They called you *King?* Really?" she asked.

He nodded a reply and obliged her request, scooting his chair back and moving it a quarter turn, so that he faced her head-on. His thighs were parted, and she hesitated, then stepped between them, the better to unwind and roll up the bandage as she went.

"I can see you as a child," she murmured, "facing down all those other boys with your chin in the air and your fists ready to claim your place in their midst." Her skirts brushed against his legs and he gritted his teeth. "No wonder they named you as royalty," she said quietly, her hands warm against his skin.

Her breasts were inches from his face and he closed his eyes, aware not only of the firm, rounded bosom before him, but the scent of her skin as her hands and arms moved mere inches from his face.

He gripped his thighs with both hands once his arm was released from the binding, and held firmly to the muscles that tightened beneath his palms. Two days with the woman and he was behaving like a boy still wet behind the ears. Thirty-three years old, and randy as an old goat.

She hummed as she worked, and he winced as the poultice was removed from both front and back of his shoulder. "Aha!" she said quietly, and his eyes snapped open.

"Aha, what?" he asked, his voice husky, causing him to clear his throat.

"Aha, it's healing nicely," she told him. "I don't see any sign of infection, and that's better than I expected. I've never treated a gunshot wound that mended so quickly." She backed away and deposited the soiled poultice and dressing in the trash, then turned to the pantry to retrieve her bag.

Another piece of white fabric was folded, a smear of carbolic salve from a flat tin was spread on its surface, and she placed it on the back of his shoulder, where she'd cut the bullet from his flesh. Another piece of material was daubed and stuck on the front, where the small entry hole had already begun to close.

"You must be healthy," Rebecca said in an undertone, apparently caught up in her bandaging. She stepped back and considered him. "I'm trying to figure out how I can fasten this without you losing the use of your arm. Once you have the freedom of moving it, you'll be able to be on your way."

"I won't be able to lift my saddle for a couple more days," he reminded her. "I don't mind paying for my keep, if you'll let me stick around a bit longer."

"You needn't pay me anything," she said. "I didn't expect that of you."

"I know, but I'll just charge it to the railroad. They pay my bills, and you might as well receive just due for your doctoring." He smiled up at her. "I'm enjoying your cooking anyway, if you must know. It sure beats the hotel in town."

She shrugged, a small movement of her shoulders. "All right, if you like. You can stay for a few days."

CHAPTER FOUR

Korosol—1872

"THEY'VE LOCATED THE MAN in question, sir." The aide to Prince Jon was subservient, bowing low as he spoke the message.

Iron-gray hair and chiseled features bespoke the prince's regal beginnings, and an expression of satisfaction filled dark eyes as the king's brother heard the news. "Have they disposed of the problem?" he asked quietly, as if the matter was of small import. Yet, an observer would have noted the quickening of excitement that brought ruddy color to dwell on his high cheekbones.

The aide shook his head. "They're on his trail. It seems he works for a railroad."

Prince Jon lifted an eyebrow and his lip curled, perhaps in derision at the thought of a man with royal blood being so occupied. "And what does he do for this *railroad?*"

"The communication said the man, Alexander Carr, is a scout, working in the Dakota Territory, arranging for the railway to be constructed. Our people believe they've located him, and the plan is underway."

"Alexander Carr." Prince Jon repeated the name. "The woman at least gave him a name. Too bad she was drawn into the situation to begin with. If Quince had done as he was told, none of this would have been necessary. Her involvement has caused more trouble than she was worth." His hand lifted in a dismissive gesture. "Not that she was worth much, when all was said and done."

"It was fortunate that we even discovered her identity, sir," the aide said, his demeanor, as always, deferential as he spoke with his superior. "Does the king have any knowledge of this?"

Prince Jon shook his head. "Of course not. He's too involved with the process of dying. It was pure happenstance that this puzzle came to my attention. Quince has paid well for his disobedience to my orders." His mouth twisted as he spoke the name of his former underling. "The woman betrayed him. That in itself was not remarkable," he said harshly. "Women have long been connivers of the worst sort."

He folded his hands on the desk before him and looked up at his aide. "If you receive any more information, I'm to be informed immediately. This must be resolved before the king dies. There can be no chance of Alexander Carr's appearance here."

"I doubt he has any knowledge of his birth, sir."

"The medallion the foolish woman took with her can be identified. It must be retrieved at any cost. And the man disposed of."

"The men we've sent are able to handle this task, sir." The aide's words were intended to soothe the would-be monarch, and yet they seemed to have little effect.

Prince Jon rose and stalked to the window, looking out upon the early blooms of spring that covered the palace grounds. "Haste is of the essence," he muttered. And behind him, the aide nodded in mute agreement, then turned and left the chamber.

Creed—The Dakota Territory

REBECCA SLEPT ON THE SOFA in the parlor, confident that Alex's wound had healed sufficiently to merit her removing her presence from the bedroom. It was wearying to nod off in the armchair, and two nights of a stiff neck and sore back made her tired enough to sleep soundly on the horsehair sofa.

The sun was rising over the barn when she peered from the kitchen window, and Rebecca yawned widely, casting away the sleepy seeds that lingered to cloud her mind. It was late. The horses and chickens could wait for feeding, but the cow would be mournfully sounding her distress if she wasn't milked soon.

Three chunks of wood in the stove and a judicious stirring of the coals made the fire ready for the coffeepot. She filled it from the pump and settled it on the hottest section of the broad, black surface, inhaling the scent of the beans as she ground them. By the time she'd gathered up her clothing and dressed behind the parlor doors, the pot was heating nicely and she opened the oven door, testing it to see if it was ready for the coffee cake she'd left to rise overnight.

Snatching her hand from the heat, she lifted the tin of sweet dough and lowered it into the yawning maw of the oven, then closed the door and wiped her palms on her apron. Milking and gathering the fresh eggs came next, and the coffee cake would be about done by the time she returned. After breakfast would be time enough to turn the animals out into the pasture and the chickens out to scratch in the field next to the house.

Thirty minutes later she entered the back door, the brimming egg pan tucked into the curve of her arm, carrying the pail of milk, topped with thick foam, in her other hand.

"You've been busy," Alex said, turning from the stove. Protected by hot pads, he held the pan in both hands, and Rebecca raised her brows in consternation.

"Should you be using your arm that way?" She hung her shawl and approached the stove, drawn by its heat and by the man who stood before her, shirtless and arrogant, uncaring that he defied the rules that forbade such intimacy between men and women outside the boundary of marriage. Her gaze turned from him, paying mind instead to her cold hands. She held them over the stove's surface, rubbing them together.

"I need to get my shoulder back into motion," Alex said. He watched her reflectively, she decided, as if he admired her early-morning appearance. His words verified her thoughts as he placed the coffee cake on top of the warming oven and murmured his deliberations aloud.

"A lady who used to come to the orphanage had a brown velvet dress just the color of your eyes," he said quietly. "And your hair is almost the exact shade as the leaves on a red maple tree. Did you know that?" His gaze seemed focused on the loose braid she'd formed upon arising and he stepped closer, his hand lifting to wind a loose tendril around his index finger. As though she could feel each individual strand clinging to his calloused skin, she shivered, and his gaze became more intent as it shifted to meet her own.

"When I finally see it undone—" His voice broke, the words unspoken that might have sent her fleeing, and she drew away from his touch.

"You won't," she stated flatly. "I rarely let my hair down. It's unseemly."

"Not when you're..." His pause was long, and then he reached for her, his palm against her shoulder, curling to deliver warmth to her flesh beneath the dress she wore.

She shivered again, a trembling that owed its existence to—fear, perhaps? She thought not. Anticipation was more like it. If he should again kiss her, if his arm should surround her, bind her to him, would she object? Would her voice raise in protest? Or would she allow him the liberty of taking her mouth beneath his, invite his caress with a subtle movement of her body?

He was addictive. Not just the masculine attributes he exuded, but the man he'd revealed himself to be in the short days of their acquaintance. She'd learned much about Alex Carr already, and yearned again to hear his voice offer memories and dreams into her hearing. Her body betrayed her even now, she realized, as he bent his head to touch her lips with his. Tilting her chin, she gave him access, and he accepted the gesture. Not snatching at the gain he'd made, but leisurely, as though they had the entire day in which to savor this hushed moment, this blending of lips.

"Alex?" Was that her voice, that wispy thread of yearning that spun between them? It seemed so, for he lifted his head and his smile was one of satisfaction. Not triumph, for that would have sent her flying but, instead, a sweet, joyous acceptance of the gift she'd offered.

"Fate must have decreed this, my coming here to you," he said quietly, his other hand sliding gently around her waist. She winced, lest he harm his wound with the movement, but he shook his head, a small, quick motion, as if he would allay her fear. "I can bear the ache if it means holding you in my arms," he said quietly. "I won't open the wound or cause the healing to go awry, so long as you…just stand as you are and let me do *this*."

This, it seemed, involved his mouth touching her throat, his other hand moving from her shoulder to clasp the braid, tugging her head a bit, guiding her where he would. And she, silly fool that she was, allowed it.

Allowed it? That was hardly the word for her behavior. She hadn't known she could be so compliant, so charmed by the touch of a man, so ready to bend, to sway like a long-stemmed flower in the wind. Until she was plastered against him like the paper on the parlor wall. And then he set her away, but only for a moment, as one hand reached out to draw a chair from the table. Lowering himself to the seat, he took her with him, and in two seconds flat, she was sitting on a man's lap for the first time in her life.

"Alex!" This time her voice spoke his name with overtones of distress, a sound of dismay that turned to delight as he whispered her name against her ear.

"Rebecca." He repeated it, softly enough to halt her breathing so she might hear what he would say. "Rebecca, let me have your warmth. Give over to me. Offer me the sweetness of your mouth…lend me your embrace."

He inhaled and his head lifted, his emerald eyes entreating her. "Put your arm around me and lean into me. As if you liked me, as if I were the man you've always yearned for."

There was no *as if* about it, she thought, her mind awhirl with the words he spoke. And who would know, who would it hurt if she did as he bade her?

Her arm slid around his neck, measuring the width of his shoulders, her other hand meeting it, her fingers lacing together. She was careful not to disturb the padding that lay in place, both front and back, held there only by the salve that held it loosely to his rapidly healing flesh. And her words were of that when she spoke.

"I think we could take off the dressings tomorrow, let the air get to your wound."

His lips curved in a smile and his eyes crinkled at the corners. "Do you think so?"

"You're laughing at me," she said, accusing him with a pout.

"You're flirting with me," he said quickly. His finger touched her mouth. "I've never seen you pout before. You do it beautifully."

"I don't flirt."

"You're learning." He rubbed his index finger over her lower lip, and it relaxed beneath his investigation. The callus teased her, the pressure of his nail tickled her upper lip and she laughed aloud. "See what I mean?" he asked, and as she watched, his eyes darkened, his lids drooped a bit, and his jaw firmed, as though he became more intent, more focused on the woman he held.

As if that were possible.

And then his palm cupped her chin and he tipped her head a bit, arranging the slant of his own in order to mesh their mouths in a kiss that was unlike the others they had shared. He released her chin, and in a movement she had not anticipated, that palm cradled her head, holding it firmly for his careful invasion of her defenses. His tongue touched her upper lip and she jolted, wary of the caress. He soothed her, tiny nibbling kisses that took the moisture he'd left behind.

And then, again, he brushed his tongue against the crease of her mouth and her eyes flew open.

His voice was husky, sounding as though he'd

poured raw whiskey down his throat, making it vibrate darkly. "Open your mouth, Rebecca." She hesitated, then parted her lips as he had asked. He was being so polite, so well-mannered about this whole business, and yet she was in a most vulnerable position and probably well on her way to being a victim of seduction. And wasn't that a word she'd never considered could apply to her?

Her heart beat rapidly, a thumping she was certain he could hear, for it seemed her chest vibrated with each measure. Languidly, she lifted her hand to thread her fingers through his darkly golden hair. It seemed just the act of breathing took all her concentration, and her eyelids were heavy. She closed them and felt his mouth descend again to cover hers, felt the warm, rough edges of his tongue as he explored the inside of her lips and then the heat of its length tangling with her own.

Heat. Warmth such as she'd never known invaded her body, and when his hand touched her waist, then shifted to cup the underside of her breast, she only whimpered, a puny protest indeed for such an indiscretion. It felt…she could not think of a word to describe the thrill of that curving palm holding her breast, as if he weighed its firm contours. Her muddled mind exploded with sensation, as if unable to contain the pleasure offered by those agile fingers brushing against the puckered crests.

Her lips whispered his name and she trembled, turning her face into his throat in a futile attempt to somehow return the delight he offered. Her mouth opened against his jaw, her tongue touched the rough whiskers of his beard, for he had not shaved in several days, and she heard his voice vibrate from his chest, against her ear.

"Sweetheart." His grip tightened on her, and as he moved her in his embrace, he groaned suddenly, a sound at variance with the murmured endearment.

"You've hurt yourself." She sat upright, careful not to jar him, her hand touching his shoulder gently, uncaring of her disheveled clothing, her flyaway hair.

"No, just put too much strain on the dratted thing," he said, his voice irritable, as if, for the first time, he resented the indignity of bowing to the pain inherent in being wounded. He'd suffered pretty much in silence, she thought, but now he was upset, almost petulant, as he faced the indignity of her fussing over him, when he'd obviously rather have the upper hand.

He'd had the upper hand, she reminded herself, rather too long for her own good, she thought, looking down at three buttons on the front of her dress he'd managed to undo, unbeknownst to her. She slid from his lap, her fingers awkward as she replaced the buttons in their moorings, then tucked the errant wisps of hair behind her ears.

His smile was crooked, as if he could not form his lips into anything signifying pleasure. A line of sweat rimmed his upper lip, and she placed her palm on his forehead. He felt clammy to the touch, and she shook her head in mute dismay. "You're going back to bed, Alex. I'll bring your breakfast in there. And no arguments, you hear?"

It was to his credit that he didn't dispute her orders, but rose and leaned against her shoulder as they made their way toward the bed. "Undo my britches?" he asked, standing beside the footboard.

She shook her head. "You can manage, I think. You got them on. Getting them off should be easy." Her shoulders squared as she walked away. He'd almost coaxed her into disaster, she thought. The man should be outlawed, and all his kind with him.

And yet, her lips felt swollen, her breasts tingled, and as she spooned up his scrambled eggs and poured coffee into a mug, she fought against the memory of his hands and mouth and the musky aroma of male flesh. The scent of Alex Carr.

IT TOOK TWO DAYS FOR HIM to gain his strength once more. Two days in which he slept, ate, and rose only to tend to his needs. Rebecca spoke out crossly when he refused to use the chamber pot in the corner of her room. There was no way on earth he would allow her to cart his leavings off to the outhouse. The thought angered him, and his words were harsh as he denied her vow to keep him indoors.

"What if your assailants come around looking for you?" she asked, hands on hips as she blocked the back door.

"Don't make me lift you out of the way, sweetheart," he said quietly. "You'll damage my shoulder if you don't move."

She shot him a look of aggravation that might have threatened a lesser man, but Alex held strong notions about certain things, and about this issue he was adamant. "I'll go outside if I need to," he told her.

"Furthermore, tomorrow I'm going to try picking up my saddle and see how strong my arm is."

"I don't think that's a good idea," she said, stepping away from the entryway and allowing him to shove the screened door open. "You need to give it another couple of days before you try something so strenuous."

He turned around and grinned at her through the wire mesh, noting her frown and her pursed lips. "And here I thought you were trying to get rid of me." He moved back a step, and she bolted out through the door.

"You'll fall down the stairs if you're not careful," she said sharply, catching at his arm as if she feared he would take a tumble if she didn't look after him.

"Walk with me, then," he offered.

"As far as the chicken coop," she said. "I need to feed them and gather the eggs."

"I can lend a hand, or else let the horses into the pasture."

She seemed to consider that idea for a moment, then agreed with a nod. "All right. You need the exercise, and that shouldn't put a strain on you."

He was more stable than she realized, and for a moment he was ashamed that he'd leaned so heavily on her over the past days, letting her wait on him when he was gaining back his strength in leaps and bounds. But he'd enjoyed her fussing over him, reveled in the softness of her caresses as she dealt with his wound, and, most of all, stored up memories of each conversation they'd shared.

He'd come to know the woman better than any

other human being he'd encountered in his life. He'd told her of his army days, of the men he'd fought with, of the battles they won and lost, and in so doing had rid himself of dreams that haunted him on occasion during the midnight hours.

Now, Rebecca held out her arm, as if he might need her strength to trod the stairs from the porch to the ground, and, beguiler that he was, he took hold of her forearm, then slid his hand to grasp hers. She glanced up at him quickly, then smiled, as if she saw through his stunt and allowed him the small victory. It was with reluctance that he released her fingers, allowing them to trail across his palm, tempted to cling to that small connection.

She hastened ahead of him to the henhouse and as he watched, she opened the chicken yard gate and allowed the hens to traipse past her to the backyard and garden space. They bustled about, pecking for small insects in the grass, several of them squatting for a dust bath, wings flapping and downy feathers flying. It was a scene of domesticity such as Alex had never known on a firsthand basis, and he watched as Rebecca held her skirts aside, entering the coop in search of eggs.

When he returned, minutes later, she stood again in the yard, surrounded by the clutch of dusty-looking hens, all busily scratching at the ground, noisy in their endeavors as they picked at the food she'd spread before them. With a splash of water, she filled a basin for their use, then walked from their midst to where he waited.

"They look like a bunch of little old ladies, don't they?" he asked, amusement alive in his voice.

"Act like it, too," she agreed. "But they're not old. They're mostly in their second year of laying. I've got a broody hen inside the coop I'm going to have to move to the barrel in a day or so, once I know she won't leave her eggs if I shift locations on her."

"The barrel?" he asked, looking about for the destination she had in mind for her mother-to-be. And then he spotted it. A keg placed on its side, a hole in one end, surrounded by a small fenced-in area.

"The fence keeps critters away from the cluck," Rebecca explained, "and keeps the hen secured and safe while she hatches her young ones. Once they're hatched, I'll keep her with them for a while, then let them have the place to themselves till they're big enough for the henhouse."

"How many batches do you hatch in a year?"

"Several. I need enough young roosters to put up in jars for the winter, and the pullets will be my prime laying hens next year."

They walked on toward the barn and Alex stood in the doorway, inspecting the interior. "You keep it clean," he said, the comment slight praise for the condition of the place. The aisle was swept, the tools hung neatly, and even though the scent of horses and the lone cow was ripe with droppings, it was a fresh aroma, not unpleasing to his nostrils.

"There's no one but me to tend it," she said simply. The cow lowed, turning her head as far as possible, caught in place by the stanchion, and Rebecca approached the animal, laying a hand on her flank. "I'll turn you loose," she said quietly. "I'll warrant you'd like some fresh grass, wouldn't you?"

"I'm glad you didn't put them to pasture when you milked earlier," Alex said. "I've been wanting to take a look at my mare."

"She's fine," Rebecca said. "Fat and sassy with all the heavy grass she's been eating. I haven't given her oats since the night you arrived."

"She doesn't need them with good pasture," he said, moving into the stall where the dark mare turned her head to greet him. Her whinny was soft and she nuzzled him, her head butting his chest.

"Have you missed me, girl?" he asked quietly, loosening the rope that held her in the stall. His hands were deft as he ran them over the sleek animal and, with a click of his tongue, he led her toward the back door, opening it to the outdoors.

"I'll bring my gelding after I chase the cow out behind you," Rebecca called out. "Just walk on ahead and open the pasture gate. They'll go right on through."

Alex walked through the open door and a chill of apprehension shot the length of his spine. "Stay back, Rebecca," he said sharply, his voice low, but no doubt carrying to the stall where she tended her horse.

He looked carefully at the trees and brush in the pasture, then scanned the hedgerow beyond to where a hayfield flourished. Something was nudging him, as if a finger tapped his shoulder in warning, and he knew better than to ignore his instincts. Trouble was afoot, and even though he hadn't spotted its source, it was out there.

"What's wrong?" Rebecca was behind him, just inside the barn, and he turned quickly to push her from the exposed opening.

As he did, a sharp sound rang out, a rifle shot if he was any judge, and a hole appeared in the siding beside the doorway. His quick movement, his need to protect Rebecca, had probably saved his life. He pushed her roughly into the first stall, and kept her behind himself as he listened, holding his breath, the better to hear sound from outside the walls of the barn.

Only the sharp whinny of his mare and the gentle lowing of Rebecca's cow met his ears, and he uttered a word beneath his breath. He wasn't given to swearing or using profanity of any kind, but the anger that swept over him seemed to warrant this venting of his frustration.

"You could have been killed," he said harshly, turning to her, scanning her stunned expression and the ashen hue of her skin.

"But I wasn't," she said quietly, her lips trembling, her hand lifting to touch his cheek, as though she must reassure herself that he was unharmed. "It wasn't me being shot at," she said quietly. "They were after you."

"Only one, I think," he said. "I only heard one shot, anyway. And I'll almost guarantee he's skedaddled by now. That kind don't usually stick around once they've made a botch of things."

"A botch." She repeated his chosen word, and her

eyes closed as if she would conceal the emotion that shone from her gaze. "You say that so calmly," she said. "You could have been the one killed." She repeated his words, her voice quivering as her eyes opened. Her hand slid from his face, fingers splaying wide against his chest. "You might have died, Alex, right in front of me, and I would have been sorry to my dying day that I didn't..."

"Didn't what, Rebecca?" His heart accelerated as he spoke the words, and already he knew what she would say, knew the message her eyes had given, felt the emotion that vibrated from her hand to his heart.

"There are things I need to say to you, Alex Carr." She clutched at his shirt, her fingers seeking purchase in the fabric as she spoke. "I care for you, more than I ever thought I could. I know you're not going to be a part of my life much longer, and you don't need to say anything. I just want you to know that you've given me something over the past days I thought I'd never—" Her lips compressed, effectively halting her words of confession.

"I've given you nothing, Rebecca," he said softly. "I've only taken from you, and I can't deny I'd probably do the same thing again, given the chance. You saved my life, and I've done nothing but take advantage of you."

She shook her head quickly, tears forming as she denied his claim. "No, Alex. What I gave you, I offered gladly. I can't help what I feel for you, and I won't even try to withhold what's in my heart."

Aching to return her words, he stepped back,

watching as her fingers lost their grasp on his shirt, aware that his silence would serve to deny the hope radiating from her dark eyes. Unwilling to make promises he could not keep, he turned his head aside, only too aware of twin trails of moisture that stained her cheeks.

She clutched her gelding's halter and turned aside with a furtive movement, brushing awkwardly at the mute evidence of her distress as she moved past him toward the door.

"Wait a minute," he said harshly. "Let me look around first before you go out there."

"No one's going to shoot me," she told him flatly, ignoring his cautioning hand and leading her mount into the fenced passage that led to the pasture gate. Shooing the cow before her, she opened the pasture gate, allowing the animals to meander through the opening to where a waving sea of green grass stretched beyond them.

She carried the rope back with her and hung it over her gelding's stall, then walked on out the front door of the barn into the yard beyond. His heart aching at her vulnerability, Alex followed, her words echoing in his mind.

There was no time today to mend his fences, to make amends. If he truly wanted what was best for Rebecca, he'd leave before his being here invited more violence to tinge her life. She'd forget him, perhaps, go on with her daily routine and forget Alex Carr had ever darkened her door. And he would forever regret his inability to make her a part of his life.

It couldn't be helped. He'd traveled alone up until

now, and his commitment to the railroad would not allow him to take a woman along on his trek. Even if she were willing to leave all she owned behind for the sake of a man she cared for. His footsteps echoed her own as they crossed the porch and entered the house.

She'd given him her father's old clothing to wear after his own shirt was declared unfit for mending, and his trousers were stained beyond scrubbing. Within ten minutes he could be on his way out of here. In an hour or so, he could be the other side of Creed, saddlebags snatched up from his hotel room and well on his way to the nearest telegraph operator to recruit help from the head office. The railroad would send men to protect him, of that there was no doubt. And if that was what it would take to get this job done, he'd call on them.

For now, his aim was to take Rebecca out of the range of trouble. Once he was gone, she'd be safe. And perhaps, he thought yearningly, when things were different, he'd make it his business to return.

SHE WATCHED HIM, turning to him as he followed her inside the door, saw the grim determination on his face, and recognized the resolve he wore as another man might wear a lawman's badge or a set of holstered pistols. He would leave. As surely as she knew her own name, she knew he'd decided to protect her by removing his presence from her house. And as she watched, he turned toward the hallway.

"Don't go, Alex." She would not plead overmuch, but she must ask, this once.

He halted his long strides and turned to her, his jaw taut, his eyes narrowed, his nostrils flaring as if he allowed himself this one, last look at her—before he set her aside. With an abrupt movement of his hand, he signified his inability to explain his actions, and she nodded, accepting his decision.

"All right," she whispered. "It's all right. I understand."

His voice was harsh, his features grim. "I have to leave, Rebecca."

He didn't call her sweetheart, she noticed, and her heart ached for the loss. "I know."

"I won't bring harm to you by staying any longer. I'm heading east for help from the railroad people. I'll wire them and wait for their men to show up. I'd be a fool to fight this mess on my own. And I'm not a fool."

"No, you're not." Her agreement was quiet and she brushed past him. "Shall I find you another of my father's shirts to wear back to town? Yours was only good for the rag bag." That it was folded, neatly mended and tucked away in her drawer was a secret he would forever be unaware of.

"Thanks. That would help."

"Don't worry about returning it," she said quietly. "I'm glad his things came in handy for you while you were here. Get ready, and I'll fix you something to eat to take along with you."

"I'd be much obliged, Rebecca."

Again he eschewed the use of the endearment that had fallen from his lips with such ease over the past days. And she bit her lip, lest she whimper aloud and make a fool of herself.

Quickly, she sliced bread and spread butter over the surface, then cut meat into small pieces and added pickles for flavor before putting the sandwiches together. Wrapped in a clean dish towel, they fit nicely into a sugar sack and she tied the top, leaving twine aplenty to fasten it to his saddle horn.

Behind her he shuffled his feet a bit, as if to let her know he stood there waiting, and she turned, offering the food, forming her lips into what she hoped was a pleasant smile. "I'll come out and help you catch your mare," she offered. "You might need me to saddle her."

"I can do it," he said. "I don't want you out of this house until I'm gone, do you understand?" She'd never heard that harsh note in his voice before, and she could only nod in agreement, aware that he would not falter should she deny him the right to be in control over this issue.

"I won't step outside until you've been gone an hour," she said obediently, and then turned to him. "Will you—" Gritting her teeth against tears that threatened to betray her, she approached him, lifting her face as she spread her fingers against his chest.

"Tell me goodbye properly, Alex. Words won't do it, not for me." She waited, unmoving as he took her measure, his eyes glittering shards of emerald.

And then he gripped her shoulders, his fingers biting into the flesh, and she rejoiced silently at the marks he would leave upon her skin. His head bent and a sound almost of pain accompanied the touch of his mouth as he kissed her. Kissed her as if it were the last time he would know the sustenance of her mouth, took from her the sweetness within her lips, leaving her to taste the defeat she owned with his leaving.

"Goodbye, Rebecca." He held her a long moment, then grasped the sack from her hand and was gone.

CHAPTER FIVE

REBECCA SPENT TWO DAYS alone, tending the animals, doing the daily chores that required her attention, yearning for the sight of a man atop a tall mare. He would return, she told herself, grasping firmly to that belief as she sought her bed after sundown. She wore his shirt, carefully mended, ironed, and still containing the faint essence of his scent.

As a talisman, it served the purpose. As a covering against the cool night air, it lacked somewhat, covering her only to the knees. As panacea to her aching heart, it provided comfort and held the promise of his return.

In the morning, she removed it reluctantly, donning her clothing. Then, folding it meticulously and placing it in her drawer, she straightened her shoulders and faced the day. "He'll be back," she said aloud, looking toward the town road as she sipped her morning coffee and recognized the sorrow in her words.

And though the sun rose into the sky each morning and settled beneath the western horizon each night, she found no joy in the beauty she'd been wont to bask in during the hours of the day. Blue skies and billowing clouds overhead were ignored as she trudged to the barn and beyond. The brilliance of the sunset late on the second day totally escaped her notice as she shepherded her flock of hens back into the chicken yard and thence into their coop for the night. She closed the door, barring it against any nighttime marauders and let herself out of the pen.

The sound of horses at the front of the house caught her notice and she halted as she neared the back porch, then felt a twinge of unease as she thought of the shotgun she kept in the pantry. It was too late to climb the steps and enter the house, she decided, turning as two men rode around the corner and one held up a hand to gain her notice.

"Madam? Are you Rebecca Hale? We heard from a fellow in town that you were the doctor in this part of the territory."

"I'm not a doctor," she told him, turning to face them head-on. "I deliver babies for the women in this area and occasionally tend injuries when I can. My uncle was the doctor in Creed until he died a couple of years ago."

"Well," the elder of the two men said, with a twist of his mouth that might have passed as a smile, "you're just the person we wanted to see."

"What can I do for you?" she asked. "Are you ill?"

"No, madam," he said, swinging his leg over the saddle and tying his mount to the hitching rail. "We are well, thank you. But it happens we are in search of a man we think took refuge here." He spoke the English language, but with odd hesitations, as if he chose each word with care.

"Really?" She felt a chill of apprehension slide the length of her spine as the second man dismounted and handed his reins to his partner.

His accent was even heavier, rolling the words from his mouth slowly. "The news we have gathered in this town is that Alexander Carr is staying here with you."

"I'm afraid you've been misinformed, gentlemen. Mr. Carr has been gone for two full days. I have no idea where he might be."

A harsh sound escaped the first of her visitors, and he shot her a look of anger that stunned her with its message. "I do not think I believe you, madam." His steps as he neared her were heavy, and she stood immobile, as if frozen in place, watching as he reached to grasp her arm and turn her toward the porch.

"A gentleman who is named Ted Duncan assured us we would find this man here."

Long fingers gripped her, digging harshly into her skin, and she was steered up the steps and across the porch as he spoke his threat. "We want this man from you. Show us where he is, or we will make you most unhappy."

"I couldn't be much unhappier than I already am," she told him sharply, tugging to free herself from his hold, but he only increased the pressure of his cruel grip. "Mr. Carr is not here. I told you already," she protested as her captor shoved her onto a chair in the kitchen. "Go look for yourself."

"Thank you, I intend to." His bow was mocking, and with a look from beneath lowered brows, he stalked across the room, leaving Rebecca to watch his progress.

Next to the back door, the second visitor stood at attention, holding a gun in one hand. Rebecca shrank from the tiny, lethal-appearing hole in the end of its barrel. Aimed directly at her chest, it didn't waver an inch, its owner focusing his unblinking stare on her face, as if he were fascinated by the sight of brown eyes and the pallor of fright she knew must be apparent.

For frightened she was. In fact, terrified might be more to the point, she thought, holding back a reckless burst of laughter. How foolish to be on the verge of cackling like a hen in the coop, when she was looking at what might well be the weapon of her destruction. And yet, she was caught up in the grip of hysteria such as she'd never known.

Only the fact that Alex was two days distant, that these men could not have any knowledge of his whereabouts, else they would not be seeking him here, kept her from dissolving in helpless tears.

"He is not in the other rooms, Gerard," the first ruffian said, reentering the kitchen. He turned his harsh gaze on Rebecca. "You will tell us where he has gone. We must know right now."

She shook her head in a defiant gesture. "I can't tell you what I don't know. He left here two days ago."

A blow from the flat of his palm cracked across her face and she cried aloud. Never in her life had she been struck by another person. And to have a complete stranger enter her house and assault her in this way was more than her aching heart could handle. Tears flowed freely, although she was silent now, swallowing the sobs that begged for release.

"I can't tell you what I don't know," she whispered, her fingers touching the stinging flesh, her eyes closing as if she would erase the sight of the man before her. Her tears, she realized, were not merely because of the pain she'd been dealt, but were, in part, for the heartache she'd held in abeyance since Alex's departure. Now the hot, salty evidence of her pain fell, streaking her cheeks and staining the front of her dress.

"So quickly you weep," the elder of her two visitors said, his voice mocking her. "I had no idea you would be so puny, so…what is the word? So weak? Yes, you are weak," he said scornfully. "And I thought to have the enjoyment of seeking the truth from you."

"You have the truth already," she said, finding strength in his mockery. "I can't tell you anything more."

"I think we will leave you in another room for the night, and we will see how brave you are in the morning when we decide what we will do to coax your help."

His hands were rough, certain to leave bruises as he jerked her to her feet, dragging her across the kitchen and then to her bedroom. She tripped, almost falling through the doorway and, placing his hand in the center of her back, he pushed her over the threshold. Her knees slammed against the wooden floor and she knelt where she fell, waiting for a blow that would surely come.

Instead, the closing of her door announced his departure and she bent her head, shuddering breaths racking her body. In mere moments, from outside her window, voices caught her attention and she listened as words spoken in a foreign dialect called back and forth from house to barn. In moments, the whinny of horses sounded from the direction of the barn, and she listened as the barn doors opened and closed.

The back door slammed shut only a minute later, and strident tones called out harsh, unfamiliar words once more as the two men dragged chairs from the table and clanged the stove lids noisily.

Rising from the floor, Rebecca stumbled toward her bed and perched on the edge of the mattress, her hands pressing against her lips, lest she sob her pain aloud. Yet she could not halt the whisper of his name, and she spoke it as a talisman into the darkening shadows.

"Alex. *Alex.*"

THE WORDS WERE TERSE, the message to the point. "Backup requested. Returning to Creed. Alexander Carr."

Short and succinct, Alex decided, and if the powers that be were on the job, he should find help waiting when he rode back into the town of Creed tomorrow. His horse stood just outside the telegraph office, and for a moment, Alex rued the hard ride he'd given the animal. And now he must expect a repeat performance from his mount once they'd both been given a decent meal to tide them over and a few hours rest.

The livery stable was just down the street, and he led his horse there, leaving orders for hay and grain and a brushing down. Now, he thought with a weary sigh, he would attend to his own comfort.

The hotel offered a dining room and, only too aware of his rumpled appearance, he paid for a room in which to wash up and change his clothing before he made an appearance there. Saddlebags over his shoulder, Alex slowly climbed the staircase to the second floor and scanned the room numbers as he trudged the hallway.

His was halfway to the back of the hotel, and he slid his key into the lock silently, then stepped to one side as he turned the knob and pushed the door open. With the degree of caution that had been his constant companion over the past days, he entered and scanned the surroundings.

Closing the door behind him, he crossed to look inside the wardrobe, then bent to take a quick peek beneath the bed. His saddlebags landed on the mattress and he opened one side with deft movements, removing a change of clothing. A basin stood on the washstand, a pitcher of water beside it, and in moments he'd stripped and scrubbed himself sufficiently to pass muster in the dining room downstairs.

The urge to begin his return journey nudged him, but his good sense reminded him that his horse needed more than an hour or so to recuperate his stamina for the long ride ahead. He walked down the stairs and entered the restaurant, where a pleasant young woman showed him to a table. Roast beef was the offering he chose and he ate quickly, then returned to his room.

A look through the window revealed busy sidewalks and a number of wagons lumbering down the street, farmers and ranchers holding the reins as they traveled the main thoroughfare. A simple scene, yet one he knew could hold danger should he forsake caution and blunder forth, perhaps into the path of those who sought him out.

And for what reason? Surely not because he was a scout for the railroad, although that had been his first conclusion. For most communities welcomed the coming of transportation to their towns. Surely there must be another motive behind the shooting he'd survived, one he determined to seek out.

And in the meantime, he'd left Rebecca alone on the farm, where she was open and vulnerable. He shook his head, regretting the choice he'd been forced to make in leaving her alone. There'd been little else he could do. The argument he'd given her was still valid. He needed assistance, and in order to obtain the help available…

Circles. He'd been thinking in circles, questioning his decision, yet accepting the necessity of leaving her. His presence in her home had put her in peril. Given the circumstances of his gunshot wound, he'd known that to be a fact. But now, some sixth sense provoked an urgency that prodded him to return, to forsake the comfort of his bed and be on the way.

Another hour, he decided, if not for his own benefit, then for that of his horse. He'd sleep an hour, then leave for the return trip. Even as he sprawled across the mattress, he placed his gun near his right hand and cast a last look at the door. The lock was in place, and he closed his eyes, aware that his long training would allow him to awake when the allotted hour had passed.

THE ROPES BINDING HER arms behind her back were tighter this time, and Rebecca rejected the urge to seek her release. She'd nearly made it through the bedroom window late last night before they'd caught her and sent her flying with harsh blows. Her attempted escape had earned her the ropes that bound her now, and though struggling against them was futile, her fingers clenched in defiance.

Contemplating the future her captors had painted with vivid detail, she stifled a groan. They'd threatened her with pain, and she'd gritted her teeth in defiance. They'd laughed at her tears, taunted her unmercifully as they refused her any of the food she cooked for their meals today, allowing her only water as they ate at her table. And then binding her again, they'd returned her to her bedroom.

Now she lay on her side on the bed, listening as the two of them spoke in guttural phrases, their words barely audible beyond the closed door.

"Alex." She whispered his name, as though the sound lent comfort, closing her eyes as she envisioned his face before her. He was in peril, and should he return now, it would be awaiting him, twofold.

As much as she yearned for his presence, she

cringed at the thought of his flesh again being marred by the wounds these men would no doubt inflict should he appear here. *Stay away.* Unspoken, the words vibrated in her mind and she closed her eyes, willing the message to seek him out. Tears slid from beneath her eyelids as she contemplated the next hours to come.

Sleep hovered mere moments from her as her senses roused her once more into wakefulness. A soft rapping was repeated, catching her ear and she turned her head, squinting through the darkness toward the window.

He was there. Just beyond the pane of glass, he rose to his feet, a shadow against the faint light of stars illuminating the night sky. She shook her head, a silent entreaty she knew he could not see. Fearful of calling out, lest the men in her kitchen hear, she waited, and watched as the window slid upward. Alex bent almost double, his long, lean body fitting through the oblong space as he stepped over the sill and into her bedroom.

She could not stifle the small gasp that acknowledged his presence, managing only to struggle upright on the bed, her hands secured behind her back. Her movement in the dark room caught his attention and he strode with silent steps across the floor, then bent to brush gentle fingers across her brow.

"Rebecca." Only her name, but it was enough to send warmth throughout her shivering body. Bending lower, his mouth touched her ear and his whisper was almost soundless. "I wasn't certain you were in here when you didn't come to the window.

"Are you hurt?" Even as he spoke his palms ran the length of her arms and his fingers worked at the knotted rope that bound her. In mere seconds she was free, her hands beginning to tingle, then ache and burn as blood began flowing more freely.

She heard a whimper escape her lips and she bit down to silence the small, revealing sound. Alex's hand was there, his palm containing her involuntary cry, and she leaned her head forward, pressing her mouth against his calloused skin. Quick tears flowed, silent expressions of both pain and relief, released from the fear she'd lived with throughout the past day and the night before it.

"I'm here. It's all right, sweetheart." His husky whisper vibrated against her ear and she nodded.

"There are two of them," she murmured.

"I know. I watched them through the kitchen window for a minute." He lifted her from the bed and she swayed, held upright by his strength and the promise inherent in his words.

I'm here. He'd managed, with those two reassuring words to instill hope in her heart. Now he spoke again, and the beating of that vital part within her breast increased as she heard his voice.

"I want you to call out, make a noise," Alex said softly. "I'll be behind the door. No one will touch you." He lifted a candle from the bedside table and lit it with a match from his pocket, then replaced the candle, the glow casting a soft light that illuminated the room.

Rebecca watched as he crossed to stand at one side of the door. One hand rose to touch her throat, and

Alex waved a cautioning palm, motioning for her to join her hands behind her back. Her captors must think she was still tied or, at the sight of her, they would be warned of Alex's presence.

She clasped trembling fingers together behind herself and did as Alex had asked, calling out, her voice wavering as her words sounded aloud. "Please. Will you come and help me?"

For a moment, silence followed her cry. Then, through the heavy panel the sound of a chair scraping against the floor could be faintly heard, and Alex nodded, his satisfaction clear as he shot her an encouraging look.

The doorknob turned and one of her captors stepped across the threshold. His second stride into the room was his last as Alex closed the door behind him and pressed the muzzle of his pistol against the man's throat. Eyes widening in abject horror, the intruder froze where he stood, until Alex thrust him to the floor, then bent and scooped a gun from the waistband of his captive's trousers.

"Don't move," he muttered, his voice a dark threat that elicited a hasty nod from the man who huddled against the floor. His eyes narrowed, glaring a message of hatred toward Rebecca. Strident words burst from his lips, words whose meaning she could only surmise, bringing swift retribution from Alex. His booted foot slammed against the ruffian's thigh, and the man's lips thinned, releasing only a muffled groan.

From the other side of the door, a voice called out, and Alex turned swiftly in that direction, nodding quickly at Rebecca. She responded with another cry, her voice trembling now in earnest.

"Help me. Please help me."

Before she spoke the final phrase, the second of her captors burst into the room, catching sight of Alex and then spinning to search out his fallen comrade. One hand held a gun, and he lifted it in a smooth motion toward Rebecca. Even as she looked into the weapon's muzzle, Alex fired. His shot spun the gunman in a half circle, and his arm flew upward, sending a wild shot into the wall beside the window. Without a murmur, he sank to the floor, his body a crumpled heap. Blood flowed, pooling beneath him, and Rebecca turned away, unable to stomach the violence before her.

"I want the truth, damn you," Alex snarled, lifting the cowering man who had watched in silence as his partner died. "Who are you? Who sent you?"

Quivering lips pressed together and his head shook in a negative movement as the captured man refused to speak.

Alex shot a measuring look at Rebecca. She was pale, trembling, and only the wall beside her held her erect. Questioning her assailant must wait. There seemed no doubt that these two had worked alone, and for now he would lend his efforts to cleaning up the mess before him and then take care of Rebecca.

"YOU'RE BRUISED...HERE..." His fingers barely grazed her cheek then moved to caress the shadows beneath her eyes. "...and here," he said, his voice a solemn condemnation of the purple splotches marring her skin.

"Did they molest you, Rebecca?" He could not speak aloud the question that burned in his mind. If she had been brutalized, if those two had sullied her with—

As if she understood his reluctance, she hastened to assure him. "No, they didn't hurt me, not *that* way," she said quickly. "They only slapped me and pushed me to the floor. They were rough and they made threats—"

She closed her eyes. "I don't know what they would have done tomorrow. They were determined to find you, and I was so thankful you weren't here."

His sigh was heartfelt, and he gathered her to himself once more. "I wish I had been. They'd have had me to deal with, instead of a helpless woman."

"Where are they?" she asked quietly, leaning against his strength as if she would gather courage merely from his touch.

"I've tied the second man in the barn. I fear I wasted one of your blankets on the other. He's in the yard, where he'll stay till morning, when I take them both to town to the sheriff's office."

He held her on his lap, rocking her to and fro in the big wooden rocking chair, next to the parlor window. His mouth pressed against her brow, and quiet whispers lent her the assurance that all was well.

"I couldn't stay away, sweetheart," he said quietly, his fingers threading through her hair as he spoke. "I tried. Then, fifty miles down the road, I found a town with a telegraph office and sent the message on its way. My horse needed some rest, but I cut it short in order to come back to you.''

His kiss was warm against her brow, and his words were a terse condemnation of his actions. ''I exposed you to danger, and I'll never forgive myself for that.''

And then he set about with the plan he'd put in place during the journey he'd made over the past hours. Choosing his words and phrases carefully, willing her compliance, he spoke the message he'd vowed would change both of their lives forever. A message he'd prayed, during the long ride, he would be given the chance to utter in her hearing.

''I want to marry you, Rebecca.'' As she jolted upright in his arms, he quieted her with a hushing sound.

''No, just listen to me. I know what I'm doing here. I thought about this all the way back to Creed and I know this is the right thing for both of us.''

''You don't owe me anything,'' she protested. ''You didn't intend exposing me to those men. You wouldn't have knowingly caused me harm, Alex. I know that.''

He nodded in agreement. ''You're right, but the fact remains, sweetheart. Just my being here brought disaster down on your head.'' His arms tightened their hold, and she relaxed once more against his warmth. ''I'm going to take our captive to town, along with his friend, and when I come back we'll decide on our plans.''

''Not till morning.'' She held her breath, waiting,

it seemed, for his assent; and it was not long in coming.

"We won't go anywhere tonight," he agreed. "And now we need to take care of your cow and feed the horses." Tending livestock was not beyond his capabilities, but milking the cow was a venture he'd never tackled before. "Come with me to the barn, will you?"

She nodded, sliding from his lap to stand upright before him. "I'll be so glad when this whole mess is in the past. I never in my life thought I'd be in the midst of so much turmoil."

"I'll keep you safe from now on," Alex told her, sliding one arm around her waist as he led her from the parlor and into the kitchen. "Get your shawl over your shoulders. I'll locate the milk pail for you."

The ruffian was where Alex had left him, tied hand and foot. Rebecca shot him a look of anger mixed with apprehension as they entered the barn, and he turned his head aside, his bearing reduced to that of a man without hope.

The horses welcomed hay and a bit of grain, and then Alex stood by her side as Rebecca stripped the final sprays of milk from her Guernsey. Hay to keep the animal content throughout the night was placed in her manger, and Alex picked up the milk pail as Rebecca opened the barn door. He carried the lantern with them, watching as she closed the door and latched it firmly.

The stars peppered the sky and the moon cast a pathway across the yard, lighting their way with an ethereal glow. He felt Rebecca's hand next to his on the handle of the bucket and glanced down to where she shared the load he carried. She needn't have, for the weight was barely enough to cause his muscles to flex, but the symbolic touch of her smaller palm lifting in harmony with his own wide hand touched a chord within him.

They would share the future, he thought, walking side by side, no matter what they faced in the years ahead. His heart swelled with a depth of emotion he could not describe, only that this woman brought forth from him a longing to cherish her for the rest of his life. He was both possessive and protective of her, and if she would agree to his plan, they would nevermore be apart.

The night air was chilly, and Rebecca shivered beneath the cover of her shawl as they climbed the porch steps. "Open the door for me," Alex said quietly, "and I'll cover the milk till morning."

She obliged, holding the screened door wide as he passed beneath the lintel and into the kitchen. The lantern lit the room, exposing the dirty dishes on the table and the pot of half-eaten food on the stove. Alex placed the bucket on the floor in the pantry, covered it with a towel and turned to her.

"Have you eaten?" he asked, searching her face and finding it wan, her features pinched.

She shook her head. "I'll have a piece of bread, maybe."

"Go in the bedroom and get undressed," he told her. "I'll bring in warm water for you to wash with and fix you something to drink. Coffee? Or would you rather have a cup of tea?"

"Tea sounds wonderful," she said thankfully. Without argument, she placed the lamp on the table and, with the experience of living long years in this house, made her way through the dark hallway to her room.

He heard her movements, heard the dresser drawer open and close, noted the sound of shoes hitting the floor with a soft thud, and then in the silence, listened to the rustle of clothing as she undressed. The sounds were hushed, bearing a degree of intimacy he relished.

Alex moved the teakettle over the hottest part of the stovetop. Opening her tea canister, he spooned leaves into her teapot, located a cup for her use, and then waited, listening for the telltale sound of water boiling. His hand lifted and his fingers touched the medallion he wore.

He'd felt the rustling of warnings within him from the first, and throughout the whole of his time in Creed. From the moment he hit the ground the night he was wounded until now, he'd felt an almost dreamlike quality blending his days together. Perhaps it was meant to be; the bullet wound, the time here in this house. As if his destiny was being woven in the tapestry of these days with Rebecca.

The blank wall that formed the beginnings of his existence somehow had to do with the medallion he wore, and the name he'd been given must, in some way, be connected to the person who had left him on the orphanage steps, all those long years ago.

He'd been formed from a different mold than most of the men he'd met over the years of his life, had accepted the knowledge of his harsh, almost foreign-appearing features and the cast of his very being as unique. He'd accepted the nickname his childhood mates had given him, and used it to his benefit over the years. *King*.

The boiling water caused the tea leaves to swirl in the pot, and he watched as they colored the water, then set the lid in place. He sliced the bread quickly and buttered it lavishly, and then he cut the offering in thirds, arranging the pieces on a small plate. A tray from the kitchen buffet held the simple repast and he lifted it, leaving the lantern behind to light the kitchen.

King. Again the name rang in his memory, and his smile was cynical as he recalled the sound of childish voices, raised at first in cruel taunting, then later in respect as he'd earned the esteem of his friends. It had been a talisman to him, marking him as special, even if only in his own eyes.

All of this, all that he was and would ever be, were what Rebecca must accept when she spoke the vows that would unite them forever. And on this night, he must cement that relationship, so that there would be no doubt in her mind that his intentions were right and honorable. She was the woman he wanted in his life, no matter where his destiny should lead.

His footsteps were firm as he walked toward the bedroom where she waited. His mind set on the plans they would make, he passed through the portal into the room where he'd slept in her bed alone while his body healed.

Tonight, he would sleep with her in that same bed, and neither of them would ever be alone again, God willing.

CHAPTER SIX

SHE SEEMED SMALL AND fragile, standing in the shadows within her bedroom, clothed in a white nightgown, one he'd seen before during her hours of nursing him to recovery. Alex crossed the threshold, then looked up to where she stood, a pale figure, with arms upraised as she braided her hair in preparation for bed.

"Come here and eat first," he said quietly, determined that her endeavors to conceal the splendid beauty of long, waving locks should be halted before he was given the privilege of touching the unbound length of it. Settling the tray on the bedside table, he pulled the sheet and quilt aright and then lay them aside, inviting her to perch against the pillows.

She did as he bid, quietly crossing the room to sit beside him. The tea had steeped long enough, he decided, and poured her cup half-full, then handed it to her. She sipped appreciatively at the fragrant brew and sighed.

"You fixed me something to eat," she said quietly, eyeing the plate he'd prepared. "I'm not used to being waited on."

"Then it's about time someone saw to that." He

offered the plate. "I'll share it with you. It's been a while since I snatched a bite to eat."

She lifted a wedge of buttered bread and bit into the crust, closing her eyes as she savored the flavor. The teacup was held in her other hand and he reached for it, sipping and swallowing a mouthful of the pungent brew. Their eyes met, and in the silence, he returned the cup to her keeping, almost as if there were a ceremony being observed.

There was about the setting an intimacy he had not known before, as if their lives were in fact being blended by these moments of eating and drinking from the same plate and cup. As if they were setting up a communion of hearts with the elements of food and drink, shared in the quiet of the midnight hour.

He poured more tea and they sipped it slowly, passing the cup back and forth, their eyes meeting, his frankly appreciative, hers darkly inviting, long looks of awakening passion and desire that were only held in abeyance by the knowledge that their future was being woven together by the intimacy of this night.

And then they were finished, the bread eaten, the tea having satisfied their need for warmth. Alex carried the tray back to the kitchen and returned to her, carrying the lamp with him. Rebecca watched from the bed, showing not a trace of wariness or apprehension in the serene glow of brown eyes that examined him with approval.

"Are you sleeping in here?" she asked politely as he lowered the lamp to the table and stood beside the bed. His nod was answer enough apparently, for she slid beneath the sheet and pulled it up to her waist, transferring the second pillow behind her to the other side of the bed for his use.

"All right." As if it were an everyday occurrence, this sharing a bed with a man, she folded her hands atop the sheet, and only the subdued movement of her fingers as they slowly pleated the fabric gave notice that her calm facade was concealing some small bit of unease.

Alex stripped from his shirt, tossing it to a nearby chair, then sat on the edge of the mattress, his voice soothing, his manner as casual as if he were in the habit of thus behaving every night of his life. "We'll get an early start in the morning," he said. "Once the sheriff takes custody of our friend in the barn, we'll go see the minister of the little church I saw on the east end of town."

"We'll have to make a stop at Mr. Bradford's place first, I think," Rebecca told him. "He's the undertaker," she explained quickly as he shot her an inquiring look.

"I wasn't going to mention that tonight, sweetheart. I don't want you any more upset than you already are." His fingers slowed in the process of sliding his stockings off and he turned to her. "I wouldn't have killed him the way I did if his gun hadn't been pointed at you. I might have aimed to wound, but he left me no choice."

"I'd have done the same," she told him. "I won't tell you it didn't bother me, because it did. I was sickened mostly by the waste of human life. I found myself not wanting to walk on the floor, there by the door, where he lay bleeding.''

"I tried to wash the stains away," Alex said. "I ended up just covering most of it with that braided rug." He stood, clad only in drawers. "I think this is as far as I dare undress for tonight. I don't want to scare you off before I put the ring on your finger."

Rebecca smiled, and allowed her gaze to sweep from his face to where his arousal was prominently displayed through the soft fabric of cotton underwear. "I'm not afraid of you, Alex. I think I know what to expect."

He lifted the lamp globe and blew out the wick, then lowered the glass in place. "Have you agreed, then, to marry me? Because after tonight there won't be any dillydallying around about this, sweetheart. We'll be seeing the preacher tomorrow."

Sliding between the sheets, he settled his head on the pillow she'd provided and reached for her, drawing her to his side, noting how neatly her head fit the hollow of his shoulder. Her arm slid across his chest and she snuggled close, the warmth of her breath sending shivers over his flesh, radiating the length of his body.

He was quiet, simply holding her in his embrace for several minutes, bending his head to press soft caresses on her forehead and across her cheek. She was alive, her life spared, when it might have gone so terribly wrong. He trembled without and within as he recognized the close call they had escaped, when he realized how nearly the brilliance of her smile, the glow of her spirit might have been snuffed out.

When he was certain his voice would not betray the shattering sense of relief he felt, he spoke. "I thought I might not get here in time. I wasn't certain what I'd find, but I knew, deep down, that something was wrong, that I never should have left you to your own devices."

Her breath was a shattered sigh as she spoke. "I prayed for you to come back, and then I prayed that you'd stay away." Confessing her wishy-washy thoughts to him without a qualm, she murmured words that tumbled from her lips as though she'd held them too long within. "I only knew I needed you more than I've ever needed anything in my life. But at the same time, I feared they'd kill you if you rode up without knowing what was going on."

"Give me credit, sweet," he said, admonishing her gently. "I've dealt with their kind before, and something told me I was riding into danger. Those men were sent here to get rid of me. I don't know why and I have no idea who sent them, but I'm convinced this whole mess has nothing to do with the railroad and the problems I ran into here in Creed. This plot has to go way back to my beginnings."

"Why would someone seek you out now?" she asked. "After so many years, I'd have thought whoever abandoned you would have given up on ever finding you again, even if she'd changed her mind."

"Maybe it wasn't a woman," he suggested. "But, you're right, it seems like something a woman would do. If a man wanted to rid himself of a child, for whatever reason, he'd just as likely dispose of it another way."

She shivered in his embrace. "I can't imagine anyone wanting to hurt a child, especially a helpless babe."

"That's because you have a soft heart, sweet. There are those in this world who wouldn't even flinch at killing a child."

Her arms tightened their grip on him and she sighed. "The men that were here would have thought nothing of killing me, would they? Even though they were looking for you in the first place. I don't like to think someone is on your trail after all these years since your childhood. Perhaps you're wrong. Maybe, after all, it was because of the fuss over the railroad coming through. They could have been just hired assassins."

He shook his head, a slow deliberate movement. "No," he said after a moment, "as I said, I thought at first this had to do with the railroad, but now I've about made up my mind that it's another thing altogether. The men who came here aren't native born. Their accents were strange, although they spoke English well.

"I suspect if I can find out where they came from, I may have the answer to questions that have puzzled me for years. If we can get that gutless wonder out in the barn to come clean, we should be able to figure this whole mess out."

She trembled in his arms, and he rued his words. "Forget him, Rebecca. Try to forget everything that happened here tonight. I want you to sleep now."

The silence drew out into a taut thread of expectancy as she clung to him, and he felt her breathing quicken, then abate, as if she would speak, only to lose her courage.

"What is it?" he asked. "What's wrong?"

She shifted against him, her mouth nuzzling against his throat as she turned her face upward, her arm tightening its grip across his chest. "I thought you might...."

"You thought I planned to make love to you?" He closed his eyes as he spoke, envisioning the picture created by her words. "I certainly thought about it. In fact, I think about it on a regular basis," he admitted. "It's getting more difficult by the minute to keep my hands where they belong."

"You needn't," she said quietly. "I told you before—"

"I know what you told me, but I won't claim your body until we've spoken the vows of marriage, sweet." His discomfort increased as they spoke, the throbbing of his arousal mocking his resolve. Turning on his side, he faced her, one palm pressing her against his lower body, seeking some small amount of relief.

Her indrawn breath alerted him, and she whispered his name, the single word a query.

"I suspect you know I'm having a hard time here," he admitted, his words teasing, even as he swallowed the frustration that threatened to drive him to distraction. "Maybe I could just—" His fingers slid her buttons free as he spoke, opening the front of her gown until the soft flesh of her breasts was bare beneath his fingertips. "I'll only..."

He bent his head, his mouth warm and damp

against her skin, and she held her breath, aware of each brush of his lips, each touch of his tongue as he investigated those two feminine parts. He was thorough, blessing each with equal fervor, his mouth pursing to enclose the tender crests, his lips tugging in a rhythm that brought tingles the length of her spine. She shivered, her hands clasping tightly behind his head, holding him in place, lest he cease his exploration and abandon her to her virgin state.

His male member pressed against her thigh, and she recognized the imperative thrust, knew the movement as one that would surely lead to his taking of her woman's flesh, given his apparent readiness. Surely she could not contain an organ of such size, certainly she was not equipped to accommodate a male part such as was even now seeking to bury itself within her.

"Alex?" She spoke his name in a hushed tone and he stilled his movement, as if he awaited her desire, as if he were prepared to accept her denial of his need should she voice it aloud. "Alex, I didn't think it would be so—" A hiccup swallowed her next word, and he clasped her even closer, nodding as he waited for her apprehension to be spoken in his ear.

And then, as if he took pity on her, surmising what she was unable to express, he whispered words that would supply the descriptive phrases she sought. "Noticeable?" he asked. "Large, maybe?"

"Something like that." Her words were mumbled, as she sought to bury her face against his chest. "I should have known. You're a big man, Alex. I don't know what I expected. You'll think I'm foolish."

Her lips played havoc as her words whispered against the muscles of his chest, her mouth moving against the upper ridges of taut skin, beneath which his body had hardened in preparation for the act of mating.

"You're not foolish, Rebecca. You're a virgin, and you have every right to be frightened." He nudged her face upward and his mouth found hers, blessing her with gentle kisses that asked no more than the privilege of tasting and savoring the softness of her lips.

"I'm not afraid of you, Alex," she whispered. "I offered—"

"Hush," he said, stifling her midsentence. "I told you then, and I'm telling you now, I won't ask that of you. Wait until tomorrow, though, and I'll want more than you may be prepared to give." He held her firmly in place, only too aware that his good intentions would be for naught should she wiggle much more against his aching groin.

"I'll do whatever you ask of me," she promised, returning his kisses with fervor, opening to the thrust of his tongue, her teeth touching his lower lip in a tentative gesture, then suckling it eagerly, as if she'd discovered some new, enchanting pastime.

He could not resist. She was like a witch, taunting him with word and deed, tasting her triumph as he submitted to the game she played. His hand left her breasts and slid lower, until his fingers cupped her through the folds of her nightgown. He felt the warmth, the dampness that met his touch and knew the triumph of having aroused her to a state of readiness.

"Rebecca?" The single word was spoken into her mouth, and she moaned aloud, her hips rising against his hand. This would never do, he decided, only too aware that he would soon be beyond the point of no return, that his own arousal was at the peak of readiness. "I'm sorry, love. I'm sorry. I've gone too far."

He gasped the words, releasing his hold on her gown, and drawing her away from the seeking masculine part of his body that would have sought pleasure within her depths, given any more encouragement. "Please, sweetheart, I want you to turn over and let me cuddle you while you close your eyes and sleep."

"All right." Trembling, as though shaken by the momentum of her own escalating desire, she did as he bid, turning until she was spooned against him. Her sigh was deep as she snuggled into the bend of his body.

"Don't wiggle," he said harshly, and she froze in place for a moment. Then a giggle escaped and she drew her pillow beneath her head a bit, relaxing against him until she was molded closely to the warmth of his belly and chest. Their legs tangled together and he savored the intimacy of small, cold feet pressing against his shinbones.

Her hair was fragrant, its texture like that of silk, and he wrapped his fist in its length, then lifted it to his face, inhaling the sweet smell. The strands slid through his fingers and shimmered darkly in the faint gleam of moonlight from the windows. Smoothing it against her shoulder, he drew out a lock, then released it, allowing the waves to curl around his fingers.

Tomorrow night, he vowed silently, he would have a lamp lit or a candle glowing on the table beside the bed. And in the morning, he would brush her hair in the sunlight and revel in the delight of knowing his would be the only eyes given the privilege of seeing her thus. Reluctantly, he tucked the waving lock between them then circled her waist with one arm.

His hand strayed, caressing her skin through the open bodice of her nightgown, then moved upward until he clasped the weight of her breast in his palm. Her indrawn breath and the soft laughter she made no attempt to conceal warmed him. His Rebecca would provide all the passion he'd ever yearned for in his lonely days and nights. She was all woman, every splendid inch of her a tribute to everything that was feminine.

And for the first time in his life, he ignored the evidence of desire to focus instead on the thrill of holding the woman he loved.

He could wait.

"THIS SOUNDS KINDA FISHY to me," the sheriff said, nodding toward the body outside his office door. Alex had placed it in the back of Rebecca's wagon, the second gunman, securely bound, beside it. Rebecca's story had been told in stark detail, and as she spoke, the sheriff had nodded, apparently accepting her tale.

And then he turned to Alex. "Why would somebody send these fellas clear out here to the Dakota Territory to settle your hash? What were you up to back east, anyway? Seems like you brought a whole heap of trouble on Miss Rebecca here.''

"I'll agree with you there," Alex said amiably. "And I don't know why they were after me. I took a bullet a couple of weeks ago on the road out of town, and I'm not sure if it was from one of these men or a gunman from Creed. I don't pretend to know if there was a connection."

"Well, it seems to me you brought a mess along with you," the sheriff said sharply. "I can't say that I appreciate having our town connected with this sort of thing. We're a pretty peaceable bunch of folks."

Rebecca bit her tongue, wondering what fairy tale the sheriff had been reading to come up with that scenario. "I've been having trouble with Ted Duncan for a while now," she said. "He knew Mr. Carr was staying at my place. Why don't you question him to find out how these men knew where to look for Alex?"

"And that's another thing," the sheriff said, his words blustering in their condemnation of Alex's whereabouts. "This fella has made you a laughing-stock in town, girl. He's living in your house and giving you a bad name."

"She'll be my wife after today," Alex said, his words a warning. "I've done nothing to harm her. She's a respectable woman."

"Well, she used to be." Grimly, the sheriff met Alex's gaze. "As to getting married to the girl, I'd say you *owe* her your name, after spending two weeks and better with her.''

His face ruddy with anger, Alex drew Rebecca to his side. ''I know *exactly* what I owe Rebecca. And as soon as you take these men off my hands and put them where they belong, we'll be on our way.''

''I'd say one of them belongs in the cemetery outside of town, but I don't know who's gonna pay for the undertaker to haul him out there. The other one I'll put in a cell until the circuit judge comes by. Since he was holding Miss Rebecca in her own home by force, we'll call it kidnapping, I guess.''

''Attempted murder is more like it,'' Alex said harshly. ''And I want to question him again myself.''

Rebecca thought of the man's stubborn rejection of Alex's queries as he'd loaded him on the wagon. His jaw set, his eyes dark with fury, the stranger had refused to open his mouth. She suspected her own presence had been all that saved the wretch from punishment at Alex's hands, and now she wondered privately if they would ever discover the origin of her assailants.

The sheriff took custody of the prisoner, shoving him into a cell. The body of the second man was brought from Rebecca's wagon and left just inside the office until the undertaker could be located.

With averted eyes, Rebecca walked past the body, and out into the sunlight, Alex behind her, his hand on her shoulder. They approached the wagon, and, without a word, Alex lifted her to the seat and climbed up beside her. Aware of sidelong looks mixed with open, skeptical stares, they traveled the length of the main street to where the small church sat on the outskirts of town.

Creed was not a town known for its forward thinking, the citizens rigid in their standards, and her actions over the past weeks had put her beyond the pale, Rebecca decided, ignoring the snubs offered by the townsfolk.

"You don't plan on staying here in Creed, do you?" she asked, and caught a glimpse of relief in his look as Alex turned his head toward her.

"Not unless it's what you want, sweet. There are lots of places more cheerful than this to live in the world. I think you'd be happier somewhere else. And I'd feel safer."

"I'll go wherever you like," she told him, feeling a sense of freedom heretofore unknown to her. "I was raised here, but I've never felt a part of the place."

"You could have married any one of a half-dozen men hereabouts, I'd think," Alex said. "But you're too much woman for these people."

She sent him an arch look. "But not for you?"

His eyes touched her with knowledge gained from the night spent in her bed. "Not for me, honey. Your property might have been a big draw for the men who courted you, but it's not important to me."

"I've never wanted any of the men who hung around me after my folks died." She lowered her gaze to her lap where her fingers twined together. "Maybe I was waiting for you." Her voice softened as she spoke. "Do you believe in destiny, Alex?"

"You mean that some greater power decided we should be together?"

She looked up quickly, seeking a trace of mockery in his face, but finding only an intent expression that bade her reply. "Yes, something like that, I suppose. I used to pray that God would send me a man I could love."

"And did He?" His eyes bored into her gaze, expectant and yet accepting.

She nodded. "You know He did. There was a reason for you finding me that night you were wounded. It wasn't just happenstance. I firmly believe that it was meant to be, that we were destined to live our lives out together."

"I've always had a sort of sixth sense," he told her, his words muted, the confession offered in a tentative fashion. "Do you believe in such things?"

"Yes, I suppose I do." And then she spoke more strongly. "I think there's more to your background than what you realize. That pendant you wear, the symbols on it, the whole story of your beginnings, is incomplete. Maybe we need to go back to the place where you were left as a baby and find the answers."

He nodded in silent agreement as he pulled the horse to a halt before the small, white church and jumped from the seat, tying the reins to a hitching post. Then he turned to face her, the sun shining brightly down upon the small oasis where they had paused for this moment of decision.

"Are you ready for this?" he asked quietly, as if he would give her one last chance to change her mind should she have second thoughts.

"More than ready," she told him, rising to her feet and waiting for him to come to her. He moved quickly, reaching up to grasp her waist as she stepped down from the wagon, swinging her to the ground. His hands were reluctant to leave her, and she looked up inquiringly. "Are *you* ready?"

"You bet, sweetheart," he said, a grin touching his mouth as he swung her to his side and led her to the small parsonage that sat beside the community church. "Let's go see the preacher."

It was a short ceremony, the minister's wife being called on to witness the event. Alex used a ring from his little finger to make the union official. With it on her left hand, Rebecca left the smiling preacher and his wife behind, certain she must have an aura of new respectability shrouding her as she and Alex walked back to the wagon.

"I'm really your wife," she said quietly, turning the simple signet ring, the better to view its surface. It was inscribed with a number and an insignia, one Alex said referred to the company he'd served in during the war. Given him by those who'd served under his command, it was a cherished possession, and she gloried in his desire to have her wear it.

"I'll buy you a gold wedding band when we find a jeweler who has a good selection," Alex told her, watching as she held her hand up, allowing the sunshine to glitter against the gold insignia.

"This is fine," she told him. "It's a little large, but I'll make it fit with some yarn."

"It'll do for now." His arms were strong, lifting her to the wagon seat, and she watched as he walked around to untie the horse. Backing the wagon, he turned it and headed on the return trip to the farm.

"I doubt the sheriff will go for my questioning the prisoner. We may never know who sent them here," he said as the wagon passed the lawman's office.

"I don't think it would do any good anyway. That man was on a mission, and he's not about to tell you anything," Rebecca said. "He made my skin crawl, just looking at him. I'll warrant he was a hired killer."

She bit at her lip as fear cascaded throughout her body. "Who would want you dead, Alex? I think you're right. This has nothing to do with the railroad. It's something bigger than that."

"We'll find out," he promised her. "Tomorrow, we'll begin delving into the whole matter, and somehow, we'll come up with answers. I can't have you living with danger." His look swept her from top to bottom as he cracked the harness over the horse's back. "For now, let's just concentrate on the first day of our marriage. We'll make it special."

"For you?" she asked, looking up at him with anticipation.

"It's already special to me, just knowing I have the right to love you and live with you for the rest of our lives."

And may it be for a long, long time. The words rang, unspoken, in Rebecca's mind as she reached for him, grasping his hand, the phrase becoming a prayer that resonated in her mind, then flew upward to the heavens.

The day was half gone by the time she put together

a meal. "Will we move from here soon?" she asked, moving from stove to table and back in the familiar routine she'd established during his stay.

He watched her, impatient with the slow-moving hands on his pocket watch, anticipation rising with each movement of her slender form as she arranged the table for their meal. Her hands were graceful, her profile serene, and he tried in vain to be patient, intent on giving her the whole of the daylight hours to prepare herself for the night to come. Rebecca was worth waiting for, and he was a far cry from the callow youth who would have hustled her into the bedroom without preliminaries, had he married her years earlier.

Now he anticipated their time of loving with the forbearance of maturity, aware that she had known no other man, that he would be the first to give her the pleasures of the wedding bed. Shifting in the chair, he directed his mind to other thoughts, yet it strayed back, time and again, to the woman who reached across him now to place a platter in the middle of the table.

She returned to the stove, ladling vegetables into a bowl, then placing it near his left hand. Her fingers trailed across his shoulder as she passed behind him and he felt a thrill slide the length of his spine.

Rebecca was flirting with him. Trying her wings in the new game they played. Deliberately seducing him with each step she took, each gesture of slender fingers as she served the food, each twitch of her skirt and tilt of her head.

And then she faced him, her smile holding an element of promise as she carried the coffeepot to fill his cup to the brim. The blue-speckled enamel container was replaced on the stove and she returned to the table, sliding into the chair across from him.

"You're a piece of mischief," he said, his words husky, his throat dry with desire that rose quickly to roughen his speech.

Her eyebrows rose in an innocent manner. "Me?" She smiled again, reaching for her napkin and unfolding it across her lap. "I can't imagine what you're talking about."

Soft words of thanksgiving spilled from her lips as she closed her eyes, offering a brief prayer for their food, and then she handed him the bowl of potatoes. "You must be hungry, Mr. Carr. You'd better eat well. Supper is going to be a bit of this and that."

He spooned a helping on his plate and speared a piece of beef from the platter. "Did you can this meat?" It seemed tender, and proved to be just that as he cut it with his fork. He'd seen rows of meat in jars in the pantry, along with fruit and vegetables left over from her preparations for the winter just ended.

"I got half a beef from one of the neighbors when I nursed his family through a bout of sickness last fall," she said. "Along with my garden and bushels of fruit from the store in town, I manage to feed myself pretty well."

"Is there someone who would benefit from your pantry when we leave here?" he asked her.

"Leave here?" She halted the movement of her fork. "Are you planning to go right away?"

"As soon as we get your animals good homes and

get your things packed,'' he told her. ''I think your idea about going back to the orphanage and seeking information there is a good one.''

Excitement welled up in her as she considered the thrill of traveling across the country with Alex, of standing beside him as his wife. ''I've promised to deliver a child for a neighbor,'' she told him. ''It's past due already, and I don't feel right about leaving before I've done that,'' she told him.

''It had better not decide to make an appearance tonight,'' he said, selecting another piece of meat.

As if he'd heard the threat and dared defy Alex's words, Homer Dooley showed up only an hour later, hat in hand, his eyes peering through the screened door to seek Rebecca.

''Ma'am?'' His voice was querulous as he called out for her, and she hurried from the bedroom where she'd been sorting through her belongings. Alex gained the barn door and headed for the house, eyes narrowed as he watched the visitor, his hand on the gun at his side. Homer ignored him, his manner harried and anxious, and without asking, Rebecca knew his mission.

''Is Winnie ready?'' she asked, setting aside all else as she put her mind to the task ahead. Babies were not considerate of even wedding nights, it seemed, and she hastened toward the pantry to seek out her bag, as Homer paced the porch.

''What's going on?'' Alex leaped the steps in a single stride as Homer stood aside, wisely moving from Alex's path. The screened door slammed behind him as he crossed the kitchen. ''Is that the ex-

pectant father wearing a path across your porch?''
His gaze touched upon her black satchel, then met
hers as his query was silently answered.

Rebecca nodded. ''I won't be too long, probably.
Winnie already has four children. This promises to
be a quick delivery.''

''I'll take you,'' Alex said decisively. ''Wait until
I saddle my horse.''

''You'll take me?'' Rebecca halted midway
through the bedroom doorway.

''You can ride on my horse with me,'' he said, a
grin transforming his face to a look of youthful satisfaction.

''All right,'' she said agreeably, and was pleased
to see that she'd surprised him with her easy acqui-
escence. Closing the back door behind them, she
waited on the porch with Homer until Alex appeared,
leading his horse. He rode beside the porch and
scooped her up in one arm, settling her across his
lap.

''Don't make me drop my bag,'' she said, hugging
it close as the horse bounded into a quick canter.

''You're safe,'' he said, and then waved to Homer,
who watched, openmouthed and anxious, as they set
off to the neighboring farm, Homer's own mount following behind.

Alex waited outside the house, leaning against a
tree in the farmer's yard, surrounded by four young-
sters who'd been banished from the house while their
mother produced the newest addition to the family.
He slid to the ground after a few minutes, and drew
the younger boys into conversation. Speaking to

them of the battles he'd survived and the places he'd been, his words mesmerized the little boys with tales of soldiers who fought bravely. Wisely, he left the bloody details from his recounting of those years, yet his audience clung to every word.

He was becoming hoarse, and had about run out of material to cover, when they finally heard the first cry from the newborn infant. Only two hours, he figured, looking down at his watch, relieved that his time of waiting was over.

"Well, she sure didn't mess around this time," the oldest child said. A young girl, probably twelve or so, Alex judged, stood and gathered her younger siblings together.

"Thanks for the stories, mister," she said to Alex. "It helped pass the time."

He rose, watching as the four entered the back door, then followed them to the porch to wait for Rebecca. Homer joined him there, his face drawn, but his eyes bright with relief as he settled beside Alex. "Had us another girl," he said. "I was lookin' for a boy, but guess we'll settle this time."

"This time?"

"A man needs boys to run a place," Homer said flatly. "Winnie done her best, I expect."

"Is Mrs. Carr about done in there?" Alex asked smoothly.

Homer's head turned quickly, as if it were on a swivel, and his mouth fell open. "Mrs. who?" he asked loudly. "You talking about Rebecca? She's not married."

"She is now," Alex said. "She married me this morning in town."

"And you let her come over here on your wedding day?" Homer snorted inelegantly. "Seems to me you'd have found another way to keep her at home and busy."

"She felt an obligation to your wife, I believe," Alex told him. "Rebecca is a woman who honors her promises. We've got the rest of our lives to worry about being together. Babies don't wait on anyone, so far as I've heard."

"You're right there, Mr. Carr," Rebecca said from behind him. She stood in the kitchen door, rolling down her sleeves and buttoning them at the wrist. "Are you about ready to go home?" Her attention turned to Homer as Alex rose to his feet. "I've given your daughter instructions about caring for Winnie. I hope you'll see to it she stays in bed for a few days to get her strength back."

"A day or two, I suppose," Homer agreed grudgingly. "There's work to be done around here. I can't afford no slackers on the place."

Alex bit his tongue as he heard the harsh words from the new father. Perhaps if Winnie had managed to produce another boy it might have been different, he supposed. As it was, Homer was not celebrating in earnest.

"I'm ready," Rebecca announced, stepping onto the porch. Alex lent her his hand as she descended the steps, wary of the broken boards that creaked beneath her weight.

They walked to where his horse waited beneath

the tree and he swung into the saddle, then reached to lift her onto his lap. "You all right?" he asked, turning the mare in a half-circle and heading toward the road. "Old Homer wasn't too pleased with having another girl, I understand."

"He'll get over it and have her pregnant again before you know it," Rebecca said tautly. "Miserable man." She turned her head and eyed him with purpose. "You'll be pleased that we had this interruption on our wedding day, Alex. I talked with Winnie for a few minutes. She told me something you'll be interested in."

"Yeah? What's that?" he asked, his gaze alert as he scanned the countryside.

"You were right about one thing. Those men have nothing to do with the railroad. They've been asking questions about you while you were healing and staying with me. She said they gave Homer money to take a shot at you that day in the barn."

"That rotten—" His words broke off abruptly. "What else did she say?"

"She told me Ted Duncan and his bunch have about given up on stopping the railroad. I don't think they had anything to do with your getting shot that first night, either."

"Was it Homer that time, too?" And if it was, he was half tempted to turn around and go back.

Rebecca shook her head. "I don't know. Winnie didn't say. But she did tell me that the men who broke into my place were staying at the hotel in town. I wonder if they left anything behind when they came to visit me the other day."

CHAPTER SEVEN

HALFWAY UP THE CURVING staircase that graced the hotel lobby, Rebecca cast a last, long look at the lobby below, and then turned her attention to the man who climbed the stairs beside her. "How did you manage that?" she asked quietly. Ignoring her query, he grasped her elbow, allowing no slowing of her pace as they reached the second floor. Room numbers graced each door they passed, even digits on one side of the hallway, odd on the other. Halfway down the corridor, Alex looked behind them briefly and then relaxed his hold on her.

They'd caused no commotion, raised no brows as they climbed the open stairway, Alex appearing confident, smiling at her as though he had every right to be heading for the second floor. It seemed to Rebecca that their sneaking into someone else's hotel room should have made them appear furtive, or at least suspicious. Instead, Alex had halted by the desk, spoken briefly to the clerk while she stood off to one side, trying to look inconspicuous, and then turned to her, offering his arm.

"I paid for a room for the night," he said, bending to speak quietly into her ear. "And while I was at it, I checked the register for names."

"How did you know what name to look for?" She was feeling rushed and frustrated, and with a jolt, pulled free from his grip.

"I didn't. But I caught sight of a precisely written signature that seemed pretty out of the ordinary for this town. Gerard Fortenay. Does that ring a bell with you?"

"Gerard?" Her heart jolted in her chest, as a sharp, vivid image shot into her mind. *So quickly you weep...I had no idea you would be so puny...* Her hands clenched, fingernails digging into each palm. "Yes, one of the men called the other by that name."

"They were registered in room 207," Alex said quietly, his gaze focused on her. Taking her arm again, he led her quickly to the next room. "Hang on, sweetheart. I need you to keep an eye out," he said in an undertone, "while I see what I can do with this lock."

Searching his pocket, he withdrew a set of narrow, metal forms, fingered them quickly, then chose one. He slid it into the lock and Rebecca looked away, leaning in what she hoped was a casual stance against the wall beside him as he worked.

Breaking and entering was a crime, one she'd never been in close contact with, but was certainly aware of. And beside her, her brand-new husband was deeply involved in a criminal act. If the sheriff could see him now, she'd be spending her wedding night in a jail cell. For wherever Alex went, from this point on in her life, she'd be right beside him.

"That does it," he said, satisfaction alive in the words as he turned the knob and opened the door.

The room smelled musty, with an overlying odor of stale food and the appearance of a hasty departure.

Alex hustled her over the threshold with a last look down the hallway, then closed the door behind them. He lifted a satchel onto the bed. "Are you up to this?" he asked as she inhaled, recognizing with distaste the scents she associated with her captors.

"I'm fine," she said sharply, and with another assessing look he nodded briefly. "Then take a look over there, Rebecca," he told her, waving a hand at the dresser. "See if there are any papers or messages, anything that might tell us something."

She poked at the jumble atop the ornate piece of furniture, sorting through the various coins and bits of clutter left behind. One scrap of paper had the number of the room scratched on it, another held names she was unfamiliar with, and a time and date scrawled at the bottom.

"I'm not sure what this means, Alex," she murmured, picking it up and turning to him. "It's just names, mostly."

Then a second bit of paper caught her eye, another, more formal-appearing document, this one folded and refolded, until the paper was worn in the creases. As she lifted it and spread it open before her, she felt Alex approach, was aware that he stood behind her, peering over her shoulder.

"Look here," she whispered. "It has your name on it, and the name of the railroad company."

He grunted, apparently absorbed in the printed message. The hand was meticulous, the words carefully drawn, and she shook her head in dismay. "It's in a foreign language."

"I can read some of it," he said. "I know a little Spanish and some French. Some of the words are much alike." He pointed with his index finger. "Murder sounds the same in any language if you know what you're looking for. A lot of the European speech comes from old Latin."

"Latin?" she asked, the look she gave him uncertain, as if she wondered at his knowledge. "What does it say?" she asked, aware of the rapid beat of her heart, conscious of standing on the brink of some new discovery.

"The bottom line is the most interesting," he said. "It's signed by the crown prince of Korosol. Prince Jon."

"Korosol? A crown prince?"

"That's what it says," Alex muttered. "And unless I'm mistaken, this is an order for my death."

"Someone ordered your death?" she asked, stunned by the very thought. "Why would anybody do that? Why would a crown prince know who you are? And where on earth is Korosol? I've never even heard of the place."

Alex shook his head, reaching past her to pick up the incriminating letter. "I'm not positive that's what it says, but I'd say it's pretty close. Your guess is as good as mine, sweetheart. I'm not dead certain of the location, but it's somewhere on the Mediterranean, I think. My best interpretation is that someone there wants me dead."

"Did you find anything in the satchel?" she asked.

"Not much. Just clothing and some personal papers." He folded the message he held and slid it into his pocket. "I think we need to get out of here. If that sheriff is half as smart as he ought to be, he'll be showing up here sooner or later, and I'd just as soon not be caught red-handed."

One hand on the doorknob, the other on his gun, Alex listened intently as he cracked the door open a few inches. From the lobby below, sounds of voices drifted upward and he motioned Rebecca to his side.

"Let's get out of here," he whispered. "The room I took is just across the hall and down a bit."

They slipped through the doorway, and as Alex silently turned the knob and closed the door behind them, Rebecca inhaled deeply of the untainted air. Half a dozen steps brought them to another door, where the number 210 on the door proclaimed it to be their destination, and he slid the key he carried into the lock.

"You did just as well with your little set of tools," Rebecca said, stepping into the room ahead of him, watching as he locked the deadbolt behind them.

"Ah, but this is legally ours for the night," he told her. "I have the key, remember? You know," he said quietly, "I probably should have carried you over the threshold."

"Should you? We're really staying here?" she asked, looking up at him.

He shrugged and grinned. "Why not? No one knows where we are except for the desk clerk, and I'm not sure he noticed you. And if he did, I gave him enough of a tip to keep him on our side for the night.''

"How can you just forget that letter we found, Alex? Is it that easy for you to set it aside and think about other things?'' The man was the picture of serenity, she thought, and full of surprises, whereas she was filled with doubts about such mundane matters as their safety and fears of what tomorrow might bring.

"Rebecca.'' He spoke her name quietly and she looked up at him, nearly choking with emotion as she beheld him, standing there in the shadows, looking down at her.

His jaw was set in a firm mold, and his eyes held depths of feeling she could not fathom as he leaned against the closed door and folded his arms across his chest. "I've had to learn in my life to take what pleasure is to be found in the moment, Rebecca. If that means setting aside everything else to enjoy my bride tonight, then I can do it.'' He allowed his mouth to curve in a half smile, and his eyes delivered a message she could not fail to decipher.

Alex was contemplating a wedding night, and she was to be the focus of his attention for the next several hours. It would behoove her to set aside her doubts and fears for the future and join him in this small time set aside for that celebration, she decided. If Alex could rid himself of care, she would do her best to do the same.

He watched her, green eyes darkening as she deliberately smiled at him. Truly, the man was elegant. Even clad in everyday garb he managed to exude the image of a gentleman. His bearing was almost regal, she thought, his stance that of a military man. She'd come to love him as he lay wounded, yet unwilling to yield to the pain of that wound. She'd found him desirable as he'd struggled to keep his dignity intact during the days of convalescence, and had discovered passion and desire in his arms.

If a wedding night was what he wanted now, she would do her best to make that desire a reality.

"I feel…" She paused, stepping away from him, her heart pounding rapidly as his gaze followed her. And then she turned in a slow circle in the middle of the room, twirling twice so that her skirts wrapped around her knees. "It's as though I'm in the middle of a stage play, Alex."

Halting abruptly, she looked up at him. "I've never actually seen such a thing, only read about them, of course. You'll think I'm silly."

Her cheeks flushed and her hands rose to cover them. "Here we are, up to our necks in danger, and I'm acting like a fool, dancing around as if I haven't a care in the world."

Then she sobered as another thought hit her. "Does this seem like a dream to you?" she asked. "Or is it just me? I can't believe that I'm caught up in a plot like the one we've just stumbled upon. I keep wanting to pinch myself so I'll wake up."

"I wish it were a dream, and all we had to worry about was whether or not our wedding night will be spent in a hotel room instead of back at your farm." He took three steps toward her, then covered her hands with his own and clasped her fingers, drawing them to rest against his chest.

"I'd like to do something about the danger I've put you in, love." His jaw firmed and his eyes narrowed as he sought her gaze. "But right now, I can't change things that have happened." He bent to touch her lips with a tender kiss and she sighed, her mouth forming to accept the caress.

"Just for tonight, shall we take what we can?" he asked. "Putting aside the thought of what lies ahead and concentrating instead on the pleasure we can find here in this room. Can you trust yourself to me?"

"Implicitly," she said quietly. "You're my husband." She tilted her head back, her eyes widening as she spoke aloud the title he wore and wholly considered, for the first time, the implications of his place in her life. "We're really married, aren't we?"

"If we aren't, that preacher has a lot to answer for," he told her, one corner of his mouth lifting in a teasing smile.

This was the Alex she loved, the man who could bring her happiness with a single look, a gesture of caring. Her fingers were warmed beneath his, and she flexed them into the fabric of his shirt. His gaze narrowed a bit, as if he felt each small nudge of fingernails against his chest, and his hands slid to encircle her throat, even as his mouth touched hers.

The kiss began as a mere brush of lips; but the desire he made no effort to contain touched her with its flame, and she was caught up in the caress. With delicate touches of his tongue, he sought the tender flesh of her mouth and she opened to his urging, anticipating the thrill of his invasion. Her lips widened to allow his entry and she was caught up in a frenzy as his hands cupped her head and held her in place.

Heat enveloped her, a flash fire of passion she could only submit to, allowing the breathtaking intimacy of a man's mouth and teeth and tongue possessing her in a way she had only lately begun to imagine. She clung to his wrists, tilting her head first one way, then the other, as he prompted her obedience to his will. Deep within her body a coiling warmth brought a throbbing delight she could barely contain, and she sighed, murmuring soft moans, signifying her pleasure.

As if it were a signal he'd awaited, his hands released her head, then moved to clasp her shoulders for a moment. From there, they spread wide on her back and his nimble fingers worked quickly at the fastenings of her dress.

They urged her buttons from the bound buttonholes, one by one, and in mere moments she felt the cool air against her bare shoulders. The dress dropped, and she slid her arms from the sleeves, until the bodice rested against her hips. Long fingers gathered her chemise, sliding it upward until she lifted her arms over her head, breathless as she considered what he would see beneath that bit of intimate apparel. The garment fell to the floor, and Alex looked down at her.

His eyes gleamed as his gaze traced the soft curves he'd unveiled. ''I knew you were well-formed, sweetheart,'' he murmured, ''but this—'' He shook his head, as if in awe. "I wondered, the first time you bent over me with that white nightgown on, what lay beneath all that material." His smile was quick, his teeth flashing in the dim light that shone from the window into the room.

He bent, his mouth opening against her skin, his tongue touching with delicate movements against the rise of her breast. She felt the shivers of delight, welcomed the puckering of tender flesh as he nibbled and murmured his satisfaction aloud.

"You taste like sweet cream and honey," he told her, lifting his head to meet her gaze. "You're perfectly formed, sweetheart. You fit my hands as though your breasts were made to rest in my palms."

She listened to his words with a sense of wonder, that this man should so blatantly admire her body, so gently touch her with calloused hands, bringing a new and glorious pleasure to each increment of flesh he explored. Silent, not knowing where he would lead her in this game they played, she bent her head, her gaze following the movement of his hands.

They were deft, his fingers reluctantly abandoning her breasts, pausing only to untie her petticoat before he slid her remaining clothing to the floor. She looked down at the jumble of fabric surrounding her feet—feet still clad in shoes and stockings—and somehow, that fact made her even more aware of each particle of skin that felt the warmth of his gaze.

"Sit down," he said, backing her from the array of cotton and bits of embroidery she'd been wearing. The edge of the bed pressed against the backs of her knees and she sat, feeling vulnerable before him. Her breasts were damp from his caresses, and she fought the urge to cover them with her arms. She would not play the prude. Alex apparently enjoyed looking at her, and a sense of pride rose within her as his gaze focused there and his smile widened.

Flustered by his perusal of her breasts, she folded her hands in her lap, suddenly conscious of the lack of covering, there where her thighs met and the triangle of curls protected her feminine parts from his gaze. Excitement conquered modesty as she waited for his next move, and it was not long in coming.

"It's my turn," he said quietly, evening the odds as he stripped from his clothing with economical movements, tossing his garments aside until even his drawers disappeared, and she was presented with the vision of a man set on a path from which there would be no detours.

He knelt before her, and his hands were deft as he removed her shoes, then rolled her stockings down her legs and set them aside. His fingers brushed the curls she'd managed to hide with her folded hands, and he clasped her fingers in his, bringing them to his mouth, kissing the knuckles in a small ceremony.

"Now, put your head on the pillow, sweetheart," he told her, his voice husky, as if his throat was taut and the sounds would not readily come forth. "I want to look at you."

"You *are* looking at me," she whispered. "I feel very naked, Alex."

"You *are* very naked." His voice was amused now and he smiled directly into her eyes. "I planned it that way." His hands lifted to cover her breasts as

she arranged herself on the bottom sheet. "I wanted
to do all of this last night, you know. It was all I
could do to keep you inside your nightgown and let
you go to sleep."

She nodded. "I thought you might—when you..."

"I almost did," he said. "But I'm glad I waited."
He bent to her, his fingers gentle as they formed and
molded the contours of her breast, his mouth covering the crest, then suckling it firmly until her hips
rose from the bed and her mouth opened with a keen
intake of breath. "Did I hurt you?" he asked, lifting
his head.

"No." She shook her head. "You just...I felt that
all the way to—" Her voice broke midsentence, and
she gestured weakly with one hand, unable to put in
words the destination of that sharp sensation.

"All the way here?" he asked, one hand cupping
the curly mound, where even now fragile tissue tingled with a moist heat.

"You touched me there through my gown last
night," she said, peering down to watch the movement of his fingers as he explored further.

"I know, but now that we're married, I've dis-
pensed with the gown. I needn't be so polite," he
teased. "I can watch your face and see what pleases
you."

One palm circled the peak of her breast and he
pressed his index finger there, nudging it a bit, sending more shards of sensation to the depths of her
body. "You like that," he said quietly, bending to
nuzzle the swollen peak, suckling it with firm movements of lips, teeth and tongue.

His fingers pressed deeper between her legs and she allowed it, relaxing as he murmured soft words of instruction. The pad of his index finger circled and stroked, and her eyes widened as her hips rose to capture the momentum of his caress.

"I think you like that, too," he whispered, lifting his head to meet her gaze. As if she could not bear to miss one movement of his hands, she held her breath in anticipation. His gaze softened and he bent to kiss her lips with a tenderness that brought tears to the surface, and she blinked her eyes, forcing one salty drop to slide down her cheek. He watched its progress and spoke her name. "Rebecca?"

"I can't believe this is happening to me," she whispered. "I love you so much, Alex." Her head turned to the side, and as though she must return his caress, she reached to place soft kisses against his shoulder and chest, her mouth forming around the flat, brown circle that was a male replica of her woman's flesh.

She suckled it into her mouth and he inhaled sharply. "I won't be able to wait for you if you keep that up, sweetheart," he warned her.

"Wait for me?" she asked, looking up quickly, releasing her prize as she sought his gaze. "I don't know what you mean."

"You will. I'll see to it," he promised. "Move over a little. Make room for me."

She did as he asked, and he settled beside her, his hands touching, fingers more brazen now, exploring her curves and folds of flesh, his palms pressing against her, lifting her, guiding her and holding her firmly in place for the tender loving he'd promised. His name whispered past her lips, his hair was threaded with her fingertips, and he was guided by the murmurs of pleasure she made no attempt to muffle as her inexperienced body absorbed the gentle caresses he bestowed.

Caught up on a wave that seemed to surpass all those that had come before, she knew a moment of madness, of ecstasy so piercing it seemed she could not contain the words that poured from her lips. His own were there, opening to capture the cries of sheer pleasure she offered, and he kissed her with fierce abandon, his tongue and teeth again taking possession of her mouth.

Her body was not her own, but his, to do with as he would, and she surrendered to his heat, to the weight of him as he rose above her, pressing her thighs apart as he sought the very heart of her feminine being. She felt probing fingers venture inside the untried opening he'd only begun to explore, and then the nudging of that thick, heavy part of him, a movement that promised delight, should she be able to absorb it within her.

Stinging pain caught her unaware and she cried out, smothering the sound with the back of her hand. "I'm sorry, sweet. I'm sorry," he whispered, his face beside hers, kissing her palm. "I tried not to hurt you."

"It's all right now," she said, catching her breath and circling his neck with both arms. His body was over her, his arms beneath her shoulders, and wonder of wonders, he was, at the same time, within her, the firm pressure of his manhood stretching her almost beyond bearing. She inhaled deeply, forcing her muscles to relax from their hold, aware that he was holding himself rigid above her, lest he cause her more pain.

Slowly, he withdrew a bit, then gently regained the ground he'd surrendered for that small moment. It was a rhythm he repeated, and she shifted to meet each thrust, her hips lifting as he slid one hand beneath her to guide her tentative movement. From deep within his chest, she heard a groan and his head thrust back, the pace of his driving momentum increasing.

Deep inside, muscles she'd not known existed responded to each tantalizing touch, and she lifted her hips in an attempt to capture him as he would have withdrawn from her, aching for a fulfillment that seemed just out of reach.

"Stay with me, sweet," he whispered, his voice harsh and rasping, his movements more rapid, thrusting into her until she could only cling to his neck, winding her legs around his as she gripped him with all her strength.

A low groan met her ears and he uttered another cry, burying his face next to hers on the pillow, as if he would stifle the sound. He stiffened, and she felt the impetus of his seed as it filled her, knew the joy of holding him fast as he collapsed against her.

"Sweetheart." He crooned the syllables against her ear, then whispered the tenderest of all messages. "I love you, Rebecca. I love you, sweet."

Her tears flowed in earnest now, and still she held

him, unwilling to allow his weight to lift from her body. "It's not what I expected. I didn't know I could feel so much a part of another person, Alex. We're truly one flesh, aren't we? The way it says in the Bible."

He lifted his head and his lips touched hers, a delicate caress that spun a bewitching web. She was caught up in it, knew the ache of love and the knowledge of her vulnerability to the depths of her soul. Lifting a corner of the sheet, he wiped her tears. "You belong to me now, Mrs. Carr. No matter what comes or goes, you're mine."

It should have gone against the grain, she thought, his claiming her as a possession. And yet, it was glorious, knowing that he had chosen to own her as his bride. As she had taken him to her heart, feeling the same sense of ownership, secure for this moment in the knowledge that she loved and was loved.

"And you're mine, Alex," she told him. "No one can ever take this away from us, can they?"

He shook his head. "No, never."

"THE MAN IS GONE, Mr. Carr." The sheriff's blustering facade was shattered as he admitted the escape of his prisoner. He lifted his shoulders in a gesture of defeat as he told of his discovery just an hour since. "I opened the door to my office and saw right away that the window in the cell was gone. Somebody pulled it right out of the wall during the night."

"Are there any horses missing?" Alex asked harshly. "What about your guns?"

"He took a mount from the corral over at the livery stable while Stan Holt was sleeping, and stole the gun ol' Stan kept in the tack room while he was at it.''

"There'll be hell to pay for this," Alex said, his voice quiet, radiating a controlled anger that was a living force within the walls of the small office. "You'd better get ahold of every sheriff in the territory, mister, and alert them that a man bent on murder is loose. And then you'd better round up a posse and see if you can find a trail to follow."

"Yessir, I'll surely do that very thing," the sheriff agreed, nodding his head as he listened to Alex's dictates. "I hope you can keep Miss Rebecca safe, Mr. Carr. I'd hate it should that fella catch up with you and hurt her."

"And if he does, her blood will be on your hands," Alex vowed.

Rebecca thought he looked every inch a warrior as he tightened his gun belt and checked the knife he wore. His jaw was firm, his eyes glittering darkly as he stood in the office doorway and surveyed the main street of town. She stood behind him, sheltered by the powerful strength he exuded. She placed her palm on his back and he turned his head, meeting her gaze.

"I'll be fine," she assured him. "It isn't me he's after, Alex. It's *your* life I fear for." She stepped onto the sidewalk and backed up against the building, her legs trembling as she waited for Alex to decide on their plan of action. In the distance, the sound of a rattling harness and the shrill neighing of horses announced the coming of the morning stagecoach.

From the ornate door of the hotel, a man emerged, announcing the arrival of the stage, declaring in the same sentence that it would be departing in half an hour to points east.

"Chicago," Alex said quietly. "We'll take the stage to the nearest railway, and go to Chicago. Once there, we can catch a train to New York City."

"New York City?" Rebecca repeated the words as if they were a magic incantation, her voice an awed whisper. "We're going to New York?"

"Yes." His voice spoke the single syllable firmly, and Alex turned to her, grasping her shoulders and almost lifting her from the sidewalk. "Listen to me. We're leaving now. This is the way it has to be. I'll buy you everything you need for a day or so at the general store and we'll fill in the rest when we reach Chicago."

"What about—"

Her words were cut off by his upraised hand. "I'll pay someone to go out to your place and take care of your animals, Rebecca. We don't have time to tend to it ourselves." His grip tightened. "You told me you trust me. Now prove it."

"Your shirt," she said, thinking of the memento he'd unknowingly left behind, that stained, mended garment she'd slept in…remembering the comfort it had bestowed.

"What's wrong with my shirt?" His brows gathered as he glanced impatiently at her.

"Nothing's wrong," she said. "I just thought of something, but it's not important." She could leave it behind, along with every stitch of clothing she owned, every stick of furniture she'd tended so carefully. Walking away from the farm and the ties that bound her to house and barn was a small price to pay for a future with Alex. Without a trace of regret, she acceded to his will.

"Ask the storekeeper to find someone who'll be willing to close up the place," she said briskly. "Winnie Dooley will appreciate having my chickens and the cow. I don't want that husband of hers to lay hands on my horse, but perhaps the banker would take him in lieu of payment for selling my place and putting the money aside for me."

Alex cocked his head and grinned. "Aren't you the businesswoman all of a sudden? Just like that, you've got things lined up neatly, and here I thought I'd have to take a stand and corral you into my way of thinking."

"I told you before, I'd do anything you asked of me, Alex," she reminded him, and was ready for the level glance he shot in her direction.

"We were talking about something entirely different, as I recall," he said, just the trace of a smile touching the fullness of his lower lip. "And you did, sweetheart. You offered more than I asked of you."

She felt a blush rise from her breasts to sweep the length of her throat, then cover her cheeks with its heat. Its warmth was not eased by his next statement.

"You were perfect, Rebecca. I couldn't have asked for a more beautiful, desirable bride, had I searched the world over." Tenderness etched each word, and she met his gaze, aware of tears hovering at the rim of each eyelid.

"I mean it," he told her quietly. "All teasing aside, you fulfilled every dream I'd ever dreamed, answered every need I possess."

He overwhelmed her with his words of praise, and she fumbled for a reply, snatching at a more neutral subject, yet one she knew might affect their future together. "What about your job, Alex?" she asked. "What will your employers say if you abandon this project?"

"I'll send a wire to the president of the line. Once he knows my life is in danger, there won't be a problem. The powers that be can arrange for someone else to take my place here. I learned a long time ago that no one is irreplaceable, sweet.

"The folks here will come around, and if they don't, the railroad will still be built. Maybe north a mile or so, but it will go through, and if the people in Creed are smart, they'll court the business and count their blessings."

She nodded, content with his resolution of the problem, knowing that Alex was already looking ahead to what must be accomplished in the days ahead. With a possessive grip, he took her arm, and together they made their way to the general store.

Alex chose three dresses and assorted undergarments from the store of ready-made articles on the shelves, including a new pair of shoes, a luxury Rebecca barely protested, once she saw the stylish, leather footwear in place. A valise was selected from the sparse selection available, and he filled it with the items he'd purchased, adding changes of underwear and shirts for himself.

Stepping farther down the length of the long counter, he paused, and his index finger pointed at soap, a shaving mug and razor, and tins of talcum and tooth powder. Then, in rapid order, he added both toilet water and soap in a delicate fragrance.

Rebecca watched, dazed by the take-charge attitude he exuded, standing aside as he packed each item into the black leather bag. Money from his purse paid the bill and he added a bonus for the storekeeper, pledging his cooperation in sending messages to the banker and to Winnie Dooley. The man smiled widely, delighted with the surge of business he'd run into, and promised to do as instructed as soon as his wife arrived to take over the running of the store.

"Is he honest?" Alex asked Rebecca as he escorted her through the double doors, out onto the wide sidewalk. "Will he do as I asked?"

"My father trusted him implicitly," she said. "Mr. Dugan's been in business for a long time, as far back as I can remember."

"Well, that's all settled, then," Alex said, as if he mentally closed the door on the last of their connections with Creed. "Now we'll check out of the hotel and purchase our seats on the coach."

CHAPTER EIGHT

CHICAGO. FROM THE MOMENT the conductor called out the name of their upcoming destination, walking through the railcar as it jerked and jolted its way down the track, Rebecca had been seized with a sense of expectation. She'd never thought to see a town larger than Creed in the Dakota Territory, and now she was faced with the reality of a city so large she could scarcely take it in.

It was magnificent, she decided from her perch on the seat of a hansom cab, this wonderful, waterfront town, where horse and buggies dashed hither and yon, and pedestrians scurried about like ants in a hill of sand. Alex seemed unimpressed by the hubbub, and she strove to equal his indifference to the splendid atmosphere with an attitude of nonchalance she was far from owning.

Alex took time to show her around, varying their adventure between the ride from the train station to the hotel where they would stay, to an afternoon of walking past banks and stores and offices of every sort imaginable.

New houses and storefronts were being erected. The sound of men laughing as they worked, hammers pounding out a staccato rhythm of progress, and visible signs of life everywhere she looked, made her feel wide-eyed and much like a child being given her first glimpse of a candy counter in a general store.

It was a fairyland, this bustling, dirty, noisy city, with odors from the stockyard blending with the fresh scent of water as they walked along the beach of the enormous lake to the east.

"Seen enough?" he asked, his amusement visible in the grin he shot in her direction. She held her newly purchased hat tightly to her head as the wind picked up from the lake, glorying in the fresh air and sunshine, certain she would never live out so perfect a day again in her life.

Aching to hug him, to throw her arms around his neck in an impetuous display of joy, she clutched instead at her reticule, a dainty bit of crocheted frivolity he'd purchased in a big department store, simply because she'd picked it up and run her fingers over the knotted string.

"Do you like it?" he'd asked casually, and she'd nodded, her smile of pleasure at the extravagant little item prompting him to nod at the salesclerk. "We'll take it," he'd said, gesturing at the blue bag, and pulling his pocket book forth to extract coins.

She'd never been so pampered, so cosseted in her life, and within her a wellspring of love flooded her being, a joyous celebration that encompassed the whole of this adventure. Beginning with the man himself, and circling to include the memories she would forever carry from their outing, she stored away each segment of the afternoon.

"Are you ready to go back to the hotel?" he

asked, as if aware that she was almost beyond the saturation point, that her mind and body were weary from the onslaught of beauty and excitement he'd provided.

"Yes," she said readily, smiling up into green eyes that narrowed a bit, then glowed with a light that was fast becoming familiar. Alex was thinking again, and she knew the focus of his attention was already aimed at what he would do once they were inside their hotel room, in the privacy of that elegant suite of rooms he'd engaged for their use.

They climbed the stairs to the second floor, each step covered with navy-blue carpeting, the bannister gleaming as though recently waxed and polished by one of the uniformed maids who glided noiselessly about, performing their duties.

"You take this all for granted," she whispered accusingly, one hand on his arm, the other holding aloft her skirts. "I think you're much more used to this sort of life than what you've told me."

He grinned down at her. "I traveled a bit with my railroad friend, sweet. He lives well, and he owed me much."

"He did?" she asked, slowing the climb lest they reach the second floor before he had fully explained his statement.

"A small matter involving the war and one of the last battles we fought," he said. "I don't often blow my own horn, but this once I'll oblige your curiosity. I saved his life, and in return, took a bullet meant for him. He chose to show his appreciation in several ways."

They walked the length of the hallway, and he slowed his steps to her shorter stride. "I told you before that I lived with him after the war for a time. Remember?" At her nod, he continued. "He's my friend, Rebecca. And he's rewarded me over the years."

They stopped before the designated room and Alex used the key he held to open their door. Then, with an extravagant gesture, bent to lift her in his arms, carrying her with a flourish over the threshold.

"I should have done that back in Creed," he reminded her. "Is it too late to remedy my oversight?" His grin was boyish and she brushed at a stray lock of hair that fell against his brow.

"I feel like a bride," she told him, sliding to stand before him, her skirts falling into place as his hands released her. "You've made this a perfect day for me," she said. "I can't thank you enough."

"Oh, I think you can manage," he said, turning around to lock the door. As he faced her again he was already unbuttoning his coat. Tossing it aside with a careless gesture, he smiled again, reaching for her. With deft touches, he busied himself, first removing her jacket, then working at the buttons of her dress. "I'm certain we can come up with a suitable reward for my generosity," he crooned, his smile becoming a crooked smirk that amused her.

"Generosity?" she asked, wondering at this foolishness Alex had never before indulged in.

"I've been exceedingly generous," he told her judiciously. "I've given you a tour of the city, not to mention buying you a new hat and bag in a department store and a nice luncheon in a fancy tearoom. I've managed to get sand in my shoes and—''

He broke off, laughing and dodging the swats of her new purse as she assailed him, her pouting mouth spitting forth denials of his generosity. ''You enjoyed it, every bit of it, Alex Carr. Don't try to get on my good side by—''

His hands lifted her by the waist and he held her inches from the floor, his strength beyond any man she'd ever known. ''Is it working?'' he asked, his smile causing his eyes to crinkle at the corners as he looked up into her rosy countenance.

''Oh, yes, I'd say it's working,'' she said, her words a gasp as she bent her head to press her lips against his. She was still almost virginal in her loving, he thought, still a bit shy and more than a little modest. But she suited him as no other woman he'd ever encountered in his lifetime had been able to do.

He lowered her to her feet, his hands still clasping her firmly, drawing her to lean against himself, and then he tilted his head, the better to return the bantering caress she'd instigated. What had begun as foolishness on her part became a serious exploration of her mouth on his. He inhaled her gasp of astonishment, noted the clamp of fingers she pressed into his shoulders, and even as she whispered small endearments past his open lips, he stripped her from the rest of her clothing.

She kicked the fallen garments aside and he lifted her with ease, carrying her across the parlor and into the bedroom alcove of their suite. Wearing only stockings caught up at her knees with pink garters, and the soft kid shoes he'd purchased in Creed, she lay on her back, one knee bent, resembling a voluptuous painting on the wall of a mens' club he'd visited once in New York.

Her lips were moist, rosy and swollen from his kiss, her hair appealingly disheveled from his hands delving through the upswept curls. And her breasts were round and firm and peaked with excitement.

He shed his clothing, aroused almost beyond bearing, recognizing the teasing gleam of dark eyes and the seductive smile she'd worn for the past days. Sliding her shoes from her feet, he tossed them across the room, eliciting a burst of laughter for his efforts. And then he sought her warmth.

She welcomed him, holding up her arms to accept his weight, adjusting her legs to contain his hips and thighs between hers, and he settled against her, his mouth taking her lips in a probing, heated kiss that brought him to the brink of passion. With barely harnessed desire, he wooed her, his caresses urging her acceptance of his manhood.

With patience he fought to maintain, he visited each place he'd become intimate with during the past days, his lips, tongue and teeth gaining access to the secrets of her femininity.

And with a skill that owed more to his natural inclination than to practice over the years, he teased and tested her limits of modesty and sensual adventure. With a delight she made no effort to conceal, she obeyed his whispered commands, moving as he bid, lifting and turning in accord with his murmured demands.

She moaned her pleasure, cried aloud as he brought her to a pinnacle of ecstasy, then another, and lifted her arms to enclose him against herself as he filled her with the power of his masculine being.

With a strength gained by years of hard work, she clutched at his shoulders, digging her fingertips into his back. Her sleek thighs parted further to clasp him with firm muscles, her hips rising to accept the gift of his seed, and he was surrounded by heat and the scent of her arousal as he sought his own pleasure— and in the seeking found a depth of love he'd never hoped to discover.

Her whispers were warm in his ear, her mouth offering the message of love she shed upon his hungry heart as manna to his starving spirit. He yawned, and a deep lethargic weariness overcame his normal caution. Eyes closing in slumber, he managed only to murmur soft sounds that made her chuckle softly, and with his face cushioned against her breast, he slept.

A FIST POUNDING UPON THE outer door of the parlor awoke him, and he stiffened, aware only that he had slept as a dead man, sprawled across the bed without a stitch of clothing on, a sheet tossed over his back. The woman who had been beneath him was gone, and he heard her voice murmuring beyond the curtain that shielded his prone body from the parlor.

"Don't open the door," he said, his voice husky and demanding as he sat upright, tangled in the sheet, feeling like a grizzly bear awakening from his winter's sleep.

"It's room service," she said quietly, pulling the drapery aside to peer into the shadows of the sleeping area.

"How…" He shook his head at her words.

"I looked out our door and stopped a maid in the hallway," she said quietly. "I ordered food. Are you hungry?"

That she had unknowingly exposed them to danger was something he needed to explain, he decided. But not right now, while she was endeavoring to please him with her resourcefulness. "Yes. I'll be right out."

"Your clothes are on the chair," she said, allowing the curtain to fall from her hand, leaving him in the shadows. Her footsteps were almost silent as she crossed the parlor, and he heard the door open and then the voice of a young man and the squeak of cart wheels as their meal was brought into the room.

With haste, he donned his trousers and pulled his shirt on, tucking it in quickly and pulling his suspenders up over his shoulders. One hand smoothed his hair as he ducked past the hanging curtain and into the parlor, his eyes narrowing as his sight encountered the brilliant light shed by the gas lamps on the wall.

The young bellboy ducked his head, tossing a knowing grin in Alex's direction and, in return, received a stifling glance. With a forlorn look at Rebecca, he backed to the door and nodded, pulling it shut behind him.

"He was waiting for a tip, sweetheart," Alex said

gruffly, and then wished the words unsaid as her face turned pink.

"A tip?" She spoke the word gingerly. "I'm not sure what that means."

"He brought the meal here and in return, you're expected to give him a small amount of money in thanks for his service." Even as he spoke the words, he recognized her embarrassment, her shame in not knowing the protocol involved in this new venture she'd undertaken.

"I'm so sorry, Alex," she murmured, hastening toward the door, opening it and thrusting her head into the hallway, as if to search for the boy.

"Come back here, Rebecca," he called quickly. "From now on, I don't want you to open that door without me right here with you."

"Are we in danger?" she asked quickly, as if surprised that it should be so.

"I don't know. It wouldn't be impossible for our friend from Creed to have followed us here. And we may have more to deal with than the threat from that one man. If he's had time to send a message to Korosol, there may be reinforcements sent within a short length of time."

She leaned against the closed door and considered him with a sober look. "We've been enjoying ourselves, or at least I have, and all this time we could be in danger."

"We've both enjoyed ourselves," he told her firmly. "I don't mean to sound harsh, sweetheart. I let down my guard and I'm blaming myself for that.

I don't expect you to be wary of every person we meet, although it may come to that.''

He approached the serving cart and lifted a silver lid, allowing a cloud of steam to escape. ''This looks good. We may as well sit down and enjoy it together.''

''I wanted to surprise you,'' she said quietly. ''I'll be more careful from now on.''

She was subdued, and Alex rued the quick reproach he'd offered, making an effort to lighten her mood. ''I must have slept the evening away,'' he said, holding her chair and seating her with a flourish. ''It's dark out.'' He circled the table to sit across from her and lifted the lid from a silver dish. ''Those look like new potatoes, don't they?''

Rebecca peered at the bowl he'd uncovered, nodding approval at the bite-sized vegetable, butter and parsley decorating the red-skinned surfaces. ''Yes. They look good.'' Spreading her napkin across her lap, she served him with a heavy silver spoon and then helped herself from a bowl of green beans. Thin slices of roast beef were pleasingly arranged on a small platter, and she used the serving fork to place several pieces on his plate.

''This gravy isn't very thick,'' she said dubiously, lifting a ladle from a steaming container.

''It's called au jus,'' he said softly. ''I think that's French for thin gravy.''

She looked up quickly, doubt dulling her gaze. ''I think you're teasing me again, Mr. Carr.''

His shrug was brief. ''Just a little. You rise so nicely to the bait, sweetheart.'' He handed her a basket of yeast rolls, and she selected one after viewing the varied shapes and sizes.

"Everything is so fancy, Alex. Who'd ever have thought of making bread in such elaborate bits and pieces? And look at the stuff they've got mixed in with the green beans." She poked at the tidbits of color that had caught her attention.

And then her eyes lit with pleasure as she caught sight of the small squares of butter on another small plate. A knife, shorter than those she had at home in her drawer, with an oddly shaped blade, took her attention. "What's this for?" she asked, lifting it and turning it over in her hand.

"It's a butter knife," Alex said. "A really formal table setting would have more than one teaspoon and a couple of forks for each person. That's made especially for serving butter from the serving dish to your bread plate."

"I need a separate plate for bread?" she asked dubiously. "Whatever for?"

"Fashion demands a lot of dinner guests," he said with a chuckle. "I'll fill you in as we go."

"I'll never understand all the things that are going on around me," she wailed. "I'm a farm girl, Alex. I'll never fit in if you decide to live in the city."

"You'll fit in wherever we end up," he said firmly. "You're my wife, Rebecca, and I'm proud of you. We'll worry about all the small stuff later."

They ate, and he watched her from beneath lowered lids, his own pleasure in the meal enhanced by her innocent enjoyment of each bite she took. She made it an art, tasting as if each item on the table were ambrosia and she the recipient of leftovers from the angel Gabriel's table.

"Are you used to eating such elaborate meals?" she asked, spearing a bite of fruit on her fork. "You must have thought my cooking was the end of the line."

"On the contrary," he said quickly. "Nothing hits the spot like a home-cooked meal, Rebecca. And you excel at every part of cooking and baking. They have a chef in this hotel for each part of the menu. They can only specialize in one area, whereas you are talented beyond imagination, putting together a whole meal and having it on the table while it's still hot."

"That's easy," she said, scoffing at his words of admiration. "I'd never be able to make pretty things like this."

"Do you think I care?" he asked, leaning across the table to snatch up her hand. Lifting it to his lips, he kissed the back, brushing his lips across the surface and looking up at her with amusement. "I'm more interested in how responsive you are in the bedroom than what you're capable of in the kitchen, sweetheart."

"Responsive?" Her brows lifted and her nostrils flared a bit. "I'm not sure I know what you mean. I heard from the storekeeper's wife one day that men would rather get fancy loving from women other than their wives." She looked bemused for a moment. "I wonder if she was talking about her husband?"

"Well, that theory doesn't apply to me," he vowed. "I'll take your kisses and teasing any day of the week, lady. What you did this afternoon with your index finger still gives me shivers."

Her blush was immediate and she looked toward the door, as though someone might be listening from the hallway to his words. "I don't think you're supposed to talk that way, Alex."

"Why not?" he asked airily. "We're married, and according to the experts, we can do anything we like in the privacy of our own home."

"What experts are those?"

"Mostly the men I've known over the years," he admitted sheepishly. "They've all had their own opinions about such things."

Making a face that left him in no doubt of her exasperation, she put her fork down on the table with a clatter and stood. "I don't know how we got on this subject, but I think you've pulled my leg long enough, Mr. Carr. I'm ready to talk about serious things."

He leaned back in his chair. "What things are you worried about?"

She counted off on her fingers. "First off, are we going to stay here for a while, or is this just a stopover until we catch a train to New York City? Second…" She tapped her index finger. "Do we stand a chance of having a life without looking over our shoulder for someone out to harm you?" Her mouth drooped and she bit at her lower lip as she threaded her fingers together. "I feel like we're treading water here, not accomplishing anything."

He rose and walked around the table to grasp her shoulders, halting her list of anguished queries. "Not accomplishing anything? Haven't you ever heard of a honeymoon?''

"Honeymoon?" Her mouth dropped open as she looked up at him in astonishment. "Is that what this is?"

"A honeymoon is the time allotted for a newly married couple to spend time alone, getting to know each other," he explained. "I'd say this is a good spot for it, wouldn't you?"

"When will we go on to New York?" she asked stubbornly.

"In a few days, as soon as I hear from a lawyer friend of mine."

"You've contacted a lawyer?"

He nodded. "He's the man who negotiated my contract with the railroad before I began this job. I had to notify him that I was backing out of the deal. I'm certain I'll have to make restitution to them for quitting my position and leaving them in the lurch. No matter the friendship between myself and the president, when it comes to this, business prevails," he told her.

"So, while I was at it, I asked him to make some inquiries for me. We'll wait here until I hear from him."

"Inquiries?"

"He's checking at the orphanage where I lived for my early years, to see if anyone there has any records I haven't been privy to before this. And to find out if anyone has been nosing around, asking about me during the past few months."

"Ah…" she said, as if understanding had come

calling and found her at home. "I wondered myself if that might not be a good idea. I didn't know if they would be willing to tell what little they might know."

"I think it's our best bet for now," he said, holding her closer, dipping his head to brush his lips over hers. "You taste like raspberries."

"I do?" And then she grinned. "Of course I do. I just ate half a bowl full of them. They were wonderful." She returned his kiss with a degree of enthusiasm he found encouraging. "So are you, Alex," she said softly. "Wonderful, I mean."

"You've given me one of the happiest afternoons of my life," he said, grinning with delight as her blush reappeared, tempting him to investigate how far south it went. His fingers touched her buttons and she bent her head, watching as he slid them from place.

"What are you doing?"

"What does it look like?"

"We just did that," she said smartly. "Surely you don't—"

He tucked her against himself and her eyes widened in disbelief as his arousal nudged her with awakening potency. "Oh!" The single syllable held a wealth of meaning and she smiled again. "Well, I guess you do, don't you?"

"Yes, ma'am," he answered meekly. "I surely do. In fact, just as soon as I push this serving cart out into the hallway, I'm going to hang a Do Not Disturb sign on that door and we'll take up this honeymoon where we left off a couple of hours ago.''

THE MESSAGE WAS WAITING at the desk the morning of the third day. On their way to the dining room for breakfast, they paused as the desk clerk called out Alex's name. ''Mr. Carr. There's a wire for you. Came in this morning, early on.''

Alex detoured to take the folded paper from the clerk and thanked him as he turned away, already unfolding and reading the printed words. He handed it to Rebecca. ''Here, read this.''

She scanned the abbreviated message quickly. ''Someone *has* asked after you,'' she breathed softly, her eyes lighting with expectancy. ''This sounds promising, doesn't it?'' Looking down at the message again, she spoke aloud the final line. ''Investigation continuing.''

''He's a good lawyer,'' Alex told her. ''He's probably already hired a private firm to follow up on things.''

''Detectives?''

Alex nodded. ''No doubt. There may be news by the time we reach New York.''

''When will we go?'' she asked, her gaze sweeping the dining room as they paused in the wide doorway.

''Today.'' He ushered her to a table against the far wall, where he could see anyone coming or going through the entrance, and then looked up as a formally dressed waiter approached. ''We'll have a full breakfast, please. Eggs, bacon and toast.'' Glancing across the table toward Rebecca he asked her preferences. ''Orange juice? Or just coffee?''

"Coffee," she answered, smiling up at the waiter. "I'd like my eggs scrambled."

They waited for their coffee, both lost in thought, and then Alex lifted his cup and sipped with appreciation. "I was ready for this an hour ago."

Rebecca poured cream into her cup and stirred it slowly. "I can't quite get used to being waited on like this. I keep thinking I should go out in the kitchen and lend a hand."

"They'd probably be able to take a few lessons from you," Alex said agreeably.

"How soon can we catch a train?" Rebecca unfolded the heavy linen napkin and placed it across her lap as the waiter approached again, bearing two plates of food.

"I'll ask the desk clerk if he has a schedule." Alex cast an appraising look at the meal he'd ordered and nodded his approval at the hovering waiter. "This is fine," he said, and then picked up his fork. "Eat up, sweet. We'll need to pack and get things organized without delay. I imagine there will be a morning train heading east, and we'd do well to be aboard."

His thoughts proved to be accurate, and within an hour they were standing in front of the hotel, waiting for the doorman to whistle down a hansom cab for their trip to the train station.

THE ORPHANAGE WAS a square, brick building that had seen better days. It sat adjacent to the sidewalk, with three steps leading to the front door. Alex eyed the bell and hesitated before he lifted his foot to the first riser. "Isn't it strange to be so hesitant at this point?'' he asked Rebecca in an undertone. ''I've been anxious to get here, and now I'm dragging my feet.''

''Not so strange to my way of thinking,'' she said stoutly. ''I'd think anyone would be apprehensive, given the circumstances of your past.''

He inhaled deeply and climbed the steps, then reached out to turn the bell. It rang loudly and he straightened his shoulders, as if gearing himself for whatever might come to pass in the next moments. The door opened slowly, and a white-aproned woman stood before him.

''Yes, sir?'' she asked, deference alive in her voice. ''Can I help you with something?''

''My name is Alexander Carr,'' he began, ''and I have an appointment with the person in charge of this establishment. A few years back it was run by a lady named Mrs. Montgomery, I believe.''

Her eyes brightened and a smile curved her lips. ''It still is, Mr. Carr. Won't you come in? We've been expecting you.'' She held the door wide, and Alex turned to take Rebecca's hand, escorting her through the doorway into a wide hall. The scent of strong soap met their nostrils and the wide boards of the foyer gleamed with well-applied wax.

''At least it's clean,'' Rebecca murmured beneath her breath. ''I'll bet that's not an easy feat to accomplish with a houseful of children.''

''We're proud of our home,'' the maid said. ''Mrs.

Montgomery sees to everything herself, checks up on everyone, every day.''

She led the way to double doors halfway down the corridor and opened one, leaning inside to speak to the room's occupant. ''Ma'am? Mr. Carr is here to see you.''

Alex stepped into the room, allowing Rebecca to precede him. It was obviously a former morning room, with wide windows placed to catch the sunlight, and comfortable chairs arranged before a large desk. The woman seated there rose as they approached and held out a hand in welcome.

''Alexander. It's been a long time since I saw the back of you.'' Amusement rode each word, and Rebecca heard with surprise the chuckle that escaped from Alex's throat as he reached to take Mrs. Montgomery's fingers in his. He lifted her hand to his lips, and as Rebecca watched, the lady's eyes widened with surprise.

''Quite the gentleman, aren't you?'' she asked. ''Won't you sit down?'' Motioning with her hand, she offered Rebecca a choice of several cushioned chairs, their upholstery bright with yellow and lavender flowers, and their green leaves providing a cheerful accent against the cream background.

''It's been a lot of years, Alexander. You were always one of my favorites, you know.''

''No, I suppose I wasn't aware of that,'' he answered. ''I remember being called on the carpet right here in front of this desk, more than once, as a matter of fact.''

''Yes. Well, you were a bit impetuous. But well-loved by the rest of the boys, and the teachers, too.''

''I was a rebel.'' He stated the fact dryly, and Mrs. Montgomery smiled in agreement.

''Yes, you were. But you were independent and had a good head on your shoulders. Always determined to be in charge, as I remember. I knew you'd be a success, no matter where you chose to go, Alexander.''

''Stubborn, is what she means,'' he said, turning to Rebecca with a quick glance. And then he introduced the two women with a few words, and Mrs. Montgomery nodded approvingly.

''You've chosen well, young man. She does you proud.''

''I think so.'' Alex sat down and lifted one booted foot to his other knee. ''I have some questions for you.''

''I've expected this visit for years. I'm surprised it took you this long to come calling. Actually,'' she said, leaning to one side to pick up a box, ''I've gathered every bit of your past I could find in order to give it to you when the time came.''

The box was tied with butchers' string, a plain, brown package that drew Alex's eyes to it in the same, abrupt manner of a magnet attracted to metal filings. He placed both feet on the floor and reached across the desk, hand outstretched. ''May I?''

"Certainly." She placed it in his palms and settled back in her chair as he placed it on his lap.

He untied the string and handed it to Rebecca in an absent movement. Then he removed the lid and peered into the box. A folded blanket lay on top and he lifted it, examining the binding, where close, careful stitches told of some woman's adherence to loving details. Rebecca took it from his hands, running her fingers over the soft fabric as she placed it on her lap.

A book was beneath it and he opened it, then after perusing the first few lines, looked up at Mrs. Montgomery. "You wrote this, didn't you?"

"Yes, it's a detailed report of the day you were discovered on the steps out front. What the weather was like, the time of day and a description of exactly what you were wearing, and even the note that was left with you."

"Did you do this same thing for each child left here?" he asked, scanning the script that gave him insight to his past.

"We're considered unusual, Alex," she began, "in that we truly care about the children in our care. We've been funded by people who contribute heavily to this place. Many children are lost in the shuffle in the institutions out there, but we want each of our boys and girls to have some small memento of their past to take with them when they leave us."

"And I left too soon for you to send this along with me," he said, his grin sheepish.

"Yes, you did," she answered. "But you were a rare child from the beginning, Alex. We've found very few children on the doorstep. Most of our infants come from doctors who deliver babies to young women who can't keep them for one reason or another. You were a challenge, because we knew so little about you.

"You were probably two months old when you arrived here. We've never been certain of your exact age, so we just gave you a birthday we thought might fit."

"This note is not written in English," he said, disappointment rife in his tone. "In fact, I'd say it's the same language as the letter we intercepted," he said, turning to Rebecca.

"We had it interpreted by a scholar at the university," Mrs. Montgomery told him. "The translation is on the following page."

Alex turned the page and read quietly. "This child is Alexander Carr. He is of royal blood, but his life will be forfeit if his whereabouts are discovered by those in power in his homeland. Take care of him and protect him, I beg you."

Rebecca's heartbeat increased with each word he read aloud. *Royal blood.* She was married to a man who carried the blood of kings in his body.

"The medallion." Softly spoken, the words nonetheless gained the attention of Mrs. Montgomery.

"Yes, there was a medallion left with him. We gave it to him to wear as soon as he was ten years old. I thought it only right that he carry that part of his heritage on his person.''

"He still wears it," Rebecca said. She watched as Alex unbuttoned three buttons on his shirtfront and withdrew the leather thong from which hung the enameled silver pendant. "It has a crown and a bird of prey on it," she said. "And another bit of ornamentation, three little things that remind me of the iris my mother planted at the edge of her garden back home.''

"They're called fleur-de-lis," Mrs. Montgomery said. "And they literally were fashioned after the flowers of the iris bulbs.'' She folded her hands on the desk and turned her attention back to Alex. "Actually," she said quietly, "the medallion is the coat of arms of a country in Europe, Alexander. I've done some research on it over the years, hoping you would come here one day in search of your past."

"I suppose I never really had a reason before now," he said. "But things have happened lately that made it imperative that I find out everything I can about my background. I've been the target of violence, and I fear for my wife's safety if we don't put a stop to whatever plot is brewing."

Mrs. Montgomery rose from the desk and rounded it to stand before Alex, who rose as she approached. "I think it is safe to assume that you are a missing heir to the throne of Korosol, Alexander. I've kept this to myself for years, and in case I was not here to let you know what I've learned I wrote down the details of my investigation in the back of that book."

"When did you discover all this?" he asked. Rebecca recognized the threat of harnessed anger in his tone. "Why wasn't I told of this when I was a child?"

"I didn't get too involved in it until you left us," Mrs. Montgomery said, her words apologetic as she continued. "I'm so sorry that your story was neglected for so long, but when you ran off, it was unexpected."

"I couldn't stand being penned up by walls and rules and restrictions any longer," he said. "My education came about the hard way, I fear."

She nodded. "I only know I felt ashamed that I hadn't been more thorough in my search for your beginnings. So I set about to find some answers, should you come back to us one day." She lifted her shoulders in a helpless shrug.

"It hasn't been easy getting information. I've met with a blank wall several times. Finally I just set the whole thing aside, in hopes that you would appear on the doorstep and inquire about your early life here.

"And then I found I could no longer keep this on the back burner when two men came to us over a month ago, searching for your whereabouts."

"Describe them," he said tersely and Mrs. Montgomery nodded, her words painting accurate portrayals of the culprits who had assaulted Rebecca in Creed.

"One of those men is dead, the other escaped from jail before he could be questioned further," Alex said quietly. "They were up to no good."

"That doesn't surprise me," Mrs. Montgomery said. "They knew too much about you, Alexander. Your age, even the actual day you were left here, and a description of you, including the color of your eyes."

"I appreciate your concern for me," Alex said. "And your being honest with my lawyer when he came to call."

"I suppose I was relieved that there would finally be contact with you after all these years," she said. "I've wondered about you many times."

"My lawyer suggested that I might be surprised at what I would find here," Alex said after a moment. "He was right."

"He told you of my visitors, then? I wasn't entirely sure they had your best interests at heart, and I didn't offer them any information."

"They must have found from government records that I fought in the war, and discovered my whereabouts from that source. If there is an ambassador from Korosol in Washington, it probably wasn't difficult to trace me from the Union Army to my position with the railroad."

"What will you do now?" Mrs. Montgomery asked.

"I don't know." Alex looked down at the box he held. "Today, I need to take this to my hotel room and look everything over well, and then make inquiries through my lawyer as to my next move."

The man she'd married was of royal blood. The phrase repeated itself over and over in Rebecca's mind as they took their leave, the words resounding in her head, surrounding Alex Carr with an aura she was not able to see beyond. Alex was descended from royalty, was perhaps meant to sit upon a throne and rule a people in some foreign land. And she had married him, assuming that he was mere flesh and blood.

"Rebecca?" His hand on her elbow tightened, his fingers clasping her firmly. "What is it, sweetheart?" he asked, settling himself beside her in the hansom cab he'd hailed in front of the orphanage.

"I'm stunned," she said. "I can't quite take all this in, Alex. Suddenly you're not the same man I married back in Creed."

CHAPTER NINE

Korosol—1872

"THERE SHOULD HAVE BEEN no problem. The fools were sent his location and description, and still bungled the job." Prince Jon stalked from his desk to the window and back, the message he'd read moments before still held between long, narrow fingers as if it were a particularly nasty bug. He lifted it, reread it quickly, then crumpled it into a ball and tossed it aside.

His aide looked down at the aged carpet, where mute evidence of incompetence had become a mere scrap of paper. Mouth trembling, hands properly folded behind his back, he faced his employer, his stance that of a man about to be executed. "Sir? Perhaps we should assign someone else to the task."

Prince Jon turned, his green eyes aiming a seething look toward the man who awaited his pleasure. "It may be too late. The message states that Alexander Carr has murdered one of my men. The second man was jailed, but has escaped from the authorities and is on the run." His jaw thrust forward, and his words were spit from between gritted teeth.

"This is unacceptable. I have been betrayed by those I trusted. The woman has been dealt with, Quince has been disposed of, and I am at the mercy of men who cannot obey simple orders."

"Sir, you must not allow yourself to—"

Prince Jon's hand sliced through the air, effectively silencing his aide. "Don't presume to tell me what I must not do. I will succeed in this. My future depends on that interloper being eliminated. I want the border guards alerted to the existence of Alexander Carr. Label him a threat to the king. Give his description to the authorities and offer a reward for his death."

The aide nodded quickly, backing toward the door. "Yes, sir. Right away, sir." His hand sought the gilded handle and eased the heavy panel open. Then, still bowing and nodding, he fled from the presence of the pretender to the throne, the man all of Korosol assumed to be the crown prince.

New York City—1872

THEY'D VISITED THE attorney's office, the man a former Union Army soldier who treated Alex with a manner of deference that somehow did not surprise Rebecca. Nothing regarding the man surprised her these days, she decided, sitting quietly in the office while the two men discussed Alex's visit to the orphanage.

The contents of his box had been shared, and together they'd pored over the small book in which

Mrs. Montgomery had written the facts and details of Alex's childhood. The lawyer had meticulously copied parts of it onto sheets of paper before he returned it to Alex's possession. And then, with a warm handshake, the men had parted company.

Their afternoon was spent at the newspaper office, where musty archives revealed little information to Alex's prying eyes. He led Rebecca from the building before sunset and they ate in the hotel dining room, Alex ever wary of those who entered and left the premises while they ate. Rebecca's legs ached as they climbed the staircase to the second floor, and she stood just inside the parlor, slowly unbuttoning her new coat. Alex shed his suit jacket in silence, but Rebecca could not contain her fears any longer.

"I fear for your life, Alex," she said, holding her coat over her arm as if it were a shield. "What if you were to go ahead and work things out without me in your back pocket. You'd be more inconspicuous without a woman at your heels, and—"

Alex cut a glance in her direction, his eyes narrowing. "Don't get cold feet now, Rebecca."

It sounded much like a regal command, she decided as she faced the man she'd married with such high hopes only a few days since. How everything could have gone so wrong, so quickly, was beyond her comprehension. Not that she would deny Alex his proper place in the history of that tiny country on the Mediterranean. Far from it. She only wished that he would listen to reason and go there unencumbered by a woman so totally unsuited to be his partner in this venture.

"It isn't a matter of cold feet," she said stubbornly. "Part of it is a matter of my lack of qualifications for the role you're expecting me to play."

"I'm not expecting anything more of you than that you be my wife." His eyes focused on her face as he stepped closer, seeming to tower over her, even viewing her as he might an underling, she thought. Truly a designation she had to agree with.

"Your future lies ahead, Alex. You may one day be the ruler of a country, sitting on a throne with the world at your feet. I don't belong in that setting." He had nothing on her when it came to being stubborn, she decided. No man alive could force her submission to his will. She'd fought for her independence for years in the town of Creed, in the Dakota Territory.

Facing up to a man who might someday be the king of Korosol was no different. She was not afraid of Alexander Carr. After all, she'd shared the most intimate of moments with this man. They stood on equal footing in some areas, and she did not fear his anger.

Only dreaded to be one day deserving of his scorn.

She could not measure up to royalty. The words flowed from her as his mouth grew taut with anger. "I can't be what you need, Alex."

"How do you know what I need?" Again his brow rose as he doubted her claim, and she smiled, a sad, small expression that only served to stoke his fires.

"You're my wife, Rebecca. It's all legal and binding." And then, as if he regretted his harsh words, he relented and his gaze turned molten as he turned it on her with the full force of his desire gleaming within those emerald eyes. "I won't give you up. Not for anything in this world."

"You didn't know what your future held when you married me," she reminded him. "I won't hold you back from fulfilling your destiny."

"I knew," he said quietly. "I've always known, somewhere in my innermost soul, that I belonged in another place, that there was something out there waiting to be discovered. I felt like a displaced spirit sometimes, seeking out the answers to my beginnings. And now..." His pause was long, and his jaw set with determination as he seemed to be forming words that would convince her.

Then, with a swift movement, he reached for her and drew her into his embrace. She balked, stiffening in the circle of strong arms and wide palms that held her fast.

"Don't use me, Alex," she said quietly, forcing her body to remain apart from his. "Don't think to coax me by luring me to bed. That's no solution, and it's beneath you to do so."

"Nothing is beneath me, if it will make the difference between our being together or you walking away from me." His words were harsh, his hands gripping her with bruising strength, and she knew a moment of temptation.

His head bent to her and his mouth was hot and open as he brought it against her throat. Her head tilted back with the force of his onslaught and she moaned aloud, her heart torn asunder as she considered a future without this man's presence. Hot tears escaped and trickled onto her temples, dampening the russet waves.

"Don't, sweetheart," he muttered, his words softening as sobs shook her frame, reducing her to a trembling creature in his arms. He thrust his fingers into her hair, dislodging the pins and combs holding it in place, causing the heavy length to fall about her shoulders like a veil of autumn leaves. And then his lips gentled, moving from the vulnerable line of her throat to settle possessively against her mouth, catching her audible sounds of grief and taking them as his own.

He kissed her, delicate brushes of his lips, as though he would comfort her and then, as she relaxed her stance, allowing her arms to rise and twine about his neck, he groaned and lifted her against himself. With the passion of a man who faced the threat of losing his very reason for living, he feasted upon the soft lips beneath his, his teeth and tongue taking possession of her mouth.

"I won't let you go," he said, the words a harsh promise as he lifted his head to look down at her tear-stained face. "You are mine...mine, Rebecca. Do you hear me?" He shook her, a quick movement that caught her off balance, and she hung in his grasp, her knees unable to hold her erect.

"No." She spoke but a single word, softly but firmly, and even as she shed tears of regret, she shook her head, closing her eyes against the passion that molded his features into harsh lines of hunger.

"I'll make you listen to me," he told her, lifting her in his arms, carrying her to the alcove where their bed stood in the midst of heavy velvet hangings and ornate trimmings of gold and burgundy fringe. It was a setting for seduction, one he'd used to his advantage over the past days, and now it represented a trap from which Rebecca feared she might never escape.

She pushed at his chest as he lowered her to the heavy spread, turning her head aside to escape his kiss, silently writhing beneath his weight, as if she fought for her very life and would not waste her energy on useless pleas for mercy. He held her beneath himself, his muscular body a deterrent to her struggles, and still she fought to free herself, knowing it to be a futile exercise, yet one she could not abandon.

"Hold still, sweetheart," he crooned, his mouth near her ear. "You'll hurt yourself." His hands gripped her firmly, though she fought his hold, twisting to free herself of his dominion. "Rebecca, don't fight me," he begged, his words pleading, knowing she would bear bruises as a reminder of this moment.

"Let me go," she demanded, opening her eyes to look up at him, and even through her tears he caught sight of the determination that drove her. "I won't allow this, Alex. If you take me this way, it will be against my will."

He felt a cold chill possess him, its icy tendrils sending a message of warning he could not ignore. Not for the world would he force a woman to his will. Even though he had a legal right to his wife's body, though the law would stand behind him if he chose to take her to himself, he did not possess the ability to harm her in any way. And though she might capitulate and be coerced to accede to his demands, he would lose the essence of Rebecca herself, would forfeit the loving spirit of the woman he had married.

His hands relaxed their hold and he rolled to lie beside her, offering her the freedom to leave the bed, to walk from this room, away from him. For a moment, she was unmoving, as if she held her breath, and then she turned aside, drawing her knees up and huddling at the farthest edge of the wide mattress.

"Where will you go if you choose to leave me?" he asked, his tone matching the hopelessness that tore him asunder. "Surely not back to Creed."

She shook her head. "I don't know. I can't think that far ahead, Alex."

"Don't abandon me yet." He despised the imploring note that took his words to the level of pleading for his very existence. Yet, without Rebecca, he faced a life of dreary days and empty nights, no matter how complex his future might be.

"All right," she said. "I'll stay with you until this thing is cleared up and you know what you have to do."

"I won't force myself on you," he told her, fearful that she would rise from their bed and leave him bereft of her presence.

Her sigh was audible and she turned over to face him. "I know that." She smiled and touched his cheek with her index finger. "You probably wouldn't have to use force, when all is said and done. I love you, Alex. I won't deny myself or you the pleasure we find here. In a day or so, when we know what your future holds, there will be time enough to lay aside our marriage, should that be the path we choose.''

He grasped her hand, capturing it and drawing it to his mouth. His lips brushed against her palm in a gentle caress, and then brought it to lie flat against his face. "You're my life, Rebecca."

She shook her head, a sad smile touching her lips. ''Perhaps for the moment,'' she agreed. ''But you must face the future. Your life will be played on a more elegant stage than this, should you truly be heir to a throne. You will live on a scale far more regal than anything I've ever aspired to.'' Her eyes warmed and her smile widened to a teasing grin.

''Don't forget. I'm the woman who didn't even recognize a butter knife when I saw one. I wouldn't know what to do with more than one fork at a meal, and I've only just accustomed myself to being waited on by waiters and bellhops.''

''See?'' he said softly, turning his head to brush another kiss into her palm. ''You're a fast study, love. We can learn all of that together. I'm a simple man, Rebecca, used to working for my living.''

''And should this come to pass, you'll work harder than ever before,'' she told him. ''Just learning the language will be a major undertaking.''

''Let's not worry about that,'' he said. ''I suspect the people of Korosol are well versed in other languages. The two examples we've met thus far spoke English fluently.''

''I hope they weren't true representatives of the rest of the people there,'' she said quietly. She cupped his jaw, sliding her palm to his throat, noting the substance of his evening beard. "When will your lawyer contact us?"

He turned his head to press a soft kiss against her fingers. "By morning, I would think. Not tonight, surely."

Her eyes met his, and he sensed the remnants of sorrow in their depths, yet a measure of hope lifted his spirits as she spoke. "Then we have the rest of this evening and all night for ourselves, don't we?"

THE KNOCK AT THE PARLOR door interrupted their breakfast. As Alex rose from the table, he drew his gun from his waist and held it behind his back, halting at one side of the door. "Who is it?" he asked quietly, motioning with his other hand toward the alcove.

Rebecca moved quickly, standing behind the draperies, peering from hiding as a man replied in a strong voice.

"I am Ambassador Gregory Lamont, Mr. Carr. I've just arrived from Washington. May I come in, please?"

Alex unlocked the door and opened it cautiously, standing aside as the gentleman strode across the threshold. Dignified in his bearing, he certainly gave the impression of being fit to represent the throne of a foreign country, Rebecca thought. White hair and sharply chiseled features gave him an aristocratic look, and his erect posture gave him a bearing that spelled out his vocation.

He offered his hand, and Alex took it with a nod, at the same time allowing his own penetrating gaze to travel the length of the visitor. "I'm pleased to make your acquaintance, sir," he said after a moment.

"I understand your reluctance to admit a stranger to your room," Mr. Lamont said. "I understand your wife is traveling with you?"

"Yes, she is," Alex told him, and then turned to where Rebecca had just slipped into the room. "This is Rebecca." Pride shaded the words, she thought, and even though she hesitated, not knowing what the proper procedure was for such an occasion, she walked forward to stand by her husband's side.

"How do you do, sir?" she said quietly. Should she bow? Or offer her hand?

The ambassador inclined his head. "Very well, thank you. I'm most pleased to meet each of you," he said, his slight accent adding a delightful tinge to his words. One that had not been present in the words of the two other representatives of Korosol she'd had the misfortune to meet.

"To what do we owe this honor?" Alex asked, ushering the visitor toward the sofa.

"I've been privy to some information that I think you will be interested in," Mr. Lamont said, waiting until Rebecca had taken a chair before he seated himself. "I received word from Korosol yesterday that may come as a surprise to you."

Alex sat down in a chair beside Rebecca, and she caught a glimpse of the veiled excitement he strove to contain. One leg crossed over the other and he rested one hand on his thigh, the other stretching just a bit to touch the arm of her chair. "I've been doing a bit of digging myself," he said. "I found out a few interesting facts yesterday, in fact."

"Ah," the ambassador said, his brow lifting a bit. "Can I assume you refer to your visit with Mrs. Montgomery?" At Alex's nod, the gentleman smiled. "I've just arrived from there myself. I fear I interrupted her breakfast, but she was gracious enough to invite me to join her. I caught the late train from Washington and went to her right from the station."

"And did she send you here?" Alex asked. "Are you come to see the box she gave me yesterday?"

"Perhaps. But more than that, I've come to tell you a story. I think you'll be intrigued with the details I'd like to share with you." His gaze traveled from Alex to Rebecca, then back, as if he waited for confirmation of their interest in his tale. He nodded then and cleared his throat.

"This goes back thirty-three years, Mr. Carr, to a day when the queen of Korosol gave birth to a son in the palace. She was told hours later that the child had died, and the whole country went into mourning. The queen died a week later, and the king remained inconsolable for several years."

"Thirty-three years ago?" Alex repeated the words, as if to confirm in his own mind the exact time that had elapsed since that fateful day.

"Yes, in the early spring of the year eighteen hundred and thirty-nine to be exact." Mr. Lamont smiled. "You are thirty-three, are you not, Mr. Carr?"

"I suspect you already know the answer to that question," Alex told him. "Go on with your story."

"It was a plot, designed by the king's younger brother, Prince Jon," Mr. Lamont said. "One I believe had been in place before the birth. Then, when the child was born, and a son's birth was verified, the babe was whisked away by an aide to Prince Jon and was purportedly smothered.

"However," he said, drawing out the word with a singular relish, "Quince, the aide, substituted another child, one who had been stillborn the same day, and made arrangements to have the young prince sent into hiding." He smiled and his face was transformed by the expression of satisfaction he wore.

"It seems he could not bear the thought of suffocating the boy, and instead sent him to America with the mother of the child they'd substituted. She nursed him and tended him as her own, but circumstances forced her to place him on the steps of an orphanage here in the city."

Alex inhaled deeply, as if he had gone without breathing during the recitation. "And you are saying I was that child?"

"Do you not believe it yourself?" He looked intently into Alex's eyes. "You have the eyes of the reigning monarch, sir. A distinctive shade of green that the men of the family have in common. You bear the physical characteristics of your father, the king, even to the color of his hair in his younger years, and the shape of his face. Your father is not well, sir."

"Not well? What's wrong with him?" Alex asked.

"He's not a young man, being the elder son. His brother, Prince Jon is ten years his junior, and there were several girl children born in the years between the two sons. However, only a male can inherit the throne. The king is suffering from a heart ailment, and even now is bedridden."

"And Jon? Is he expecting to take over the throne?"

"He was," the ambassador said, "as were all of the subjects. No one was thrilled over Jon's ascendancy to the throne." His voice lowered and he spoke with fervor. "He is not a man fit to rule. I would not be surprised if he were responsible for several near-fatal accidents that have befallen the king over the past few years."

"I have proof that he ordered my death," Alex said bluntly. "Shall I show it to you?"

"I'd be most interested." Surprise lit the ambassador's eyes and he waited expectantly as Alex carried the box to the sofa and lifted the lid. He had placed the note found in the hotel room in Creed among the rest of the contents, and he drew it forth, presenting it to their visitor.

Ambassador Lamont read it quickly and nodded. "You're correct. It is an order for your death." He looked at Alex with deference, bowing his head in a gesture of respect. "I have only one more request, sir. I ask to be shown the medallion that was left with you at the orphanage. I understand you wear it on your person."

Alex nodded, his fingers deft as they unbuttoned

his shirt, drawing forth the leather thong that held the silver emblem.

The ambassador lifted his hand and traced the blue enameled border and then touched with care the images it held on its surface; the crown, the bird of prey and the three dainty flowers that Rebecca had puzzled over. His hand fell to his lap and he watched in silence as Alex tucked the proof of his identity beneath his shirt.

And then the gentleman spoke again. "Your Majesty," he said quietly. "I offer you my aid in any way necessary to give you safe passage to Korosol. I am at your disposal. I'll send documents immediately to the king, supporting your claim to the throne."

Rebecca closed her eyes, aware that she was a part of intrigue and betrayal on a grander scale than they had imagined. Alex was truly fated to be a ruling monarch. She held her breath as he began to speak, hearing the words as a death knell to her hopes of living a quiet life in a normal manner with the man she loved.

"I appreciate your loyalty, Ambassador. If all of this is found to be actual fact, I will reward you appropriately for your service to your country." Alex rose and stepped to stand in front of Rebecca's chair, clasping her hands and lifting her to her feet.

"Rebecca? Will you support me in this?"

She looked up at him, weighing his words, knowing that he offered her no choice, and more than aware of his motive in putting her on the spot in this manner. Alex was not above a bit of manipulation himself, it seemed. And even as that thought tempted her to turn aside, she was aware of the duty to his position that drove his every action.

She could not deny him her support in the hearing of the dignitary who listened, and Alex knew it, triumph alive in his gaze, certain already of her loyalty to him.

And so she nodded, unable to speak for the lump in her throat.

CHAPTER TEN

Korosol—Three Weeks Later

ACCOMPANIED BY THE ambassador, Alex and Rebecca walked past the royal sentries. The voyage across the Atlantic Ocean had been uneventful, with several guards accompanying their entourage, herding them on board an ornate railway car when they reached the train station upon landing in France for the second part of their journey. They'd crossed the border into Korosol, being halted once inside the country, as armed soldiers searched the car for what they called *interlopers,* on the order of Prince Jon.

Gregory Lamont stood firm, guaranteeing their safety with papers drawn up by the embassy in Washington, and within hours they were in a carriage, heading for the royal palace, where the king was in residence. It was in the midst of a park, with lawns and trees surrounding the three-story building. Armed guards at the entrance stood aside as Gregory Lamont led his party through the wide front doors.

Had Alex always held himself with such assurance, Rebecca wondered? Was there something in his manner that caused attention to follow in his footsteps? Or did his face bear such a striking similarity to the features of the reigning monarch? His hand touching her elbow, he walked with an imperial manner, causing even the uniformed figures to bow their heads in deference.

"Are we expected?" he asked Mr. Lamont in an undertone, as a butler took their hats and outer garments just inside the foyer.

"Most definitely." Rebecca thought there was a shade of satisfaction in the gentleman's reply as he ushered them toward the west end of the palace. They walked abreast, Rebecca at Alex's right hand, and she barely stifled the urge to gawk at her surroundings. Portraits hung on the walls of the corridor, richly hued carpet muffled their footsteps and uniformed servants strove for invisibility, their faces exhibiting awe at the sight of the tall man who strode past.

"The council has been told that I've brought visitors to see the king. Although he has received news by courier of my discoveries, I thought it best not to advertise your presence until we had the full support of the palace behind you."

"Where is my uncle?" Alex asked quietly, his gaze focused on the large double doors ahead, where another uniformed guard stood watch.

"Prince Jon? I'm not certain. He may be in the king's apartments." The ambassador spoke in an undertone. "He's like a vulture waiting for your father to breathe his last, poised to issue his claim on the throne."

The guard stood staunchly in front of the doorway.

"May I ask if you have an appointment, sir?" he asked the ambassador. At Mr. Lamont's affirmative reply, the guard shot Alex a second look, and his eyes widened, marring the perfection of his demeanor.

"Mr. Carr is expected also," the statesman said. "The king has agreed to see both of us, and Mr. Carr's wife as well. Please tell him we've arrived."

The guard nodded. "Wait here."

"Do they all speak English?" Alex asked, surprised at the absence of a language he would have had to decipher. "I assumed—"

His words were cut off by the almost immediate return of the guard, and Alex once more noted the quick glance in his direction. "You may go in, gentlemen. And you, also, madam," he said, turning his attention to Rebecca.

He held the door wide, and they entered the small sitting room. Windows allowed sunlight to enter through gossamer curtains, and bright colors designated this room as having been lovingly designed for family use. At the far side, a door stood ajar, and it was there that the ambassador turned his attention.

"Come along, sire," he said to Alex, leading the way. He pushed the door open and crossed the threshold, coming to a halt as a man rose from beside the bed. "Prince Jon," the ambassador said stiffly.

"What is the meaning of this?" the slender, dark-haired man asked imperiously. "King Philippe is not well. You have no right to bring strangers into the royal bedchamber."

"I knew they were on their way," a voice said from within the hangings of the bed.

Alex turned his attention there, aware of the heavy thud of his heartbeat against his breastbone. For this, he had come across an ocean and left behind each part and parcel of his life, save for the presence of the woman at his side.

The voice beckoned them forward, its quality touched by age, yet vibrant with a regal undertone. Its owner sat upright amid rumpled coverlets in the center of the wide bed, and as Alex watched, a hand lifted, extended in his direction.

"Come closer." It was an edict, issued by a king, and Alex obeyed. The bed stood on a platform, and the mattress was more than three feet above that level, putting Alex almost eye-to-eye with the monarch.

"Open the draperies," the king said sharply, and Prince Jon strode to the window, snapping the heavy coverings aside, allowing the sunlight to pour through leaded glass.

Alex was torn between gazing at the man who was in all likelihood his father, and watching with care and foreboding the man who would have had him slain for his own purposes. His heart won out, and he allowed himself the luxury of envisioning himself as he would appear in thirty years time.

King Philippe, though less than seventy years of age, according to the ambassador, appeared much older, his physical being obviously beset by the ravages of illness. Lines of suffering edged his mouth and eyes, and his flesh was ashen and drawn tightly over his cheeks. Yet there was visible in his gaze a reminder of youthful vigor, the clear emerald color bringing to mind the warm days of the coming summer.

Alex bowed his head, a gesture of respect that was not lost on the monarch. The elder man reached farther, grasping Alex's sleeve and tugging at his visitor.

"Come, my boy. Sit beside me."

"Sire!" Prince Jon stepped to the other side of the bed, casting a malevolent glare at Alex, and in the process ignoring the movement of Ambassador Lamont. The statesman circled the foot of the bed and placed himself beside the prince, as if prepared for any eventuality.

Alex grasped the frail hand in his, emotion rendering him almost speechless, his heart thundering now as he stepped up onto the platform and sat beside the king. It was uncanny, the striking resemblance he bore to the man, almost like looking in a mirror at a blurred image. He'd thought himself ready to accept his identity as being that of the monarch's son, but the reality was almost more than he could absorb.

"Sire, I must protest this man's intrusion," Prince Jon said sharply, stepping forward, hand outstretched as if he would thrust Alex from the bed.

"You have nothing to say about this," Ambassador Lamont said harshly, his emotion apparently overcoming protocol as his scornful words erupted, catching Prince Jon unaware.

He turned toward the white-haired statesman and

thrust him aside, then lunged toward Alex. The king uttered but a single word. Spoken with a harshness that surprised Alex, given the man's obvious illness, it resounded within the walls of the chamber, causing the prince to retreat with haste. The king spoke again, and though the words were unintelligible to Alex, the meaning was clear. Prince Jon was not in favor. Reluctantly, he stepped away from the bed, bowed stiffly toward his monarch, then stalked from the room.

"I have not been patient in my waiting," the monarch said, as once more Alex found himself the focus of that startling green gaze. His throat tightened with a thickening that warned him of overwhelming emotion. As surely as he knew his own name, he was certain that the man before him was his sire, that over thirty-three years ago this palace had been his birthplace.

A sense of wholeness enveloped him as he beheld the king, the final link in the circle being formed. For the first time, in his own mind, he fully acknowledged his identity as the heir to the throne of Korosol.

"Sir," he said quietly. "I am here at the bidding of your ambassador to the United States. He is certain that I am your son, that the medallion I wear verifies his claim. He is certain I was taken from here after my birth and left in an orphanage in America," he said, praying that his voice would not betray him.

Releasing his hand from the king's hold, he opened his suit coat, then unbuttoned the first several buttons of his shirt, withdrawing the leather thong, from which hung the silver pendant. It shone dully in the sunlight from the windows, and the king leaned forward to better verify its identity.

"I have one identical to it," he said. "There were three of them in existence, but one disappeared at the time of your birth. Up until now only two remained here. Until today."

"I have worn it my whole life, sire. And now the ambassador tells me it is my claim to a place in your kingdom. Do you hold with that theory, also?"

That the syllables faltered a bit was to be expected apparently, for the king smiled, a look of happiness flooding his worn features as he spoke his welcome.

"Ah, yes," the king said, his voice breaking as he spoke. "My boy...my precious boy." His hands gripped Alex with unbelievable strength, and he gazed with longing at the man who bore his likeness. "I knew...I've always known that someday, somewhere, you would be found."

"You knew, sire?" Ambassador Lamont asked. "How could you have known?"

The older man looked up his trusted aide. "How does a blind man know the difference between day and night? He feels the warmth of the sun at noon and the depths of darkness at the midnight hour." He laughed aloud, his voice stronger now. "And in the same way I felt the chill of wrongdoing, deep in my heart and to the depth of my bones, when a child was offered to me as my own and my very being said it was not true."

"That child was buried in the family vault, sire," the ambassador pointed out.

"Yes, there was no proof otherwise, and his mother mourned on her deathbed for the child she'd lost," the king said sadly. And then his countenance brightened as he leaned closer to his son. "But my heart knew the difference, and I've hoped for years that this day would come."

"There is no doubt as to Alexander Carr's identity, insofar as you are concerned, sire?"

The king lifted a hand to touch Alex's face, his fingertips eager as he traced the line of his jaw and the chiseled blade of his nose. "None. None, whatsoever. I might be looking at myself, thirty years ago." He turned to glare at the ambassador. "Surely you can see what I see in him."

"Yes, sire. I saw it immediately in New York City. But I had to be certain, and that proof could only come from your own eyes. Everything else points to this man being your true and legal son."

The king looked over Alex's shoulder to where Rebecca stood, tears flowing unchecked as she beheld the acceptance of the man she loved into the royal family. "This is your wife?" Without awaiting Alex's reply, he held out a hand to her and waved her forward. "Come and let me look closer at the woman who has won my son's heart," he said, authority ringing now in his voice.

Rebecca did as he asked, stepping onto the platform and standing beside the bed. "I'm Rebecca, sir," she said simply. "Alex and I have been married for just over a month."

"You hold yourself with pride," her father-in-law said approvingly. "With a visit to the royal dressmaker and a session with my tailor for my son here, we'll have the pair of you ready to meet the people of your kingdom.''

Alex grinned up at Rebecca, but his query was directed at the king. ''My wife fears she is not adept in protocol, sire, and, I assure you, neither am I. I'm certain I can figure out how to bow, but is there someone available to show her how to curtsy? She's wary of appearing in court.''

''And you, Alexander? You have no fear of facing the people of your kingdom.''

''I fear nothing with Rebecca by my side,'' he said firmly.

''Good,'' the king said firmly. ''As to your wife, she is the future queen, and as such, her subjects will bow and curtsy to *her*. There will be no need of lessons for the princess.''

''WILL YOU BE HAPPY HERE?'' Alex asked Rebecca. They stood before a window on the second floor of the palace, looking out upon the moonlit grounds. Their room was large and furnished with pieces dating back over two centuries, and Rebecca was awed by the history inherent in such furnishings.

''I'm with you,'' she said simply, turning in his arms to face him, her gaze meeting his. ''I made a decision in New York, Alex. I told you then I would support you in this undertaking. I haven't changed my mind.''

''I'll see to it that you don't,'' he vowed. ''We'll find happiness here such as we've never hoped for. The people here will soon love you as I do.''

"Will you love me now?" she asked simply, lifting her face for his kiss.

"Now and forever," he said. "I warned you once that I would never give you up." He lifted the medallion from his chest and touched it to his lips. "I swear by all that I am and shall ever be that I will be a true and faithful husband to you. I pledge you my love and my life."

"Come with me," she said, taking his hand and leading him to the wide bed that sat in the center of the room. Holding her nightgown with one hand, she climbed the two steps provided, allowing her to sit on the edge of the mattress. "I've been wondering if sleeping in a prince's bed will compare with the nights I shared with my husband in Chicago," she said, her eyes measuring his muscular frame.

Alex smiled, his hands reaching to unbutton the front of her nightgown as he spoke. "Give me an hour and I'll give you the answer to that, sweetheart." He tumbled her back onto the thick, feather mattress and she opened her arms to accept him.

Almost in unison, they spoke the words of their love, and the whispers and soft laughter continued on into the night, long beyond the hour he had asked of her.

"I love you, Alex," she said, curling against him, safe in his embrace.

"And I you," he vowed. "You are my life, my very reason for living."

EPILOGUE

THE CHURCH BELLS RANG OUT the news on that fateful day. By word of mouth the people learned of the return of their rightful crown prince and his bride, and a suite of rooms was prepared for their use. Within days, the servants in the palace were smiling and bowing with respect as their new princess walked the hallways and spoke to them by name. She made it her business to visit the orphanage and the schools alike, where the children were encouraged to flock around her, basking in the sunshine of her smiles.

The disappearance of Prince Jon put into motion a search that encompassed the whole of Korosol during the next several weeks, followed by the discovery of his body in the lake behind the palace. His funeral was a state occasion, followed by his burial in the family plot.

The exposure of a long-hidden plot was laid at the feet of unknown traitors to the throne, and those who were aware of Prince Jon's treachery were silent, abjuring any knowledge of his conspiracy, even as they expressed sorrow at his accidental death. The lack of a hue and cry over his death, however, did not appear to cast any pallor on the plans for a welcoming ball for the return of Prince Alexander and his princess.

It was the most elaborate celebration of the century, and on that eventful night, they set the revelry in motion. Alexander, handsome in his royal uniform, led his exquisitely gowned princess through the steps of a waltz in an elegant display of courtly splendor.

Their escape before midnight was noted by many of the partygoers and remarked upon, the consensus being that Prince Alexander was truly smitten by his bride. In fact, it was said they shared a love affair of true beauty, indeed, a fairy-tale romance.

The ball was the highlight of the social season in the small, underdeveloped country and set the stage for the beginning of Prince Alexander's reign of his homeland. As the crown prince, he was revered and lifted up as an example of progressive thinking.

FIVE YEARS AFTER HIS son's return, King Philippe succumbed to a fatal heart ailment, shortly after the birth of his third grandchild. He was buried beside his queen, and mourned over the period of a year throughout the kingdom.

Alexander and his princess became the ruling monarchs of Korosol, and were well loved by their people. During the new monarch's reign, he brought about social reform that allowed peasants to become landowners, and caused the wine industry to flourish well into the twentieth century.

Seven children were born to the House of Carradigne, three of them traveling to America to make their fortunes there at the turn of the century. Three daughters married European royalty. Rebecca's first-born, a son, lived in the palace during all the years of his life, and followed his father as monarch in the early years of the twentieth century.

Alexander and Rebecca lived well into their seventies and left behind a legacy of love and laughter that is, to this day, a legend often told and joyfully remembered in that jewel of a kingdom beside the sea.

Embark on the adventure of a lifetime with these timeless tales from Harlequin Historicals

On Sale January 2003

LADY LYTE'S LITTLE SECRET
by Deborah Hale
(Regency England)

Will a wealthy widow rediscover true love with the father of her unborn child?

DRAGON'S DAUGHTER
by Catherine Archer
(England & Scotland, 1200)
Book #3 of *The Brotherhood of the Dragon* series

Passion blazes when a brave warrior goes in search of his mentor's secret daughter!

On Sale February 2003

THE SCOT by Lyn Stone
(Edinburgh & London, 1870)

Watch the sparks fly between a feisty lass and a proud Scottish baron when they enter into a marriage of convenience!

BRIDE OF THE TOWER
by Sharon Schulze
(England, 1217)

Will a fallen knight become bewitched with the mysterious noblewoman who nurses him back to health?

HHH Harlequin Historicals®
Historical Romantic Adventure!

On the lookout for captivating courtships
set on the American frontier?
Then behold these rollicking romances
from Harlequin Historicals.

On sale January 2003

THE FORBIDDEN BRIDE
by Cheryl Reavis
*Will a well-to-do young woman defy
her father and give her heart to
a wild and daring gold miner?*

HALLIE'S HERO
by Nicole Foster
*A beautiful rancher joins forces
with a gun-toting gambler to save her spread!*

On sale February 2003

THE MIDWIFE'S SECRET
by Kate Bridges
*Can a wary midwife finally find love and acceptance
in the arms of a ruggedly handsome sawmill owner?*

THE LAW AND KATE MALONE
by Charlene Sands
*A stubborn sheriff and a spirited saloon owner
share a stormy reunion!*

HHH Harlequin Historicals®
Historical Romantic Adventure!

The nights are long, but the passion runs deep...

Where the Nights Are Long

Containing two full-length novels
for one low price!

by favorite authors

BOBBY HUTCHINSON

KATE HOFFMANN

These larger-than-life stories take you to the great
outdoors of Alaska and the Yukon, where two couples
find love where they least expect it!

Available in January 2003 at your favorite retail outlet.

International
bestselling author

Miranda
LEE

Brings you the final three
novels in her famous
Hearts of Fire miniseries...

FORTUNE & FATE

The passion, scandal and
hopes of Australia's
fabulously wealthy
Whitmore family promise
riveting reading in this
special volume containing
three full-length novels.

*Available in January 2003 at
your favorite retail outlet.*

HARLEQUIN®
Makes any time special ®

There's something for everyone...

Behind the
Red Doors

From favorite authors

Vicki Lewis Thompson

Stephanie Bond

Leslie Kelly

A fun and sexy collection about the romantic encounters
that take place at The Red Doors lingerie shop.

**Behind the Red Doors—
you'll never guess which one leads to love...**

Look for it in January 2003.

HARLEQUIN®
Makes any time special®

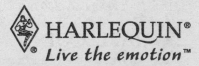